NO LOVE LOST

Recent Titles by Eileen Dewhurst from Severn House

ALIAS THE ENEMY
CLOSING STAGES
DEATH OF A STRANGER
DOUBLE ACT
ROUNDABOUT
VERDICT ON WINTER

NO LOVE LOST

Eileen Dewhurst

WITHDRAWN

YF
2002

This first world edition published in Great Britain 2001 by
SEVERN HOUSE PUBLISHERS LTD of
9–15 High Street, Sutton, Surrey SM1 1DF.
This first world edition published in the USA 2002 by
SEVERN HOUSE PUBLISHERS INC of
595 Madison Avenue, New York, N.Y. 10022.

British Library Cataloguing in Publication Data

Dewhurst, Eileen
    No love lost – (A Phyllida Moon mystery)
    1. Moon, Phyllida (Fictitious character) – Fiction
    2. Women detectives – Great Britain – Fiction
    3. Detective and mystery stories
    I. Title
    823.9'14 [F]

ISBN 0-7278-5816-5

Typeset by Palimpsest Book Production Ltd.,
Polmont, Stirlingshire, Scotland.
Printed and bound in Great Britain by
MPG Books Ltd., Bodmin, Cornwall.

One

The girl rounded on the woman, ponytail swinging.
'Don't you tell me what to do! You're not my mother!'

'You're a cruel, ungrateful girl, Susan! I know I'm not your mother, you don't have to keep telling me. But like it or not I'm in her place now and it's my duty to try and see that you—'

'Your duty! Not your pleasure!'

'Not if you won't let it be. It's up to you. If you won't allow me to—'

'I'm going upstairs.'

'Temper, temper!' This from the older woman sitting by the fire.

'And you're not my grandmother!'

'What's all this, then?'

'Daddy!' The girl ran at the tall man who had appeared in the doorway and pushed her tear-stained face against his chest. 'Daddy! She says I can't—'

'*She* has a name, Susan. It's Sandra.'

'I can't cope, Hugh.' His second wife jerked her hand through her hair and he saw that tears were lurking in her eyes, too. Tears of frustration. The older woman by the fire was turning a quizzical gaze from one protagonist to the other.

'Susan . . .' The father held his daughter away from him by the shoulders. 'If Mummy was still here, she'd

1

tell you to do this or that, the way I do. You're still a child, even though I know you don't feel like one, and you need guidance.'

'That's right,' said the older woman, nodding.

'Leave it, Etta.' The father gave an irritable jerk of his head in the direction of the fire. 'Now, Susan, what is it Sandra has said you can't do?'

'She says I can't go to the disco some of them from school are putting on.'

'The one the school's organising? We've both told you you can—'

'Big deal, that'll be as exciting as a chapel service. This is one some of the girls . . . all my friends . . .'

'Sandra's right. You can't go to that one, Susan. She discussed it with me before she told you.'

'You mean she told you to say no! Daddy, all my friends . . .'

'I'm saying no on my own account. And that's my last word on the subject. Maybe next year. Now, I must be on my way; I'm already late.' He dropped a kiss on his wife's hair, nodded to his mother-in-law, and turned back to his daughter, who stepped away from him with a toss of the head.

But she followed him out to the hall. 'Daddy . . .'

'It's still no, darling.' Smiling, he put his arms round her angrily resistant body and held it until it relaxed and she was smiling, too.

'Daddy . . .'

'Yes, darling?' There was something in her smile that made him wonder, for the first time, if she was beginning to turn from child into woman.

'Do you and Sandra really, really love each other?'

'Goodness, Susan! Of course we do!'

'Then why do you go singing with another woman, and Sandra stay late at her office and have supper with her . . .

her business partner?' Wide blue eyes, searching his for an answer.

'Well . . .' He felt absurdly shaken. Not so much by the question, he thought, as by the fact that it had been posed by someone he had seen as too young to be disingenuous. 'You know I've always gone singing some way or another, and as you've just said, Sandra and Joe are business partners. Sandra's very good at her job. And these days estate agents, like so many business people, can't always afford to stop work at half past five.'

'No. You don't always, do you? But you're always home for supper.'

'Oh, Susan. Are you still so very unhappy?'

'Most of the time. I'm sorry, Daddy.'

'So am I. But Sandra had nothing to do with our losing Mummy, so try not to blame her, darling. If only for my sake.'

'For your sake I'll do anything.'

'That's my girl. Now, I must be off.'

As he went out to his car he found himself trying to do something he had never done before: tot up the number of times in the past few weeks his wife had come home late and tired, asking him if he'd mind if she just sat with him while he ate his dinner, because she and Joe had grabbed something when they'd realised they weren't going to be able to get away at anything like the usual going-home time . . .

'Twice a week it's been for a while now,' the older woman said, as her daughter dropped wearily into the chair the other side of the fire.

'What has?'

'Those choir practices. With his secretary. Anything you ought to be worrying about, Sandra?'

'Of course not!' But the younger woman jerked upright as she felt a thin worm of doubt about her husband wriggle against her brain. 'What an idea, Mother! You're an evil old woman!'

'Just a woman of the world, darling. But if you say things are all right, then of course they are.'

'Of course they are!' But the worm had gained access.

Upstairs in her room, the child locked the door, ran over to her chest of drawers, knelt in front of it, pulled out the bottom drawer and drew a wrapped object from under a heap of clothes. She threw herself on to her bed with it in her hand, then carefully unwrapped it. Inside were a crude plasticine model of a woman and a packet of pins. There were already some pins pushed deep into the plasticine, and the child spent several minutes slowly and carefully pushing in a few more.

Two

Phyllida rang Peter to tell him she was ready to come back to Seaminster, and her work with the Peter Piper Detective Agency, late on the day a case came up for which, before her call, he had been thinking wistfully that she would be the brilliantly ideal investigator.

He was, of course, enormously grateful for the coincidence, but not especially surprised: from the start, his relationship with his female field operative had been as unique as her role of sleuthing 'in character', and as likely to take an extraordinary turn.

He wasn't surprised to learn that she was coming back, at whatever time. A few days after she had exchanged her view of the English Channel for a view of Edinburgh Castle, she had telephoned to make the promise that she would return. Promised 'faithfully', and in a strange tone of voice that at the time he had tried to describe to himself and for which he had been able to come up only with the absurd phrase 'tensely wan'.

'It could be a few months, Peter. I can't tell you at the moment. So of course I'll understand if you'd prefer to terminate—'

'Don't be absurd. I'd wait for you years, let alone months. Where would I find another woman to be a cleaning lady one day and Lauren Bacall the next?'

'You never know.'

'Oh but I do.'

He remembered he'd hesitated.

'Is anything wrong?'

'Yes. But right, too. Can we leave it there for the moment? I know I'm asking—'

'I shan't ask another question. I'll only ask that you keep in touch. And let me know if I can be helpful.'

'Dear Peter. Thank you. My house . . . You've got the keys. If you could keep an eye . . .'

'Dear Phyllida. Of course.'

He'd sat and looked at the telephone a number of times over the ensuing six months, but never dialled the number she had given him. He *had* got into a sort of rhythm of letter-writing – about one a month – telling her about the Agency's more interesting cases; developments in the private lives of his two junior members of staff, Jenny and Steve, which they had brought to his notice or he had deduced; the continuing well-being of her house, and the appearance of the sea and Seaminster generally as the weather changed. In response to each letter had come a short, grateful note, telling him nothing about her Edinburgh days apart from reciprocal weather reports.

Another thing he had deduced – and confronted her with before she left – was that her visit to Scotland was of vital importance to her. She hadn't denied it, hadn't contradicted his deliberate insinuation that the importance was personal, and as he had met her grave, steady gaze across his desk, he had been visited by the dismaying possibility that if things went well for her in Edinburgh he too would suffer an emotion of personal importance: he would find himself personally bereft.

This had been a totally new sensation, and he had tried to dismiss it before it took root, knowing that for a woman like Phyllida Moon emotional importance could exist in only one direction. He'd told her then about his recent thoughts of taking her into partnership, not as an inducement to her to change her mind about Edinburgh – he knew that nothing he offered could do that – but to reassure her that if Scotland didn't work out there was a significant place for her in Seaminster. He'd used the phrase 'business partnership' and had forced himself to smile, he remembered, at what she must have seen as the absurdity of his meaning any other kind. She'd at least responded with enthusiasm, but the unspoken qualification of *if I come back* had continued to hang heavy between them

Her voice, when she had rung him today, had been wan without the tension. She had offered no other information beyond the fact of her imminent return, and he had been disingenuous.

'I'll air your bed. And the guest bed, of course, if—'

'I'm coming back alone, Peter.'

Which didn't mean, he told himself severely as he got to his feet and moved slowly towards his closed office door, that someone else might not be following her later . . .

As he opened his door, Peter was ashamed of his surge of hope that her tone of voice might have indicated this was unlikely. 'Jenny! I've some good news for you. Phyllida'll be home tomorrow.'

'Wow! That's wonderful!'

Jenny spun round from the computer, her pleasure suffusing the careful application of pink on pearl with a natural rose, her elaborate frame of dark hair swinging as she leapt to her feet and shouted in the direction of the general office. 'Steve!'

'I heard.' Steve's usual stance in Reception was propping up the doorpost of the general office or the restroom – depending on which of them he was emerging from – but now he was standing unsupported and his pale, sharp-featured face was also tinged with colour. 'That's really great.'

Steve was a born and bred Londoner, not given to

expressing the emotions both Peter and Phyllida suspected, from his thin-skinned exterior, that he experienced in some depth, and this reaction to the news of Phyllida's imminent return was untypically expressive. Without ever putting it into words, Steve had let it be seen that he approved of Miss Moon, quite apart from his inappropriate lusting (embarrassing to him and a source of amusement to the others) after the husky-voiced American sophisticate who, under a variety of names and wigs, was a staple of Phyllida's sleuthing repertoire.

'Isn't it just?' Jenny turned back to the computer. 'I'll get some of those chocolate gingers she likes when I go out at lunchtime.'

'And I'll pop across to the Golden Lion and tell John Bright in person. He promised when she left that her room would always be waiting, but that's quite a time ago.'

The Agency's windows looked across Dawlish Square at the handsome facade of Seaminster's oldest hotel, and Peter had only to traverse the central path in a few long strides to find himself beneath its early-Victorian classical portico. A couple of years earlier he had thwarted a confidence operation that had started to cost John Bright, the Golden Lion's owner-manager, customers as well as cash, and John was still regularly expressing his sense of inadequate gratitude when Phyllida had appeared. So it was in the interests of them both that Peter had told John in confidence of her role with the Agency, and asked if a room could be made available for her in which to prepare her alter egos and if necessary sleep. Sleuthing in character inevitably led to requests to escort her home, and she and Peter had seen from the start of her unique role that the only way she could protect her real identity was to tell them that her current character was staying at the Golden Lion. Once safely delivered there, she would revert to herself and go home as the unknown Phyllida Moon. In the same way, she had always arrived at the hotel at the start of the day's (or night's) investigation as herself, parking in an unobtrusive spot behind it and going up to her small, spartan room via the back stairs, there to assume her current persona. To Peter and Phyllida's own gratitude, John had never asked any questions, even acting as Phyllida's chauffeur on occasion without inquiry as to what he was helping to thwart or assist. His young staff in Reception, schooled by him, maintained the same admirable lack of curiosity.

'Mr Piper!' Tracy and Sharon in chorus, looking pleased and interested – as far as they ever went.

'Good morning, ladies. Is Mr Bright in?'

'He will be to you. Come through.'

Peter noted the query in both pairs of immaculately made-up eyes, but neither girl voiced it.

'Dr Piper to see you,' Tracy said in the office doorway, as Peter hung modestly back.

'Peter! Come in! Come in! I hope I know the reason for your visit.'

'Yes, John. She's coming home. Tomorrow.'

'That's wonderful! I'll have the bed aired.'

'Same room?'

'Of course.'

'Good. I suspect . . . she's going to be grateful for a bit of continuity.'

'Family bereavement?'

It was the only question Peter could remember John Bright ever having asked in connection with Phyllida.

'I don't know. She hasn't said.' He had to work hard for a moment to conceal his shock. 'I suppose it could be.' Someone close . . . mother or father nursed through the final stages . . . He had perhaps misunderstood, been unduly pessimistic. Savagely Peter suppressed another absurd surge of hope. 'We seem to have got into a habit of reticence.'

'Not a bad one, I should say, in your business. Well, Peter, I know how delighted everyone here will be to have her back. The girls are as busy as ever, but I suspect life at the Golden Lion has lost a bit of its savour for them since Miss Moon went away.'

'It's the same across the Square.'

'It must be. Coffee? Or a drink – it's almost noon?'

'Thanks, but I've a spot of business.'

Peter left the hotel by the front entrance, but after a glance at the Agency building, seeing no signs of life at either the entrance or the windows, plunged immediately down one of the narrow lanes on each side of the hotel that led to The Parade.

It might have been February, but the air this morning was soft and mild, and the pale sun had roused a sparkle on the gently hiccuping sea. Peter crossed the road and the wide pavement beyond it, and rested his arms on the rail that ran out of sight to either side of him like a long, blue arrow, thinking how bizarre it was to have seen Phyllida more recently on television than he had seen her in the flesh – it hadn't been long after her disappearance to Scotland that Independent Television had shown the crime series *A Policeman's Lot* in which she had played the plum part of the policeman hero's sister, a private eye.

'Seen her' was an overstatement, Peter reflected, as he took a deep, open-mouthed breath and felt salt on his tongue. She'd worn no prosthetics, she'd been neither younger nor older than her thirty-eight years, but she hadn't looked or sounded in the least like Phyllida Moon. Not just because she was a good actress, he mused; there was also her passionate determination to protect the anonymity essential for her work with the Agency, the work she'd told him (he'd repeated her words over and over in his head since her departure) was the real stuff of her daily life.

Unless Edinburgh won . . .

It was hard to have an enemy you knew nothing about and might never encounter face to face. Phyllida had told him she was coming back, but not that she was coming back alone, or for good.

He'd surely know *something* more by tomorrow; it was futile to exhaust himself today against the unyielding rock of his current ignorance. The one thing he did know already was that she would let little time go by before asking him anxiously if he had heard anyone speculate on the likeness between the new feisty female on prime-time TV and the quiet woman who sat irregularly in Seaminster's reference library, working on a book about women and the stage. He would be able, of course, to tell her no, to assure her that even John Bright and the girls in the Golden Lion's Reception had failed to comment that the actress with the name in the credits they didn't recognize looked uncannily like Miss Moon. Who had been away from Seaminster for all those weeks in the spring . . .

No, Phyllida's TV secret was safe, Peter decided as he turned his gaze away from the fine pencil-line of the horizon. And if the studios wanted her for a sequel, as he had to face that in due course they surely would, her absence then would be nothing compared to the absence that was coming to a close tomorrow . . .

Yet he was grateful to the TV company that might take her away again: she'd come to the Agency in the first place in search of a job that would give her some hands-on experience of the role she had been contracted to play. And he had sent her away!

Peter remembered their first meeting with a catch of breath. But she hadn't taken his no for an answer: she'd presented herself as a client, the husky-voiced American sophisticate with whom Steve had fallen in love at first sight, and they'd sat together over drinks in Seaminster's ritzy Connaught Hotel, discussing her make-believe problem until she'd excused herself and come back as Miss Phyllida Moon, and he'd enrolled her then and there as a temporary member of his staff . . .

Peter swung away from the rail and walked The Parade as far as the short upward slope of road where Phyllida lived, his hands in his pockets and his fingers caressing the pair of keys he had kept in one or other of them since her departure.

It was only after she had left, and he had let himself gingerly in through her front door, that he realised this was the first time she had invited him into her house. But he had never invited her to his flat, either; all their time together had been spent in the civilised set of Agency rooms where he passed so many non-working hours and even slept sometimes on the big squashy sofa in the middle of the restroom. It wasn't that he didn't like his own place: Peter suspected it was because it reflected his chaotic private life that he felt more comfortable with Phyllida in the place that reflected his orderly conduct of business.

He'd deputed Jenny to be at Phyllida's in the afternoon, to supervise the firm of cleaners he was sending in as a welcome-home present, but the house still looked in good order, thanks to Jenny's regular borrowing of the keys to have 'just a bit of a dust round'. But he was sure it was Phyllida who had made up a clean bed before leaving. The sheets felt clammy despite his or Jenny's regular toing and froing of the curtains and Jenny's turning the electric blanket on for the half-hour or so she was wielding the duster. Peter turned it on now, deciding the bed would be nicely aired by the time he'd made a late-afternoon visit to Sainsbury's and bought in some basics and one or two other things he knew she particularly liked. He'd ring the new would-be client before the working day was out and accept the case, and then there would be the expectant tomorrow, with maybe a telephone call from Phyllida to tell them she was safely home, and the day after that she would come through the Agency door.

'You look different,' Steve said, following the few silent seconds in which Phyllida stood with her back to the door in mutual contemplation of the three-man reception committee.

'I don't know how, exactly,' Steve went on, ignoring Jenny's sharp 'Shush'.

'*You* don't, Steve. Or you, Jenny.' Phyllida's inquiring gaze reached Peter's face, and stayed there. 'Or Peter.' She moved away from the door and the committee broke ranks as Peter indicated his open doorway.

'Let's have coffee,' he suggested.

'It's ready.' Jenny had turned towards the kitchen, but not before Phyllida had noticed the look of protective anxiety in her face. It touched her, and for a moment the tears she thought she had at least temporarily subdued threatened to resurface.

'Thanks, Peter. It's good to see you all. I've thought of you every day.' That was true.

'And we've thought of you.' Steve reddened, looking surprised by his eloquence.

'Come in and sit down.'

Phyllida followed Peter into his office, took her usual chair facing his across the big desk. It was a comfort to look for Steve's usual performance when they were together in the boss's office – attempting to lean nonchalantly against the desk, failing, and drawing up a chair – but this morning he went straight to the chair, his eyes on her face as he felt for it behind him. Jenny was there with the coffee before they were settled, and Phyllida could sense that they were drawing out the play of taking first sips and choosing biscuits as long as they could.

'It's amazing,' Peter said, as the biscuit plate was finally returned to the tray. 'On Monday I had a call from a potential client and was thinking how tailor-made the case would be for you when you rang. So it's straight back to work if it suits you.'

'It does.' A slight inward trickle of warmth, if not, as in the past, the surge of adrenaline.

'I'll tell you about it when you've . . . when we've . . . I mean . . .'

'You mean when I've given you an explanation for a six-month absence. Which I'll do now.' But Phyllida lapsed into silence, staring out over the irregular roofs of buildings at the grey-white sparkle of the sea, always a source of comfort and inspiration.

It was the sound of Steve shifting in his seat that brought her back to them. 'I'm sorry. It's difficult. But I have to tell you . . . A few weeks after I arrived in Edinburgh I got married.'

'Phyllida! How wonderful!' That was Jenny, her hitherto grave face transfigured. Peter, Phyllida noted, had no expression on his face at all, and Steve had flushed and was looking wary.

'It was. It is. Although I've come back to you a widow. My husband died a couple of weeks ago. We were expecting it,' she went on quickly, over what was now a general shifting of position and a cry of rebellion from Jenny. There was something at last in Peter's face, but she couldn't read it. 'I married Dr Jack Pusey, who I met when he was Director of Seaminster's Botanic Garden before he went to work at the Botanic Gardens in Edinburgh.' Now there was recognition in Peter's face, and she caught and held his eyes long enough to extract a silent promise that he would not enlighten his other members of staff if they failed to connect the name with the man Phyllida had met in character during an investigation

14

in which he had briefly been one of a group of suspects.

It wouldn't have mattered – and not a lot mattered at the moment anyway – but she was mildly relieved that there was no change in the two young faces. Steve grunted and looked down at his knees, and Jenny said, 'Oh, Phyllida . . .' as her eyes swam with tears.

'We both knew what was going to happen.'

'Did you marry him out of kindness?' Steve asked, his head jerking up. 'To comfort his last days?'

'Send him out!' Jenny begged Peter.

'It's all right,' Phyllida intervened swiftly, as Peter sent a thunderous look in Steve's direction. 'I want you to know that I married Jack because I loved him, and I wish I could have spent the rest of my life with him. Now! I'd like to leave it at that, and I'd like to get back to work.' Phyllida smiled into each troubled face in turn. 'I hope you have some idea what it's meant to me, knowing you were here and waiting for me.'

'You'll stay with us?' Steve asked, his wary glance shifting from Peter to Jenny.

'I will.'

'I've seen John Bright,' Peter told her. 'Your room's ready for you.'

'So you're Mrs Pusey,' Jenny said.

'Yes. But let's stick to Phyllida Moon here, behind the scenes. And Miss Bowden front of house.' Miss Bowden – a no-nonsense unmarried woman ten years or so older than Phyllida – was the persona that allowed her to appear in front of clients and take her own cases without jeopardising her anonymity. 'At home, now, I'll be Phyllida Pusey.' Because, first and foremost, she wanted to carry Jack's name, but also because Phyllida Pusey lacked the past that there was always the slight risk could one day breach the precious anonymity of Phyllida Moon.

Three

'*Would it be possible for me to make an appointment to see Dr Pusey?*'

'*I'm sorry . . .*'

'*Yes?*'

'*I'm afraid Dr Pusey is on extended leave of absence.*'
Soft, clear Edinburgh voice.

'*But he's only been . . . Is he ill?*'

'*Dr Pusey is unwell.*'

'*And you can't tell me when he'll be back at work?*'

'*I . . . No. I'm afraid I can't.*'

'*And even though I'm an old friend I don't suppose you can give me his home telephone number. It isn't in the book.*'

'*Dr Pusey hasn't been in Edinburgh for very long. And no, I'm afraid I can't give you his number. You'll understand, it's standard practice . . .*'

'*Of course.*'

'*Perhaps, though, in the circumstances . . . Hold on a minute, will you, please.*'

A snatch of Vivaldi.

'*I'm sorry to have kept you waiting. I can tell you that Dr Pusey is currently in hospital.*'

'*Ah . . . Can you tell me which hospital?*'

'*Edinburgh General. I'm afraid that's all . . .*'

'*Thank you. You've been very kind.*'

'I'm afraid it wasn't very much.'
Afraid. Afraid . . .

Phyllida shook her head and made herself smile at Peter
across his desk. He was half-smiling himself, sadly, and as
their eyes met he put out his hand and she put out hers and
the hands just managed to meet and clasp, firmly enough
for him to feel the hardness of the gold ring on the third
finger of her left hand. Before her departure, that finger
had been bare.

'You'll have to forgive me if I disappear somewhere
inside myself every now and again. I promise not to do
it when I'm on the job.'

'I know you won't. Unless your character does. Look . . .
I'll just say this once. Knowing you, I don't suppose you'll
want to say any more than you've said already and I don't
know anything about your girlfriends and how helpful
they'll be. But if you want an ear . . . well, I've an idea
I'd be as good a listening post as anyone.'

'Never a listening post, Peter. But thanks. If it's to be
anyone, it will be you.'

'Thanks.' But he found himself ungrateful for the role he
had invited. 'So. You really do want to get back to work?'

'I've never been more eager. And I think you said
yesterday something had come in that would suit me.'

'I think so. I haven't seen the chap involved but I've
had a long talk with him over the phone.'

'So fire away.' Again not the usual surge of adrenaline,
but at least a sort of gentle bathing, as with a soothing
lotion, of her raw insides.

'Right.' Peter opened the thin folder in front of him and
began to read from the single sheet it contained: 'Hugh
Jordan, age forty-four, architect with office in Moss Street
and living at Venthams, Harcourt Avenue – that's going
out of Seaminster towards Billing.'

'I know it.'

'Of course. Married to Sandra Jordan, age thirty-nine, an estate agent he thinks could be having an affair with her business partner.' Peter looked up. 'No, it isn't exactly novel or exciting, but he sounded as if he might be an interesting sort of chap and he wasn't at all worked up – quite calm, I thought, unless he's an actor too. Anyhow, I thought you might get to make the acquaintance of the wife, in one or other of your personas.' Peter's eyes returned to his folder. 'They've been married for two years. He was married and widowed before, and has a daughter aged thirteen who's at Claire College, which you know all about from your first case here. Clever girl, he told me, and as he didn't puff himself or his family up in any other way, I suspect she is. When gently pressed he told me – and I quote – that "the usual practices" of married life were in place but that his wife seemed . . . distracted. He'd put it down at first to the refusal of his daughter to accept her stepmother with any grace.'

'So what's made him think it might be more than that?'

'Nothing. That's how he started off when he rang, telling me he didn't really have anything to go on beyond – I quote again – "a sudden instinct". Which had made him start to question whether his wife really needed to spend half her evenings working as well as the whole of her days. The partnership's Hardman and Andrews – Mrs Jordan was already in it when she married Hugh Jordan; Andrews is her maiden name. You'll be seeing a lot of the firm's rather tricksy signs in evidence about Seaminster at the moment. Sandra Jordan pleads pressure of business as excuse for her long working hours, including her working suppers with her business partner.'

'So Mr Jordan presented you with a suspect?'

'A chief suspect. When I questioned him, he didn't rule

out the possibility of someone else from inside or outside the office, with his wife using Hardman as cover.'

'Which suggests things aren't quite the way they should be between husband and wife, if Hugh Jordan's still uneasy even with the thought of Hardman out of the picture.'

'That's how it seems to me.'

'So you want me to be looking for a nice little flat?'

'Perhaps. First and foremost I'm seeing you – whoever you may be – asking if you can join Mrs Jordan in a crowded lunchtime café, or some such mild stratagem. The beauty of you is,' Peter went on, his expressive face illumined by a sudden triumphant smile, 'that thanks to all your incarnations, one doesn't cut out any others.'

'There's another possibility now, Peter. Jack had to rest for a part of every day, so I took a crash computer course. It was a tremendous help, and if I hadn't been . . . I think I would've enjoyed it.'

'Oh, Phyllida.'

'So I can now get temping jobs in offices. Nothing too specialised or advanced, but I can word-process and work with databases and spreadsheets.'

'That's wonderful!'

'So Miss Bowden will be able to give Jenny a hand. Tactfully, of course.'

'Of course. But I want to talk to you about your role at the other end of the scale. I want to take you into partnership, Phyllida. And not because I'm feeling so desperately sorry for you. You know I mentioned it before you went away.'

'Yes. The thought of it was as helpful as the computer course. To Jack as well.'

For the first time since she had come to work for the Peter Piper Detective Agency, Phyllida got up from her chair in its owner's office and walked to one of his windows, where she stood looking out across the marine horizon until she felt confident she could go on speaking in her normal voice.

Peter waited in silence till she was back in her chair. 'I'll make an appointment with my solicitor for as soon as possible. What shall we call ourselves?'

'What you call yourself now.' She had thought about it before she had known what Edinburgh would bring. 'We can't sound any more arresting than the Peter Piper Agency. I came to you originally because of your name and the memories it stirred of the old rhyme. And the only name I could go public with is Bowden, which is hardly a draw.'

'All right.' Peter wondered if he had managed to keep his sense of relief out of his face, and Phyllida thought with affectionate amusement that she had caught a glimpse of it. 'It's only words; whatever we have up front won't alter the fact that you'll be half the business.'

'It won't upset Jenny. But Steve?'

For a moment they surveyed one another in silence.

'I don't think so,' Peter said eventually. 'I suspect he looks up to you and he doesn't like change; he'll probably see it as cementing you in. Whatever, though, we're going ahead. So I suppose it calls for a handshake.'

This time they rose together and met at the side of the desk, and this time it was Phyllida's right hand that Peter took, and felt the pearl ring on her little finger that had always been there. When their hands dropped he hesitated for a moment before putting his arms round her, and it was a relief to feel her relax against him, the silky top of her head fitting for an instant into the curve of his neck.

'Right!'

'Right!' They sat down. 'Any more to tell me about the Jordan household?'

'Jordan's mother-in-law lives in a self-contained piece of the house, but I gathered spends plenty of time *en famille*.

He told me about her sort of warily; I got the impression she was a person, as well as a topic of conversation, that he was inclined to tiptoe around – whether because she's the mother-in-law from hell or simply a rather formidable matriarch I couldn't tell on the telephone. He's coming to see me this afternoon, so I should get a better idea of things. I'd like Miss Bowden to be around, if that won't jeopardise your making use of her when you start investigating his wife.'

'I know it's hard to imagine, but Miss Bowden comes in a number of guises so she won't be at risk. And he'll scarcely notice her. People don't.'

'I know. But they might notice Phyllida Moon Pusey, so I think you should cross the square before we go any further and assume Miss Bowden. I didn't expect to see you this morning as yourself.'

'Six months ago I'd have gone from home to the Golden Lion on a reflex, but just at the moment my precious anonymity doesn't seem quite so important. Which is absurd, seeing that without it I couldn't do the only thing I want to do.'

The unspoken *now* hung between them, and Peter accorded it a silence that Phyllida broke as she got to her feet.

'Miss Bowden's in the car behind the hotel. I'll go and put her on.'

'John and the girls will be glad to see you. There was great excitement yesterday when I went over with the news.'

'That's nice. I'm not feeling much just now, Peter, beyond . . . but I do feel that. And the welcome here.'

'That's for as long as you want it, which I hope will be a hell of a long time.' He had been going to say *You belong here*, but managed to turn his words in the nick of time. He wasn't all that strong on empathy, but even he had to be aware that at that moment she would be unlikely to see herself as belonging anywhere. 'I expect you're already on the way to deciding how you're going to approach our new subject.'

'A few ideas are turning.' Starting to bathe, thank heaven, the aching contours of her mind. 'If Miss Bowden comes back to you early this afternoon?'

'I'll be here.'

Phyllida gritted her teeth against the inevitably weakening effect of Jenny's sympathy, but even the smile and the held-out hand were enough to engender another speechless moment.

'I'm going to do what I should have done before I came in,' she managed as she started towards the door. 'Assume Miss Bowden. I'll be back by two at the latest. And Jenny . . .' This time it was the distraction of slight anxiety for which Phyllida was grateful as she continued to return Jenny's warily affectionate smile. 'I've just been telling Peter, my husband had to rest for part of each day, so I took a crash computer course. Which means I can give you basic cover if you need it, and let you have flu with an easy mind.'

'Oh, *Phyllida*!'

Now it was Jenny's eyes filling with tears; she was getting to her feet and coming round the reception desk, and it was for her sake even more than for her own that Phyllida held out her arms. 'It's all right, it's all right,' she murmured into the curly crown of Jenny's quivering head, and was astounded by the sudden shaft of anger that shot through her. No, it wasn't all right; like everything else in her life apart from the Peter Piper Detective Agency it was cruel and wrong. Every good thing had been denied her, and then when the best thing of all had appeared it had been snatched away . . .

No! Returning Jenny's hug with the fierceness of her

rejection of this would-be onset of self-pity, Phyllida reminded herself that if she hadn't met Jack Pusey she would have been as happy now as any woman alive. And would she really prefer to begin her working partnership in the emotional chill of the self she had been before she had come to love him?

'No bitterness, Jenny,' Phyllida said, as she drew back and wiped a tear from Jenny's cheek. 'Jack loved me as much as I love him, and he would never have left me if he'd had the choice, so I'll never truly lose him.' *And the dazzle of him will never fade.*

Jenny managed another smile. 'It's wonderful if you can think like that. I don't think I could, but you're . . . well, you're you, and I'm so glad you're back with us, even though you'd rather not be.'

'Without Jack in the flesh there's nowhere in the world I'd rather be than the Peter Piper Detective Agency. Now, I'd better go and put Miss Bowden on before anyone—'

But the outer door was already opening, and Phyllida slid into the cloakroom without waiting to see who was pushing it forward.

Not a cloakroom, she was happily reminded, as she stood looking round what Peter always proudly called the king of bathrooms. Almost as large as the restroom and the general office, it had all its original fittings, including a high dangling lavatory chain with flower-decked ceramic handle and a magnificent bath on dinosaur feet in which Peter had confessed to her, just before she went away, that he was wont to soak at nights before going home or dossing down on the big squashy sofa that was the centrepiece of the restroom. Jenny yearned to get her hands on the king of bathrooms and transform it, as she had transformed the old kitchen, into the last word in modernity; but Peter, with Phyllida's support, guarded it zealously. Steve had never expressed any views, but Phyllida suspected from his

23

silence each time the controversy raged that he approved of it as it was.

When she peered out, Reception was empty and she could hear voices from behind Peter's closed door, the female one veering between hesitancy and confidence.

'An appointment?'

'No.' Jenny looked up from the computer. 'But she seemed anxious and Peter said he'd see her.'

'I must go before she emerges, or someone else comes.'

This time Phyllida entered the Golden Lion through the revolving front door, and went up to Reception. Gail and Tracy were both there, and allowed their pleasure to show in their faces and remain there – a laxity, Phyllida was confident, they would not permit themselves the next time they saw her.

'Welcome back!' they said, in *sotto voce* chorus.

'It's awfully good to see you,' Tracy said. Gail told her her room was ready.

'Thanks. It's good to see you both, too.'

Phyllida trod her back route warily: she herself, now, was a character she no longer entirely knew, certainly knew less well than her Miss Bowdens and her mature sophisticates, and she was unsure of her reactions. When she had shut the door behind her and was alone in her small, anonymous working space, the utter silence with which it instantly surrounded her, its spartan fittings, its small window on to a dark inner well, seemed to underline the loss of Jack's presence, allegory of her ever-now-to-be solitude, and standing rigid against the door she experienced a moment of loneliness as intense as any she had yet undergone. She, for whom the norm throughout her life had been herself alone – even, she had learned as Jack's wife, when she had been Gerald's – had lost her self-sufficiency.

For a rebellious second Phyllida yearned to recover it

by undoing the immediate miraculous past, but as she sank down weeping on the bed she found herself gradually suffused with a confidence that it would eventually return to protect her in a warmer, far more positive guise.

Because Jack, now, would be inside it.

By the time Phyllida was back on her feet she knew she had defeated the utter bleakness that had assailed her on her first confrontation with the working solitude that lay before her, and that she would be able to rebuff its inevitable future sorties until it ceased its attempts to overcome her.

Meanwhile Miss Bowden was waiting, and required some effort of reacquaintance after an absence that felt far longer than the six months she and Phyllida had been apart. Because they were to be increasingly together, Phyllida had allowed her Agency version – the only Mary Bowden to lay public claim to her generic name – an ironic sense of humour and a trace of warmth lacking in the dry sticks who knocked on doors and asked apparently innocent questions, or sat alone at café tables, and when she was ready to leave the room Miss Bowden gave her creator a slight looking-glass smile that was not out of character.

Phyllida had wondered if there would be respite from her heartache with the assumption of another persona, and before Miss Bowden had completed her descent of the back stairs she was aware of the effect of a strong pain-killer: the acute edge was dulled. Which was probably good news for her performance, she reflected as she passed Reception with no more than near-imperceptible nods from all parties, reminded for the first time since Jack's death that she herself had an ironic sense of humour.

'Miss Bowden! Good morning!' John Bright, formal but smiling. 'Have you the time to come through to the office for a moment?'

'Of course.'

She hadn't said anything to the girls but she must tell John, and sanction him to tell them something.

'I can't say you look well, or otherwise,' he said, when they were alone and he had the sherry decanter in his hand. 'Miss Bowden forbids it. So you must tell me how you are.'

'I'm all right, John. Even though I have to tell you that I got married while I was away, and that my husband has died. So it will be good to get back to work.'

She tried to smile at him reassuringly, but when he had put the decanter down and his hand on her shoulder, both of them were unable to speak and remained in silence until he went back to the decanter, poured its pale contents into two exquisite glasses that some fragment of her mind was free to admire, and drew up a chair beside her.

'It's all right, John, really,' Phyllida managed then, looking down at the neat skirt of Miss Bowden's suit rather than into his shocked, concerned face. 'Jack and I knew from the start that we wouldn't have long, and what we did have was perfect. And now I'm going into business partnership with Peter.'

'I'm delighted to hear *that*.'

'Thank you.' Phyllida looked up, and it was John who was blinking away tears. 'And for keeping my room for me. Peter's got a case for me as well as a partnership, but I can't tell you yet how many women will be coming and going in the Golden Lion during the next few weeks, or what they'll look like, because I don't know.'

Four

'*D*r *Pusey . . .'*
      '*Ah! Good afternoon! Forgive me, I was dozing. I wasn't expecting medical attention during visiting hours.'*
      '*I'm not . . . I'm a visitor.'*
      '*For me? I'm afraid I don't . . .'*
      '*May I sit down? I'll leave if you get any . . . any visitors you know.'*
      '*Please, this is intriguing . . . I apologise for having taken the more comfortable of my chairs. And I'm not expecting any . . . other visitors. All right? Now, what can I do for you?'*
      Oh, my dear love!
      '*You can tell me . . . You've no recollection of ever having seen me before?'*
      '*Well, now . . .' Searching brown eyes. 'I've no idea of your name, but I do somehow feel that we've met. Will you enlighten me? And forgive me if I oughtn't to need enlightenment?'*
      '*You do need it. The last time we met I stopped by your table in the restaurant at Seaminster Botanic Garden, and told you how much I enjoyed visiting. Which I'm sure a lot of people did. But so far as I'm concerned, before then . . .' So hard to bring out, despite the myriad rehearsals. 'I met you as Fiona Steele.'*
      Recognition, then. Shock. Controlled anger.
      No time to fumble.

'My name's Phyllida Moon, Jack, and I'm an actress who sleuths in character for a detective agency. I joined your art class in Seaminster last year as a red-haired Scot called Fiona Steele' – cue to assume Fiona's voice – *'because I was investigating the disappearance of the two women members of the class who were found dead on a roundabout—'*

'And had been the objects of a mock courtship by two young friends of mine. Which, I now see, is why Fiona agreed to have drinks with us.' A flinching at the change of voice, but still the anger.

'Yes. But then . . . By the time Fiona had to disappear, I . . .'

'Yes?'

'I found it difficult to let her go.'

'But you did. You're a true professional, Mrs . . . I'm sorry, I forget your . . . real name.'

Her turn to flinch. *'Phyllida Moon. Yes, I'm professional. But when Fiona had gone – and Dr Pusey with her – I found . . . I discovered that it wouldn't do.'*

No more anger. No expression at all. *'So what took you so long to come and find me?'*

'I was coming sooner, but I was ill.'

'Ah . . . Fiona Steele was married. Are you?'

'Not now. Are you?'

'Not now. Nurse! D'you think you could rustle up an extra cup of tea?'

She had thought it would be hardest at home, because of her abiding awareness that if he had lived he would have been there with her; but she had discovered that it was as hard in the working space where she had been and always would be alone, and she was finding it as hard here, in the corner of the Golden Lion's smaller bar, where she had ended up with a sandwich and a glass of wine after fleeing downstairs. Doubly hard, because this was the first time she had appeared in public as Miss Bowden without the necessity for it, and during the short time that she was in the bar her sorrow mingled with a sense of professional guilt.

'The world's back to rights.' Her old friend, head barman Mick, pausing in his whip-around wiping of the empty tables. 'Though I'd sooner have served the American charmer.'

'You will, Mick, you will.' Mick's favourite, Phyllida recalled with a fresh pang, had been Fiona Steele. She herself he had met only once, when he had been helping out at Reception during the last winter's flu epidemic, and she suspected that Phyllida Moon was no more real to him than the rest of her characters.

'Everything all right now?' John Bright, at her request, had explained her absence to his staff as the necessity for a temporary shouldering of family responsibilities.

'Yes. Thanks, Mick. Everything's fine.' Draining her glass, Phyllida realised with an inward grin – unfamiliar and briefly warming – how absurd she had been to feel guilty about Miss Bowden's presence in the Caprice Bar: now that she was appearing openly in the Agency there could be no secret that she worked there, and even so austere an employee would surely cross the square from time to time for a quick lunchtime snack

Employee? As she got to her feet and told Mick he would be seeing that morning's manifestation again, Phyllida realised she and Peter had yet to discuss whether the existence of his new partner was to be made public; if it was, it could only be in the person of Miss Bowden, and her own instinct was not to look for publicity where it could be avoided.

She intended telling him what she felt as soon as she was back in the Agency, but the strange expression on Jenny's face when she turned round from the computer drove the question from her mind.

Jenny's eyes were dancing, and she made Phyllida think of a girl in school assembly desperately trying to suppress an untimely fit of the giggles.

'Share the joke?'

'I'd love to.' Jenny spoke on a snort of laughter. 'But Peter's bagged it.'

'So can I go in?'

'He said as soon as you arrived.'

Peter's expression as he rose from his chair was not unlike Jenny's.

'Dear Miss Bowden! I'm so very glad to see you.'

'And I am not amused, Dr Piper.' Miss Bowden sat primly down, and Phyllida leaned across the desk. 'So will you please let me in on the joke that appears to be creasing you and Jenny!'

'Yes. Y'know' – Peter wandered across to a window, and stood looking out – 'I've wondered ever since I started the Agency if this would happen one day.'

'*What* would happen?'

'Sorry.' Peter came hastily back to his desk and sat down. 'You know this Hugh Jordan who has an appointment for three o'clock?'

'I hadn't forgotten.'

'Well, about twelve – I think you'd just left – a woman arrived without an appointment and asked Jenny if she could see the boss. As I'd nothing on before lunch and no lunch date I told Jenny to send her in.' Peter paused, tapping another slim folder on the desk in front of him.

'*Go on!*'

'Sorry. The woman's name turned out to be Sandra Jordan.'

'I don't believe it.'

'It's not all *that* unlikely, we *are* the better of the two Seaminster agencies – well, we've got the more attractive address. Anyway, my visitor was indeed the wife of the said Hugh. She told me she was concerned her husband could be having an affair with his secretary, who's been his office right arm for several years, and asked if we could put a tail on him. As I said, I've always wondered—'

'Did you take her on?'

'Well, yes.' Phyllida had learned long ago that the sudden pleading look in the brown eyes was one of Peter's more easily assumed weapons. 'You're back, and there's Steve . . . and what excuse could I give for turning her down?'

'None. But it'll be tricky. She didn't coincide with her husband this time, but she could do another day and we'll have lost them both.'

'I know. So let's make the most of the situation while we've got it. It'll be interesting to see how we feel about them *vis-à-vis* one another.'

'You still want me to take the wife?'

'When you've looked at the file on the husband you'll see why I'd like you to take them both.' Peter slid it across the desk, then looked up at his wall clock. 'He'll be here in an hour. If you're in my office when he arrives it won't seem contrived.'

'Right. What did you think of Mrs Jordan?'

'Tense. A tad ill at ease. Rather pretty in an apologetic kind of a way.'

'Devastated?'

'Bewildered. I suppose by what she was afraid might be going on, but she also gave me the impression of someone who'd made a snap decision and was already wondering why. Unlike her husband, who I suspect had rehearsed his performance before picking up the phone. Which I know doesn't mean that he isn't genuinely concerned. It's just that both of them seemed in their different ways . . . well, more wary than angry or upset.'

'Intriguing.' To Phyllida's relief – vying, now, with a

31

sense of disloyalty she knew Jack would dismiss with a
smile – the adrenaline was flowing. And the tears, at the
sudden vivid image of that smile. 'Sorry, Peter,' she said as
she wiped them away. 'I'm looking forward to this one.'

'I know you are. So am I. And if you feel . . . over-
taken . . . any time, and the bathroom's occupied and I
don't have a client, for goodness' sake come in here!'

'I will. Thanks. I'm fine now.'

'I'd worry if you couldn't cry . . . Oh, yes – d'you sing,
by the way?'

'I was in the choir at school, and I've sung now and
again onstage.'

'Good. I'm hoping you'll cross the floor and join the
choir where Jordan sings with his secretary. All right?'

'Yes.'

'Good. Details later, but you'll be wanting to think about
what sort of chorister you're going to be.'

Phyllida was back with Peter five minutes before Hugh
Jordan was due to arrive, and precisely at the appointed
time they heard his powerfully pleasant voice through the
closed door as he greeted Jenny. Peter and Phyllida had a
glimpse of her flushed, flattered face as she showed him
into Peter's office, and as Phyllida rose to meet the tall
figure, she understood Jenny's reaction: even Miss Bowden
was blinking in the light of his intimate smile. The sort of
man, Phyllida saw immediately, who has the disabling gift
of a smile that seems intended exclusively for whomever
it lights on. 'Dr Piper? And . . . ?'

'My partner. Miss Bowden.'

The surge of anger at herself for having failed to tell
Peter of her preference for an unstated role made Phyllida
glad of Miss Bowden's slightly tinted spectacles. But as
the respect in Hugh Jordan's eyes for Peter was switched
to Miss Bowden, Phyllida conceded that what she had

thought was a reasoned preference could have been her personal shrinking from the limelight, and that Peter had been right. Whatever, the decision had been made.

'Miss Bowden.'

'Mr Jordan. If you will excuse me, I have other business to attend to. I am leaving you in very capable hands.'

'I don't doubt it.'

Outside, the flush had only partly receded from Jenny's face. 'Just imagine it,' she said wistfully as Phyllida shut Peter's door. 'Arriving at a film première on *his* arm!'

'It *is* imagination, Jenny, for the vast majority of us.' Phyllida was mildly amused to find herself unsure whether she was speaking in her own or Miss Bowden's persona. She was certainly speaking in Miss Bowden's voice, with its flat northern vowels and scarcely varying pitch.

'Peter was telling me . . . His partner's going to be Miss Bowden.'

'I'm afraid so. The Agency name won't change, though.'

'I know. It's just . . . I wish it could have been someone else.'

'So do I, Jenny.' Phyllida saw Jenny's face lighten as she reverted to her own voice. 'But Miss Bowden makes sense. We don't want a big personality. And I can vary Miss B in so many ways and still use her in the field. If we had the mature American, say, that would be the end of her anywhere else.'

'I know. It's just . . . I shall miss our lunches.'

'We'll still have them, Miss Bowden has to eat. Now, I'll take a look at the file on Mr Jordan in the general office, then see what Peter made of him and what he said to suggest the sort of woman who should be the first to scrape acquaintance with his wife.'

Phyllida had no difficulty hearing Hugh Jordan's farewell to Jenny through the closed office door, and when the outer door had clicked to she went immediately back to Peter.

'Well?'

'Sit down.' But Peter himself got up as she did so, and wandered across to a window. 'A chap very much in charge of his life,' he said to the view. 'In apparently dramatic contrast to his wife.'

'Any further clues to how he's feeling?'

'Nope. He *told* me he was cut up, but I couldn't see any evidence of it. I could hazard a guess he's the kind of man who would react pretty quickly if his *amour propre* was threatened. As for his feelings . . . if he has them, he hides them well. My instinct tells me his primary concern for approaching us is social rather than personal, but that could be a grossly unjust misreading.'

'Men who automatically charm women – and he's one of those, Peter – often fail signally to charm men.'

'Ouch.'

'I presume he gave you the customary timetable of his wife's daily doings?'

'It's all here.' Peter looked down at the new piece of A4 heading the thin file in front of him. 'She's left home by nine a.m., Monday to Friday, but can get back at night any time between six and nine thirty p.m. And she sometimes works at weekends.'

'Not a delegator.'

'Like her partner.'

'Has Hugh Jordan met him?'

'Oh, yes, they've had him to dinner, if not recently. All very amicable, but Jordan said he sensed undercurrents. Having met Mrs Jordan, though, I can imagine undercurrents being in evidence in other situations too. Not a happy bunny.'

'At home. It has to be different at work, or she wouldn't be a partner.'

'The partnership could be down to her *beaux yeux*.'

'So I shall have to be a client at some stage, to see her at work.'

'You took the words out of my mouth.' Peter surged to his feet and crossed back to the window, over the short route that must surely one day show his daily trail in the pale-gold carpet. 'I wish a million times for your sake that you weren't here, Phyllida, but for mine – I can't tell you how glad I am.' It was an effort to keep his gladness professional, but Peter had a strong sense of fair play, and even in his mind he was trying. 'Have you any idea who you're going to be first?'

'I think I'll start with an attempt at friendship, so I'll take on a sympathetic personality and save the Miss Bowden variant for a request to look at properties. I'm inclining steadily towards the American sophisticate, who might appeal to Hugh Jordan too if she gets access to the household. I'll use a Miss Bowden type for the choir, I think, as I'll be observing there rather than trying to make friends, and the less conspicuous the better.'

'I'm with you all the way. You'll see from my notes that Mrs Jordan tends to eat in the same café when she has time for more than a sandwich at her desk. Sometimes with her partner and sometimes on her own.'

'Fine. If I can't participate, I can observe.' But not that day: it was already afternoon. Barely three o'clock, and Phyllida's empty house did not beckon. 'Which are Hugh Jordan's choir nights?'

Peter opened the other slim folder. 'Tonight – Tuesday – and Friday. Seven thirty in the Aeolian Hall. Sandra Jordan told me they're always short of singers. The shortage of altos is apparently chronic. Is there any chance . . . ?'

'My voice had dropped by the time I was thirty.'

'You are the most amazing . . . You'll see in the file an advert from the Seaminster freebie asking for recruits and

35

giving rehearsal dates, so you'll be able to present yourself without arousing any suspicions. But even you . . . Can you really get someone together by this evening?'

'Of course.' The sense of relief was as warming as a cloak thrown over her shoulders. 'Another uncharismatic female but nothing like Miss Bowden except probably for her age – I'm thinking of a far less reticent woman, sort of comfortable, who'll be seen as safe by wives and unsexy by husbands. This ought to make conversation easy and at the same time give me the opportunity to learn anything there is to learn by eavesdropping as well as through chat, because she won't be giving out danger signals as she wanders around . . . I'm thinking this out as I go along. Does it make sense?'

'Yes.'

Out in Reception, Steve was in his usual position of taking the support of the general office doorpost. He looked gloomily at Miss Bowden as she emerged from Peter's office. 'Jenny tells me Miss Bowden's the new partner.'

'I'm afraid so, Steve. It makes sense.'

'I suppose so.'

'Lauren Bacall is going to be around too, in the near future.' Phyllida could see that Jenny was trying less successfully than she was to hide her amusement at the pink flooding into Steve's face, but she was helped by the fact that Miss Bowden had not seen the joke. 'We've got our first double case, Steve: a husband and wife asking for a tail on one another. You'll need to be involved.'

'He asked to see you as soon as you got in,' Jenny contributed.

'Okay.' With a shrug in Miss Bowden's direction, Steve ambled across to Peter's door.

'When I've some idea how the week's going to pan out,' Phyllida said to Jenny as the door closed behind him, 'will you come and have supper with me at home?'

Jenny's shining-eyed acceptance of the invitation was a slight help as Phyllida crossed the square to the Golden Lion and made her way up the back stairs, but when she entered her office bedroom Miss Bowden ceased to protect her and the crumpled face in the mirror was her own, grotesquely painted. Staring at it with distaste, for that moment she was glad the necessity for another version of Miss Bowden was far enough away to demand a new start, and when she had ripped off the wig and torn her way out of her top clothes, she plunged into the tiny bathroom and scrubbed mercilessly at her face. Then came back into the bedroom, flung herself on the bed, and cried herself to sleep.

When she awoke an hour later she rang down for a jug of coffee and began to think constructively of the evening ahead. She was back at work, she accepted with relief as she poured her first cup, but the new Mrs Pusey still had a long way to go before she met up with the old professional Miss Moon, and Phyllida suspected that she might never quite reach her.

Five

'*The bell . . . I must go. Shall I come tomorrow?*'
    '*I thought that would have gone without saying.*'
    '*I'm sorry, I'm afraid I tend to . . . My characters are the women with self-confidence.*'
    '*So I recall. Tomorrow at this time I shall be at home. Let me write down my address.*'
    '*Which I might never have discovered if I'd come a day later.*'
    '*So you had to come today . . . Here you are. A first-floor flat in the New Town, provided by my new employers.*'
    '*Thank you. Jack! I haven't even asked you why you're in hospital, there's been so much else . . . I'm glad you're better.*'
    '*Ah . . . I'll tell you about my health tomorrow.*'
    '*Jack . . .*'
    '*I'll tell you all about it tomorrow. I promise. And give you a better cup of tea.*'

The impressively named Aeolian Hall was Seaminster's venue for all manner of musical events, both amateur and professional. Its main space was used for performances and there was a smaller space for rehearsal, as well as half a dozen tiny sound-proofed rooms containing upright pianos that could be rented for practice. There were also a couple of civilised conveniences and, Phyllida had learned from musical acquaintances, a small kitchen with hob, sink, and power point.

The Seaminster Choral Society (established 1967), although its performers and administrators were entirely amateur, had considerable local clout, which Phyllida reluctantly recalled as the slightly smiling, slightly untidy Miss Pamela Spence pushed open half of the brass-handled swing doors that led into the building.

Within, the low-lit, pillared entrance hall seemed to be milling with people who knew what they were doing and where they were going, and it was a relief, after a few confused seconds, when her eyes came to rest on a tall, white-haired man stationed just inside the doors and offering her an inquiring smile.

Phyllida approached him, her own reflexively reciprocal smile tallying with Miss Spence's.

'You look a little lost, my dear. Can I help you?'

'That's very kind. I wonder . . . if by any happy chance you're connected with the local choral society . . .'

'I am.'

'Oh, my goodness!' Miss Spence scrabbled round in her handbag and brought out a crumpled press cutting. 'I saw this advertisement in the paper. I've sung in choirs in the past.' All fictional and all safely disbanded, Phyllida reminded herself, on an encouraging surge of awareness of her ultimate omnipotence *vis-à-vis* this unsophisticated middle-aged lady. 'It says you're particularly short of altos, and that's what I sing.'

'Ah!' No mistaking the gleam of triumph. 'I'm very pleased to meet you, Mrs . . . ?'

'Miss Spence. Miss Pamela Spence. It says there's a rehearsal this evening . . .'

'There is indeed. Let me show you through to the rehearsal room.'

'But you appear to be waiting for someone. If you tell me—'

'I was waiting for you, Miss Spence. With more hope

39

than optimism, I have to admit; but whenever we insert an ad a few days before a rehearsal, one of us takes up a hopeful stance at the door. It's early, and when I've handed you over to our conductor I'll come back, although I hardly anticipate two contraltos in one evening. I'm Ted Evans, by the way. Bass.'

'There seem to be a great many people about,' Miss Spence observed, as she crossed the entrance hall at his side.

'There's a concert tonight. Folk. Not really our sort of thing so we don't mind the clash. Here we are!'

Mr Evans had led her through an archway into a long, narrow passage lined with doors, and halfway along threw one open with a flourish.

Beyond it was a larger space than Phyllida had expected, containing a rough semicircle of chairs, three deep, in front of a music stand on which rested a wad of unopened music. A pair of windows looked out on some sort of inner garden or courtyard, and about a dozen people were standing casually about, some of them with open sheet music in their hands that they were studying or discussing. One man was standing alone in front of an upright piano on which he was arranging more music.

For an instant raw fear touched Phyllida, a sensation unfamiliar since her earliest days in the theatre. It went as quickly as it came, but it had time to warn her that one may not emerge from a watershed precisely as one was when one entered it, and that her professional carapace might need some strengthening.

'Miss Spence? This is Charles Gardner, our leader and conductor. Charles, Miss Spence sings alto!'

'How absolutely splendid!'

Big, beaming, shambling. The sort of man, Phyllida had learned both in and out of character, who in the world of the arts could be a steely perfectionist beneath the

40

surface bonhomie. So she must keep that hovering fear out of her singing voice, or, in her own eyes at least, lose her professional status as well as her chance to join the Seaminster Choral Society.

'You had better hear me, Mr Gardner, before you rejoice.'

'The professional approach, Miss Spence! I welcome it.' Charles Gardner consulted the large watch on his left wrist, its face lacily shadowed by a frayed shirt cuff. 'There's plenty of time, and we're not all assembled by any means. Shall we go into a practice room? Thank you, Ted.'

There was no sign in the rehearsal room of Hugh Jordan, and as Phyllida accompanied Charles Gardner out into the corridor, she concentrated on her relief at learning there were choristers yet to come.

A few incompatible snatches of piano passages from behind the closed doors were making up an atonal concerto that carried Phyllida back to her schooldays. Gardner put his dark, curly head to a couple of the doors before knocking on a third, receiving no response, opening the door and beckoning her inside as he snapped on a light in the small windowless space.

'I shan't need much,' he said with a cheerful smile, as he sat immediately down on the stool and opened the piano lid. For a vivid, unnerving second, the few lines of gold print inside it carried Phyllida back to the pianos in the practice rooms at school: all defined in gold as *By Appointment to the late Queen Victoria*, and each inscription painstakingly modified by some long-gone wag into *he ate Queen Victoria* . . . She wrenched her mind back to the present as Charles Gardner spoke again.

'How about a descending scale?'

Before starting to get ready Phyllida had shut herself into her bathroom at the Golden Lion and opened her throat for the first time in months, and it had been all right. As she prepared to open it now, she tried not to think of what she knew to be inevitable: that this coming few seconds would be as concentratedly taxing as any that had ticked by since she had started to work for Peter, even without her alarming glimpse of what might be stage fright.

She heard the chord. She heard Gardner's 'All right, then?' She thought of Jack and started to sing, listening in gratified amazement to the warm steady tone she could hardly believe was issuing from her own mouth. If the fear had shown itself in public in any part of her, it would have shown in her voice. So it was defeated; and she had discovered that Jack would be her professional strength rather than her professional weakness. So long as for God's sake she didn't start crying . . .

'That's absolutely super. How about a verse of a hymn?'

Phyllida sang the first verse of Crimond, in which Gardner joined her halfway through the first line.

'Lovely. You can read music?'

'Yes. If a bit haltingly at first. I'm rusty.'

'Don't worry, that goes for a few of us. We've just started working on the *St John Passion*, which we're going to perform in Seaminster's grand parish church. Know it? The *Passion*, I mean.'

'I sang in it once. Long ago.' She really had, with her school choir. But she had loved it, and it might not all have to be sight-reading.

'Better and better. We're concentrating on the chorales tonight, probably your best introduction.' Charles Gardner rose from the piano stool, and his untidy bulk loomed above the woman who was not quite as tall as Phyllida Moon. 'So consider yourself recruited, Miss Spence. Come along now and I'll introduce you to the others. Particularly your fellow altos, of whom at the moment there are only seven.'

It was a relief to see Hugh Jordan's elegant figure in the

throng. He was standing close to a tall, handsome woman and they appeared to be the centre of a small group.

'Our soprano soloist, Marjorie Turnbull.' It was the name in Jordan's file, and Gardner was nodding towards the woman beside Jordan. 'And Hugh Jordan – the tall man beside her – is one of our most reliable tenors.'

Phyllida noted respect in all eyes as they reached the group, and the slight coming to attention. 'Good evening, everyone! May I introduce Miss Pamela Spence, who is going to do us the inestimable favour of singing contralto.'

There was an approving murmur, to which Miss Spence responded with a breathy 'Hello!' and a widening of her self-deprecating smile.

'Now. Wendy, may I place Miss Spence in your capable hands? Wendy Ashton leads our slim contralto band, Miss Spence, and she will look after you.' Charles Gardner looked round. 'Are we all met? Then let us begin.'

Hugh Jordan had, of course, accorded Miss Spence no more than a quick glance; one thing Phyllida would not learn in the persona of Miss Spence was his reaction to sexually attractive women; but the woman she was confident would enter his household at the invitation of his wife would surely give her some idea, even if she was unlucky enough to light on a character who was not his type . . .

'I shall do better next week.' Miss Spence was as wary of her own achievements as her creator, and hadn't in fact done too badly after a tentative start. 'If I may take a copy of the score home.'

Wendy Ashton smiled, and Phyllida gazed with respect at the deep bosom from which such powerful sounds had a few moments earlier emerged. 'Of course. And you did pretty well this week, Miss Spence. You have a true voice, and that's a foundation on which one can always build. Now, do have some coffee before you go.' Phyllida followed the stout lady's plodding progress across the rehearsal room to a trestle table, behind which a soprano and a tenor were standing, having brought in, respectively, two large jugs of coffee and milk. 'Milk? Help yourself to sugar. Now, if you'll excuse me . . .' With another encouraging smile, and carrying a cup of coffee before her as if it were a votive offering, Wendy Ashton made her way over to a couple of fellow altos.

Hugh Jordan and Marjorie Turnbull were approaching the coffee array, still giving the impression of being a pair, and Miss Spence slipped into a chair set conveniently beside the end of the trestle table where they were pausing.

'It went well tonight,' Jordan said. 'You're in good voice, Marjorie.'

'Yes. It felt good.' Complacency in the soft, low speaking voice and the large, dark eyes. Justified, Phyllida had to concede; Marjorie Turnbull had a fine voice, and had used it well in the solo piece she had sung – as demonstration rather than practice, Phyllida suspected – just before the rehearsal broke up. And in Hugh Jordan's voice and eyes . . . admiration for his companion's musicianship and, of course, that intimate smile. Which Phyllida realised, on a dart of frustration, was going to make it difficult to divine if and when there was real feeling behind it.

As if in illustration of the task ahead, Hugh Jordan caught Miss Spence's eye as he dropped his gaze to the coffee cups, and briefly the smile flashed out, its brilliance invoking an involuntary response in kind from Phyllida as well as Miss Spence.

'Hello!' he said. 'You shouldn't be sitting there on your own, Miss . . . Forgive me . . .'

'Spence. Pamela Spence'

'Miss Spence. What will you think of our manners, to say nothing of our sense of hospitality! I hope you've enjoyed this evening enough to be looking forward to the next rehearsal.'

'I have indeed.' Miss Spence rose to her feet and moved the couple of steps necessary to form a group with Hugh Jordan and his companion.

'May I introduce you to Marjorie Turnbull?'

The inferior is always introduced to the superior. The adage from some long-forgotten manual on etiquette sprang up in Phyllida's mind. Well, in this instance it was justified, and probably instinctive. Which didn't, Phyllida severely reminded herself, have to mean that Hugh Jordan valued more than his secretary's vocal prowess; and if the three of them had met in his office, wouldn't Marjorie Turnbull have been presented to *her*?

'Mrs Turnbull. You sing absolutely beautifully.'

'Thank you.' Gratification in the fine eyes, rather than amusement at the over-the-top reaction of a provincial lady. But maybe Marjorie Turnbull lacked a sense of humour. 'It's *Miss* Turnbull, actually.'

The smiling glance the soprano turned on Hugh Jordan as she spoke made Phyllida's professional reflexes tingle: she might just have read an expression of conscious significance, as if Miss Turnbull were reminding her employer that she was unspoken for. But it could have been no more than her own abiding tendency to believe she saw a reaction she was hoping to see, and she tried to warn herself against it.

'Your standards generally are very high.' There was a wistful note in Miss Spence's voice that had Hugh Jordan, at least, hastening to tell the new recruit that she would surely help to maintain them.

Miss Turnbull merely agreed with her on another complacent smile, and Phyllida decided that Hugh Jordan must have a strong character to withstand the radiant self-belief of the woman who was so very much his inferior in their daily association.

Unless their relationship really was more than it seemed. Or simply (she told herself severely), that he was one of those bosses who are content to leave the daily running of their business lives in other, capable hands while they concentrate on the theory of their profession or slope off to play golf.

If only she could see behind that smile.

Phyllida had been dreading beyond all resumed work events the night-time moment when she would stand outside the Golden Lion and look across the square at Peter's windows. Always, before her pilgrimage to Edinburgh, she had been glad when they were alight, a beacon to tell her he was still in the office and awaiting a chat over glasses of Scotch about her evening's activities while they were still vivid.

Always, except for the one night she been glad to see them dark, the night on which, as Fiona Steele, she had had to tell Jack that she was married, and was facing for the first time the bleak prospect that she would never see him again. Now she was facing that prospect again, standing there under a starry sky with fists clenched and head thrown back, forcing herself to absorb her knowledge that this time the prospect was a certainty. She would never see Jack Pusey again.

But as she stood there, defiant, she found the challenged bleakness receding, and that there were warmth and triumph in this second loss. No, she would never see Jack again, but she knew, and the world knew, that he was hers and she was his, and they would never walk separate ways again.

Peter's windows were alight, and she was glad.

As Miss Spence plodded along the path across the square, Phyllida even caught for a moment the echo of the happy anticipation with which she had gone that way so often in the past, and had to hold herself back from breaking into a canter unthinkable for the persona she was still inside.

46

'Thanks for being here.' As always on these occasions, whatever her appearance, Phyllida had reverted to her own voice.

'How could I not be?' Peter had appeared at the window while she was standing the other side of the square, and the two drinks were ready on his desk. 'I wasn't sure right away that it was you, your new woman is so different.'

'That's a relief.'

'I rather like her; she's sort of cosy. What's her name?'

'Miss Pamela Spence.'

'So how did it go!' he asked, as he handed her drink across to her. 'Were you in good voice?'

'Yes!' Phyllida took a long swallow. 'Fortunately I didn't realise until the last moment that it was to be the trickiest moment of my sleuthing career – the moment of truth, in fact, because there's no control over the singing voice the way there is when you speak. In the end all I could do was open my mouth and listen to what came out – I doubt I had any more idea of what would emerge than the choirmaster did . . . Anyway. It was quite a good sound – well, as good as I'm capable of. I felt the most enormous relief. And don't say you knew it would be all right, because neither of us could have had any idea.'

'Very well. Jordan and secretary were there?'

'Oh, yes. Hard to picture her – Marjorie Turnbull – in her subordinate daytime role; she's the lead soprano, and aware of her position. Suits it physically, too. Tall and imposing. They at least looked the handsome couple.'

'And you're going to tell me, you magician you, that you've already discovered whether or not they are.'

'No. Moving about talking and listening is for next time, when Miss Spence has lost her novelty; but tonight I did at least get the impression – only the impression,' she said warily – 'that Miss Turnbull felt a tad proprietorial towards her boss, because when she corrected my *Mrs Turnbull* to *Miss* it seemed to me that she looked at him with a consciously significant smile. But what *he* felt . . . The biggest hurdle in the way of my discovering anything, Peter, is going to be Hugh Jordan's smile. As a man you may not have noticed, but he has that intimate smile some men turn on whoever they're talking to – well, the women at least, and I shouldn't be at all surprised if the men too. Even Miss Spence was briefly illuminated. It's the sort of smile most men would give only when the person they're giving it to is ultra-special to them, but Hugh Jordan sprays it around everyone. I foresee that smile getting in the way of my learning the thing we most want to know about him, even when I'm in his house and a deal more attractive than Miss Spence.'

'Have you decided on your next appearance?'

'Only, as I said earlier, that I want to start by investigating Sandra Jordan interactively and so I'll want someone *sympathique*. And someone sexy, to have any chance of getting behind that smile and discovering if Hugh Jordan has a generally wandering eye, even if I'm unable to find out if it's wandered in the direction of his secretary.'

'If it has, and there *is* something going on, both Jordan and Turnbull would have to be very discreet indeed not to give rise to some speculation in either office or choir.'

'That's what encourages me. So far as the office goes—'

'You're going to suggest applying as a temp, but even you can't do everything at once, especially so soon after . . . What I mean is, you haven't worked for half a year and I think you should take it a bit gently. So concentrate for the moment on choir and café. You might find yourself killing two birds with one stone in the café – learning something about the husband as well as the wife.'

'All right. So long as you promise that if I find myself feeling the least bit underemployed you'll let me branch out.'

'I promise. Another one? Say yes.'

'Yes. Are you giving yourself a field role?'

'I'm not sure as yet; I'm so hamstrung by being known to both parties and not being capable of assuming disguises. I might just talk architecture with Jordan, which could lead to an invitation to his office. Not,' Peter went on hastily, 'that I consider myself to have better interpretative powers than you – quite the opposite – but because it would offer another opportunity to see and hear boss and secretary together. And if Murphy's Law was in operation and the missus came in, she'd think I was there on *her* account . . . Complicated, isn't it? I've deputed Steve to shadow Mrs Jordan and her partner one night soon when they're working late, and am hoping that in his inimitable cloaked way he'll be able to witness their goodnights.' Each picked up their glass on an instant, and stared at each other wide-eyed over the rim. 'I know, it *is* tacky sometimes,' Peter said eventually. 'But it's part of the job they're both paying for.' He paused, long enough for the pleading look she was expecting to flood into his eyes. 'In fact . . .'

'You'd like me to try to follow Hugh Jordan and Marjorie Turnbull when they leave a rehearsal, and park where I can watch him drop her off. I was going to suggest it.'

'Dear Phyllida. I wish, I so wish, I could give Jack back to you.' For a moment, on a surge of emotionalism, Peter believed himself.

'Dear Peter. But just now, when I was looking up at your windows, I discovered that he hasn't left me.'

Six

'*Come in and sit down. Oh, but I've needed to see you! Phyllida . . .' The first touch, big gentle hand against her cheek. 'Why so glum?'*

'*I hadn't realised . . . until I was leaving the hospital . . . what sort of ward it was.*'

'*Ah . . .*'

'*Jack, though . . . you've come home. So it's all right, isn't it?*'

'*Sit on the couch here . . .' The hand now surrounding both of hers. The feel of his thigh. 'Phyllida, I've come home because I've refused treatment. It's in the family. Leukaemia. I saw my brother die. He had an extra eighteen months because of his treatment, but they weren't life, they were mere existence. I prefer to be myself for as long as I can. Oh, I've thought about it. And thought. And that's the decision I've come to.*'

'*Jack . . .*'

'*You're not going to try to talk me into going back to hospital?*'

'*No. I'm going to cry. Oh, God, Jack. To find you again. And then . . .*'

'*I fell in love with Fiona. You know that, or you wouldn't have come to me. When you've stopped crying I want you to go and check out of your hotel and bring your things here.*'

The photograph was a good one: the moment Phyllida set

50

eyes on the woman in the window of the Outlook Café she knew it was Sandra Jordan. A slim woman with dark red hair, thin pale face and large, inward-looking eyes, alone at a table for two and eating a sandwich in quick bites. So quick, she wouldn't be there for much longer; and – the adrenaline rushed in at almost its old strength – Phyllida had been right to wait for peak lunchtime: the Outlook Café hadn't a single free table.

'Forgive me . . . but may I join you? I can't see a free table.' She could, as two people rose and shrugged into their coats, but the table they were leaving was at the back of the café and not within Sandra Jordan's field of vision. Briefly compromising her American sophisticate's strolling pace through life, Phyllida had shovelled the nearest sandwich pack on to a plate, poured a black coffee, edged past the people waiting for food that needed serving, and offered the right change at the till within the space of two or three minutes, and when she reached Sandra Jordan, her subject still had a corner of sandwich to go.

'Oh . . . yes, of course. I'm just leaving, anyway.' Quick, light voice, attractive but indifferent; and Sandra Jordan was draining her coffee cup.

'Not on my account, I hope. You know' – as the American made heavy weather of her sandwich pack and forced a brief smile into the face now so near to her across the narrow, rose-sprigged tablecloth – 'I have to confess I wasn't sorry to see that I wasn't going to be able to sit alone. This is my first visit to England and I'm finding myself wanting to talk to English people – I'm sorry, I'm told I should say British – whenever I can find the opportunity. Oh, dear, I don't seem able to . . .'

'Let me do it . . . There . . . You're American?'

'Yep. Thanks. Different pressure required from the one I'm used to . . . Yes, I come from an obscure corner of Illinois.' Where she had gone with Gerald on a visit to a distant cousin of his at the time she was beginning to get seriously impatient with his regular infidelities. It had not been a happy visit and she had gone for long walks, alone but for the compliant family dog, in a variety of directions she had let the dog decide on. 'Hutton Ridge. You won't know it.' Sandra Jordan wouldn't; it was a distortion of the nearest obscure settlement that had had more than a couple of shops. Phyllida and Peter had discussed into the night the comparative dangers of the lies Mrs George Parker might tell her, and had decided that a valid excuse for a sophisticated woman to seek conversation with a stranger had to be paramount. Which meant that Mrs Parker had to be newly arrived in Britain.

On another surge of adrenaline Phyllida saw that Sandra Jordan's face was losing its indifference.

'Hutton Ridge. Sounds as if it ought to be in Yorkshire.'

'It probably is, somewhere. I've discovered since I crossed the Atlantic that Boston isn't the only American place name that has its origin over here.'

Mrs Parker laughed, and Mrs Jordan smiled as she responded. 'I have a cousin in New London, Connecticut. It's on the River Thames, and it was only when I went to visit him that I discovered it's pronounced as it's spelt.'

'If he was the least bit Anglophile he'd have been ashamed for you to find out.' The pale face briefly coloured. 'He was, wasn't he? Admit it.'

'All right, yes.' All the preoccupation gone, now, and the fleeting smile more and more in evidence. 'But he spends a lot of time in Europe. Have you been anywhere there?'

'I was in Italy for a time. A while ago, now.' Another joint decision with Peter, to help explain Mrs Parker's cosmopolitan aura. 'So I've had a peek or two at France and Switzerland.'

'Yes. Forgive me, that was nosey.' The wariness back, as Mrs Jordan started fidgeting with her bag. Because she was having to make the decision between leaving, as she would normally have done the moment her lunch was finished, and lingering? If there really were problems in her emotional life, they might be affecting her small everyday judgements.

'Not at all! I welcomed your question. As I told you, I love to speak with English – British – people.'

'I suspect most of us are a bit of a hotchpotch. My mother was Scottish.' A reminiscent smile, then Mrs Jordan's first emphatic remark. 'You must go to Scotland! It's a wonderful place! Are you . . . are you here on your own?'

'I'm afraid so. I lost my husband a while back, and eventually decided to take myself out of myself and go have a look at the United Kingdom. He spent some time in London when he was very young – before we met – and loved coming south to the coast.'

Not for the first time, Phyllida felt a frisson of shock at the ease with which, in character, she found herself almost believing in the scene she was setting. She could even see the eager young American Merle Parker's blond, floppy-haired husband-to-be, leaning over the rail on Seaminster's Parade, as Phyllida Moon so often leant, breathing deep and gazing at the sea . . .

'So you're walking in his footsteps.'

'Sort of. He came to Seaminster once.' The embellishments were all hers, but she had added them in the past and to date evoked Peter's approved amusement rather than his wrath.

'How romantic! I hope you find it a happy experience and not a sad one. You've no friends here, though?'

'Nope. The Golden Lion's pretty friendly, though.'

'Ah, yes. I think it's Seaminster's nicest hotel. But it's not the same. I wonder . . .'

Phyllida saw Sandra Jordan's sudden dismay at what she might just have implied – a moving of this nameless woman's bag and baggage into her own home – and thought she understood why she hastened on.

'Perhaps you'd care to come out to us for tea one weekend afternoon? Or a drink one evening? Make a Seaminster contact? We're on the edge of town.'

So many of Phyllida's ploys took longer to work than she had hoped for, it was sweet indeed when one succeeded both earlier than expected, and against the real possibility of long-term failure.

'I'd love to! What a kind thought! But you should know who I am. Mrs George Parker. Merle.'

Phyllida held out Mrs Parker's beringed right hand, and Sandra Jordan took it without hesitation.

'I'm Sandra Jordan. My husband's Hugh. He's an architect and I'm an estate agent. Real estate you call it, don't you?'

'We do. Sandra . . . your Hugh might not appreciate an unknown American ringing his front doorbell.' She had become adept at knowing when it was safe to appear to draw back.

'You won't be unknown; I'll have told him you're coming.' The laugh again, but Sandra Jordan had glanced at her watch. 'I'll give you a ring at the hotel.'

'Thank you. I already look forward. But now I mustn't keep you.'

'It's all right, although I must go in a moment. Have you any free time this next weekend?'

'Yes, but don't you want to ask your husband . . .'

'No need.' The hint of defiance in the soft voice made Phyllida wonder if Sandra Jordan was squaring up to make a point as well as liking the idea of seeing this charming American again. 'Sunday evening? Sixish? D'you have transport?'

'Yes.'

'Here's my card.' Sandra Jordan had reached into her bag, and handed Phyllida a white square. 'There's a tiny map on the back.'

'Thanks.'

'Perhaps we'll meet here again in the meantime.'

'It could be. I've been trying to get around a variety of places, but a friend has it over a change of décor in my book every time.'

'That's nice. Sometimes my partner's with me. Business partner, I mean.' Nothing openly significant, just a simple explanation. 'If he is, though, don't go away. And now I really must dash.'

'Of course. I'll look forward to Sunday if I don't see you meanwhile.'

'So will I.'

'That's all for now, Amy. But I'd like the report by three thirty, Mr Jordan needs it for a meeting at four.'

'Yes, Miss Turnbull.'

The Songstress wasn't a bad old stick, Amy Calder reflected as she shut the senior secretary's door quietly behind her (having been called to task for slamming it on her first day she had closed it quietly ever since – somehow one remembered to carry out whatever suggestions Miss Turnbull made). It was a pity – all the girls agreed on this – that she was so competent and carried most of the day-to-day admin load, because it meant they didn't see as much as they'd all have liked to of their gorgeous boss. Not because he was lazy, they all knew (partly from what Miss Turnbull told them, and partly from their own observation), off playing golf or having long, heavy lunches, but because he was so clever he needed lots of time to himself thinking up ('dreaming up', Miss Turnbull sometimes called it) the schemes that had already won him some national recognition. 'Heavenly Hugh' was the sobriquet among the junior girls, and needed no elucidation (that smile!). Miss Turnbull had been nicknamed the Songstress because of having given an impromptu performance of 'One Fine Day' at the conclusion of an office party, and because of the tall, generous figure that kept the now legendary occasion in the collective mind. The title was so widely (and respectfully) used it was adopted after a few days even by the temps. Whether boss and secretary were aware of their alternative names, no one was sure.

In view of the dishiness of Mr Jordan, and the fact that he and his senior secretary went choral singing together, there was, of course, as close an eye as possible kept on the two of them *vis-à-vis* one another, and a jealous fear among the junior female staff that one of them, one day, would catch them *in flagrante delicto* – or even merely kissing or holding hands – in one or other of their offices (which had a connecting door); but this had never happened, and none of the girls really expected that it ever would. Not so much because they were convinced there was in fact 'nothing between them' as because both boss and senior secretary were so obviously aware of their respective work positions (so much to lose in respect and status, especially by Miss Turnbull!), and anyway had to have ample opportunity to misbehave elsewhere. Amy Calder lived quite near Miss Turnbull, so had of course been deputed to try to find out if there was a man in her life; but occasional walks over the past three years in the vicinity of Miss Turnbull's neatly hedged detached home had yielded the sight on her front path of nothing male beyond men and boys in uniform delivering her letters or seeking to read her meters.

In public, Miss Turnbull's demeanour towards her boss was respectful but independent, and it was obvious to everyone from the latest temp to Miss Turnbull's preferred typist, Amy Calder, that Mr Jordan's professional life would be seriously affected should she ever decide to leave.

'Everything all right, Marjorie?' Hugh had put his head round the door between them, seen she was alone, and was advancing a little way into her office.

'Everything's all right. Amy will have that report for you in good time. She's competent and reliable.'

'Because you've trained her. This meeting could be important; Birch Associates have a lot to offer to whichever they decide is the right organisation.'

'They'll offer it to us. Hugh, the rehearsal tonight . . .'

'I'll pick you up at a quarter past, as usual.'

'Thank you.' She drove a car, could have taken herself to the choir practice, then said goodnight to him in view of the others and gone solitary home instead of being alone with him in the night-time darkness of his car. And perhaps, later, in the privacy of her home . . .

That smile!

Marjorie Turner reminded herself, for the umpteenth heartwarming time, that Hugh Jordan didn't have to give her a lift to and from the Aeolian Hall.

'Sorry I'm late. I met a fascinating American.'

'Ah-hah!'

'Female, Joe.'

'I'm glad to hear it.'

'Don't be silly.'

'Sorry. Fascinating, you say?'

'Well, yes.' Sandra Jordan went round the other side of her desk and sat down. 'I was surprised somehow when she told me this was her first visit to England, she seemed so sophisticated. But she has lived in Italy.'

'This is the first time I've heard of you getting into conversation with a stranger.'

'You don't hear everything about me.'

'I know, I know. Don't be so prickly. Things awkward at home?'

'That's none of your business.'

'I was thinking about Daddy's little girl. You should have married me, you know, Sandra. No complications.'

'No? How about my not wanting to?'

'I don't deserve that.'

'You do. What's come over you lately? We agreed—'

'I know, I know. It's just that I've sensed . . . I've felt things weren't right with you. And as they're pretty good here in the agency at the moment, it has to be at home.'

'Home's all right, too. Not, as I've just said, that that's any of your business.'

'But you still have your problems with Susan.'

'It'll get better.'

'After two bad years? Sandra . . .' Joe Hardman leaned across the desk, and Sandra Jordan looked up reluctantly into the glowing face she knew so well. 'I shan't say any more, I promise. I'm only jokey because I . . . We're all right, aren't we?'

'Of course, Joe. We work so well together. Don't forget it; we don't want to lose it.'

'Is that a threat?' Joe Hardman drew back a little, his colour deepening.

'No. Just a reminder. That the past is a very long time ago. Now, if you haven't anything more important on, will you come with me to my meeting this afternoon with the landlords of Bardwell Street? I'm not afraid of them, but they probably think I am, and if you're there it might save some time.'

'I'll be there. Then there are the Wallaces later . . . six, isn't it?'

'Yes.'

'If we can unload nineteen and twenty Rayner Street on to them it'll be a real weight off our shoulders. They've got the money to convert, by the way; I've just had the confirmation.'

'That's good news.'

'Mrs Wallace was more at home with you than with me. Can you do me the return favour?'

58

'Yes. Hugh'll be late tonight, too; it's his choir practice.'
Joe Hardman heard the sigh, and had to struggle against remarking on it. 'So we'll have something to eat after the Wallaces?'

'No. It won't take all that long, I'll go home for a meal tonight.'

'Whatever you say.'

When he had left her on his customary grin, Sandra sat for a few moments staring at the wall before seizing the telephone and quickly punching out a number.

'Could I speak to Mr Jordan? It's his wife.'

'Just one moment, please.'

The usual insult to Mozart. She'd ask Hugh – sometime – if he'd consider dispensing with it in favour of the simple ringing tone.

'Sandra? It's Marjorie Turnbull here.'

As it always seemed to be, these days, when Sandra tried to speak to her husband at work. A sudden vivid vision of his senior secretary in all her formidable size and self-confidence made Sandra, for an absurd furious moment, hope to learn from the Peter Piper Agency that she was not the upright figure she presented to the world. Then, shocked, she berated herself for such stupidity. She would die inside if it turned out that Hugh . . .

'Sandra?'

'I'm sorry, Marjorie, I heard someone at the door but it was only the lunchtime post. May – can I speak to Hugh?' 'May' would mean: 'Have I your permission?' 'Can' meant: 'Is it physically possible?' Not that Miss Turnbull would honour the distinction: Sandra suspected she had more than once said Hugh was out of the office when he was in . . .

But this time Marjorie said yes, he had just left her office to return to his own; that must be why the switchboard had put the call through to her.

Implying a long session together. Again, not for the first time. Whatever Hugh's feelings might be, Sandra suspected his senior secretary of being in love with him. Unless she was simply spiteful by nature, or just envious of her, Sandra's, married state? Which sounded a bit unlikely for someone as confident and competent as Marjorie Turnbull. Although she was, Sandra reflected as she waited for Hugh's voice (still, for her, the voice of voices), in a way old-fashioned, and perhaps still adhered to the one-time social belief that the proper destiny of a woman was the married state . . .

'Sandra?'

'Hugh . . . hello.'

'Something wrong?'

'No!' Oh, she had so hoped he wouldn't say that! 'Does there have to be, that I thought I'd like to talk to you? But I'm sorry if it's a bad moment.'

'No, no. What is it, darling?'

His last word flooded her with warmth, even as she reminded herself that he used it indiscriminately when addressing women. Along with his smile . . . but he had told her he loved her, and until her mother had planted the worm it was only his daughter who had made her wary.

'I just . . . Shall we go out for a meal tomorrow night? You don't have choir and I'll shut up shop early.'

'You're sure you can do that?'

Hugh's voice was without expression: she couldn't tell whether or not he was being sarcastic; but if he was, then it had to mean he was jealous of the time she spent at work. Or with Joe.

The warmth was back. 'Of course I can! Will you book at Leone's?'

'Surely. Half past seven?'

'That'll be fine. See you tonight for a late supper.' *And love you.* But she could hear Marjorie Turnbull's voice in the background, and she didn't say it aloud.

Seven

'*A re you tired, darling?'*
   'Not really. Which is a miracle when you consider we've walked the length of the Royal Mile. And . . . last night.'
   'The night of my life.'
   'No others?'
   'No.'
   'That makes me so sad for you.'
   'Don't be; I'm not sad for myself. Well, not today . . . and anyway, it's for ever. Past and future. What would you like to do now?'
   'Go home.'

With the good fortune that sometimes leavened the prevailing disappointments of her second profession, Phyllida encountered Hugh Jordan and Marjorie Turnbull in the doorway of the Aeolian Hall; but as Hugh held the door for Miss Spence she realised that his reflex smile was entirely impersonal, as was Miss Turnbull's impassive stare.

Miss Spence, though, was a good soul, and would spare them embarrassment if she could. 'Mr Jordan, Miss Turnbull, good evening to you both. I'm very much looking forward to my second rehearsal.'

'Ah! Yes . . . of course . . .' Still no reaction from Miss Turnbull but Hugh Jordan playing for time, the high, handsome forehead sporting a couple of wrinkles, then the radiance of relief shining forth and making Miss Spence blink. 'Our new alto.'

'It's good to be singing again.' He'd forgotten her name, of course, and Miss Turnbull was unlikely to have bothered to make a mental note of it. Which was, Phyllida reminded herself as she crossed the entrance hall a couple of steps behind them, welcome confirmation that she had succeeded in her prime aim of making her new persona unmemorable.

'Marjorie! Hugh! And . . . Miss Spence!'

Phyllida was glad for the same reason that Charles Gardner had had to glance down at the sheet of paper on the music stand before speaking her temporary name, and briefly happy on her own account that, when he did, the enthusiasm was still in his voice.

'Mr Gardner.'

'Charles!' Marjorie Turnbull leaned upwards, and with slow theatricality kissed the maestro on both cheeks. Already turning to melt into the surrounding group, Phyllida was aware of more than one exchange of amused looks and suspected, on a small shot of adrenaline, that the evening had already yielded one piece of information: despite – or perhaps because of? – the seriousness with which she took herself, Marjorie Turnbull was a source of entertainment to others that had nothing to do with her singing voice.

It had been a bonus. Charles Gardner was already calling them to their places, and further observation – by ear, if she was lucky, as well as eye – would have to await the post-rehearsal coffee.

As they launched into the chorale she had been practising at home, Phyllida found herself recalling her attendance the previous year at a local art class, also in the way of business. Painting and drawing, as well as singing, were activities of her extreme youth, and it was only her enforced professional attendance at the art class rekindling

62

in her the forgotten early enjoyment of sketching and using watercolour that had led her to draw and paint Jack, in the Princes Street Gardens and on the seat across the long, classical window of his drawing room. (She hadn't been able to unwrap her efforts since her return to Seaminster, but one day she would. One day she would frame one or two of them and hang them on her walls.) Now, it seemed, her enforced professional attendance at choir practice was reawakening her enjoyment of making music as well as listening to it. The enjoyment of listening was something it had been wonderful to discover that she shared with Jack, sitting hand in hand a couple of times in the Usher Hall, and many times in the flat, finding it so much more difficult not to cry when she was hearing Mozart than when there were other sounds, or silence . . .

She was starting to cry now, in the face of all her professional instincts and her professional record, and savagely she thrust her private thoughts away, reminded of why, before Edinburgh, she had been so careful to keep them at bay while she was in character. There were a number of disciplines to be re-imposed. And she would re-impose them. It would be a betrayal of Jack to fall from her high standards because he had illumined her life . . .

'Good. Very good.' Charles Gardner smiled at them bracingly as he pushed both big hands through his already untidy hair. 'But I'd just like to go over it again from that soprano E. Which was spot on, Marjorie. I don't want a real rallentando, but I'd like you all to ease back a bit. From the previous bar, please, Tom. When we've all finished coughing.'

'You all right, dear?'

Miss Spence's immediate neighbour sounded like Miss Spence herself, concernedly observant, and must have spotted the one escaped tear and Phyllida's haste to wipe it away.

'I'm fine, dear. Just a little cold in the eye.'
'It's that wind; it's been very keen these last few days.'
'I expect so.'
'All right? All ready? Thank you, Tom.'

The short break before they switched to a section of the *Passion* as yet unrehearsed remained within the thrall of the music, and it wasn't until Charles Gardner had stepped down finally from his little podium that Phyllida resumed awareness of other people beside their conductor: the sight-reading had taken all her concentration and had not been as enjoyable or as personally successful as her efforts in the art class. At least, though, Phyllida reflected wryly, as along with the rest of the singers she relaxed the tension of her throat and looked around her, in the choir her shortcomings as a musician could be hidden among the talents of others in a way artistic shortcomings could not.

'That was difficult, wasn't it, dear?'

Her neighbour again, and as Phyllida turned to smile at her, she saw that in physical appearance as well as manner she was like enough to Pamela Spence to be confused with her by the Hugh Jordans and Marjorie Turnbulls of this world; and the third finger of her left hand was bare. Phyllida Moon had at least retained her casting ability.

'Yes, it was. I'm Pamela Spence, by the way.'

'Esther Campbell. I'm so glad you've joined us. Shall we have coffee?'

'Lovely.'

Phyllida let Miss Campbell lead their slow way across to the trestle tables, behind which within minutes another pair of singers was setting down pairs of jugs.

'Do you have a rota for the coffee?'

'Oh, yes. We've a nice little kitchen, you know, with all mod cons. Though some of us can't carry two jugs at once. I'm afraid that includes me these days.' Miss Campbell gave a sigh which turned into a chuckle. 'Milk and sugar?'

'Just a little milk, thank you.' However wildly Phyllida's characters differed, all had one thing in common: their tea and coffee requirements. So far as alcohol was concerned it was not quite so simple, and one of the many reasons she enjoyed the company of her American sophisticate was that her choice of aperitif – gin and dry Martini – coincided with Phyllida's own.

'You've been a member of the choir a long time, then, Miss Campbell?'

'I think you might call me Esther. Fifteen years. When I was a mezzo.'

'I was once soprano.'

'It happens, dear.'

They had moved a little away from the trestle tables and taken up a stance, subtly engineered by Miss Spence, with their backs almost against the wall beside the door, so that the whole company was in Phyllida's view. Hugh Jordan and Marjorie Turnbull must remain that way, so that she could leave the hall immediately behind them, but so far they were showing no signs of departure, standing near the centre of the untidy group. Phyllida noticed without surprise that there was a small space around them.

'Those two' – Miss Spence waved her cup – 'Mr . . . Jordan, isn't it? and Miss Turnbull – they seem somehow larger than life, don't they? There's even a little space round them as if they were real celebrities and no one quite dared . . . but they were ever so friendly when I met them coming in. Well, Mr Jordan was; I don't think Miss Turnbull—'

'Oh, Marjorie has delusions of grandeur, I fear. Good luck to her, though; she's got a fine voice and uses it well, and if we're honest, I think we all rather bask in her aura of celebrity, the way she somehow makes the most ordinary event feel like an occasion. And she's kind as well as clever. When poor Miss Parsons fell down in a faint a few weeks ago, Marjorie was on her knees beside her in no time and knew just what to do.'

'She and Mr Jordan make such a handsome couple. Are they . . . ? I felt Miss Turnbull was making something of a point of telling me she was unmarried when we were introduced but they seem . . . well . . . so compatible, as they call it these days.'

'They do look good together, don't they? But Mr Jordan's married and has a young daughter. We tend not to bring our private lives to the choir' – Phyllida felt a jolt of disappointment – 'but I know a little about the Jordans because their daughter's in the same form at school as my god-daughter Emma.'

'Good friends, are they?'

'Not best friends, but so far as I know they get on all right. Emma told me once that Susan – Mr Jordan's daughter – has been a bit unpredictable since her mother died and doesn't seem to be reconciled to her father's second marriage.'

'Recent, was it?'

'A year or two ago, I believe. So obviously her father and Marjorie are just friends.'

'Of course.' Miss Spence might agree with her new friend that Hugh and Marjorie's relations must, in these circumstances, be platonic, but Phyllida felt she could safely assume she had seen more of the world than either of those two worthy ladies and been more painfully a part of it; and – the only real significance – Hugh Jordan's second wife had made no such assumption . . .

Phyllida was ready to move among other members of the choir, and managed it by pointing to a row of uninteresting-looking pictures hanging further along the wall by which they were standing, from where she would be able to keep an eye on the door.

'Are those pictures part of an exhibition?'

66

'Oh, yes. The local authority here's very keen about fostering local talent, and there seems to be something new every month. Not much of a showcase, of course, but it must be better than nothing to an aspiring artist.'

'Of course. Shall we have a look?'

Miss Campbell hesitated, her open face revealing her struggle between politeness and inclination. 'You go, dear; I've seen them. And I ought to have a word with Violet . . . over there . . .'

'Of course.'

'D'you have transport home?'

'Oh, yes, thank you.' *And I hope you have, too.* Here was a possible complication they hadn't foreseen.

'Ah. I was wondering if you needed a lift.'

'How very kind, but I'm in my car.' Not Phyllida's car – the car hired for both Miss Bowden and Mrs Parker from Peter's tame garage proprietor, who relished his special relationship with a private eye and, like John Bright of the Golden Lion, never asked questions. Someone other than Phyllida Moon at the wheel of her own car was a risk too far. 'Anyway, I'll look forward to seeing you next week.'

There was a valedictory note in Phyllida's voice: a few choristers were making for the door.

'So shall I, dear.'

Miss Campbell set off rather more quickly than her pace hitherto in the direction of a dispersing group near the podium, and Phyllida strolled the other way towards the pictures, which on close inspection turned out to be even less rewarding than she had feared. One of the tenors was studying them too, and after a few silent moments side by side Phyllida asked him what he thought of them.

'Is the artist a friend or relation?'

'Oh, no. I don't live in this part of the world.'

'Good. So I can tell you I think they're pretty much

crap. Sorry!' He was probably the youngest of the male choristers, and he had just turned to Miss Spence and registered that she was one of the oldest of the female. 'Sorry!' The round, rosy face reddened more deeply as the regret was repeated.

'Don't be. I tend to agree with you. I'm Pamela Spence, by the way.'

'Justin James. I hope you're going to enjoy the choir. Everyone's chuffed to have another alto.'

'Not for very long, I'm afraid. I'm only in Seaminster for a matter of months. So as you can imagine I'm . . . chuffed . . . too that Mr Gardner has taken me on. Especially as you have such a high standard.'

'Thanks. We get pretty good reviews from the local press, but it's reassuring to have a flattering individual assessment from time to time.'

Phyllida turned to look out over the dwindling throng. Marjorie Turnbull and Hugh Jordan, still side by side, were talking to one of the coffee-servers across the trestle table.

'Miss Turnbull has a splendid voice, hasn't she?'

'Very impressive, yes.'

'She's an impressive lady. Has she sung professionally?'

'Not that I know of. But she's taken leading roles with the local operatic society. She's a good stage presence, as you can imagine. Somewhat overpowering face to face, though.'

'You're remembering that I'm only temporarily in Seaminster.'

'Yes, but I don't think I'm the only one who would say that. I probably only mean that I'm scared by her aura of supreme self-confidence.'

'I know what you mean. She and Mr . . . Mr . . .'

'Jordan?'

'That's right. Mr Jordan.' It had been a mild trap, to see if this young Mr James saw her two subjects as a pair, in whatever sense. 'They make a very handsome couple. Are they . . .'

'An item? I doubt if there's anyone in the choir who knows; everything they do is so studied. I know Hugh Jordan's married, but I haven't met his wife.' Or, it appeared, learned that his marriage was a repeat, and recent; but of her own accord she was coming to accept Miss Campbell's disappointing dictum that the Seaminster Choral Society was not a place for gossip.

'Miss Turnbull isn't?'

'Oh, no. But can you imagine her consenting to matrimony? It isn't easy.'

Miss Spence laughed. 'I'm glad I came to look at these unrewarding pictures, Mr James. I've enjoyed our little chat.'

'Me too. Even though it would more accurately be called my little monologue.'

'And none the worse for that.' The golden duo was moving slowly towards the exit. 'Well, I must be on my way now, but I look forward to seeing you at our next rehearsal, Justin.'

'Me too.'

Hugh Jordan was wandering alone around the entrance hall, and after a stab of panic Phyllida went through the door marked *Women*. Marjorie Turnbull was standing in front of the mirrors back-combing the top of her thick crest of tawny hair. There hadn't been time for her to use one of the cubicles, and this time the stab was of intrigued realisation that she had come into the cloakroom merely to improve her appearance. For a mere lift home in the dark. Which implied, for Phyllida, that Miss Turnbull had hopes of the lift rather than expectations, although she reminded herself with her customary severity that there were many women who must, if they can, face every experience freshly adorned.

'I did so enjoy your solo, Miss Turnbull.'

The fine eyes in the mirror appeared to notice Miss Spence for the first time. 'Oh . . . thank you. Yes, it went well tonight.'

Close to, and in isolation, Miss Turnbull's presence was very strong, almost over life-size and heavily accented by a musky perfume. 'It did indeed.' With someone less self-regarding than Marjorie Turnbull, Phyllida might have worried that so obviously unvain a woman as Miss Spence using a ladies' cloakroom merely to survey herself in the mirror might attract surprised attention; but with this woman she had no such qualms, and washed her hands and messed about with a comb on the surface hairs of her wig until, after a satisfied nod at the glass, Miss Turnbull swept out.

Phyllida followed in time to see her and Hugh Jordan disappearing through the entrance doors, and tailed them at a discreet distance to the car park. Steve had given her Hugh Jordan's car registration, and Miss Spence had parked within sight of it but some way away.

It was ten thirty, raining heavily, and the streets of Seaminster were almost deserted. Phyllida had no difficulty keeping a clear space between the two cars all the way to Miss Turnbull's suburb, but it was there rather than in town that she had been braced for difficulty: Miss Turnbull's house, scouted that morning by Steve, commanded as clear a view of the two treeless roads on the corners of which it was situated as he had morosely reported.

At least the front gate gave on to one of them rather than the other. Phyllida turned the corner past it, and past Hugh Jordan's now parked car, slowly enough to see that the two silhouettes had space between them and that the driver was already opening his door. She drew up a little way along the angled road and loped back to the corner, carrying the camera she had been unable to risk using on her way past Hugh Jordan's car and glad of the meagre cover of the privet hedge that bounded Miss Turnbull's property as well as the one immediately short of it.

At least the downpour meant there were no other walkers, and she could see no lighted rooms with undrawn curtains. Peering round the angle of Miss Turnbull's front garden, Phyllida saw her and Hugh Jordan standing on the pavement, and took a picture. Miss Turnbull was speaking, and when she had finished, Hugh Jordan patted her on the shoulder and Phyllida took another picture, and another when he left his hand there as he escorted her up her garden path. Phyllida crouched her way to the abrupt end of the hedge by Miss Turnbull's front gatepost, from where she could see the householder fitting her key into the lock of her front door, then turning back to Hugh Jordan before pushing it open. Phyllida took another picture as they stood there for a moment motionless, and another as Hugh Jordan leaned forward and for a moment their faces blended. Cheek or lips? There had been no way of telling and it was unlikely that the camera would offer more in the rainy dark, but at least Phyllida would be able to report that Hugh Jordan hadn't entered Miss Turnbull's house and that the moment of contact between them had been very brief.

Report then and there, she hoped with sudden fierceness, as on a wave of desolation she sped towards the Golden Lion and the Grail of a lighted window in the Agency.

There was a café almost opposite the premises of Hardman and Andrews, estate agents, and the woman in the mac and floppy, wide-brimmed hat made it inside just as the few raindrops developed into a heavy shower. She had seen from outside that there was a vacant table in the window, and she sat down at it and ordered a pot of coffee

71

before getting some papers out of a briefcase and starting to study them.

'Market research?' the waitress suggested as she set the coffee pot down.

'Um? Oh, something like that.'

'Any questions for me to answer? I love quizzes.'

'Sorry. It's to do with estate agencies. I've just been over the road.' Where she had strolled along the wall of photographs inside Hardman and Andrews, and been asked by a young woman if any assistance was required. Phyllida had said no, thank you, she was just looking, because she was watching Sandra Jordan disappear from sight through a door at the back of the spacious and attractive sales area. There was no sign of her partner, and Phyllida had told the girl she would try to make it across the road before the rain got serious.

'Right. They do a good range of coffees.'

The girl in the café was equally ready to offer a commentary. 'They do fab business; you see their signs everywhere.'

'I suppose they come over here?'

The question was idle, the customer was absorbed in her papers.

'Oh, yes. Not the bosses so much, but the junior staff, regular like.'

It was twelve noon, and if Murphy was active he could well take pleasure in sending in one of the junior staff just mentioned by this chatty waitress, who would then inevitably make the parties known to one another and prove Phyllida a liar, but it was a risk she must take.

The girl was swaying from foot to foot but she was still hopefully there. If other customers came in it might be difficult to get her back and Phyllida could hardly rush out of the café in pursuit of a suddenly appearing Sandra Jordan if she hadn't paid.

72

'Could I pay now, d'you think? While you're not so busy?' The bill had been placed under the milk jug, and felt slightly sticky when Phyllida picked it up.

'Surely.'

'That's lucky, I've got the exact amount. And . . .'

'*Thanks*!'

Twenty long minutes went by before Sandra Jordan emerged from the premises opposite, during which the waitress twice asked Phyllida if she would like another pot of coffee, a couple of young women who had not gone into the estate agency during Phyllida's visit came out of it, and after a few heartstopping glances across the street decided to go elsewhere. So it was a relief to be able to get to her feet and smile a farewell before swiftly letting herself out of the café.

Sandra Jordan walked quickly to the Outlook Café on The Parade, bleakly sleek with rain. It was a little earlier than on their first encounter there, and there were a few empty tables. Sandra Jordan made her way to one already occupied by a man Phyllida recognised from the photograph Steve had taken following Hugh Jordan's visit to the Agency: Sandra's business partner Joe Hardman. The dark curly hair of the photograph was black, and the round, soft-featured face was swarthy. The eyes were noticeably dark and keen, and immediately fixed themselves on Sandra Jordan, where they quizzically remained. Without, Phyllida noted with surprise, in the least disconcerting her. Her subjects were sitting at right angles to one another, and she had been able to find a free table facing them both, close enough to hear what they were saying and read their facial expressions, and from the instant of regarding them she was aware that Sandra Jordan was a far more confident woman in the company of her business partner than she had been in Peter's office, or even alone.

After they'd smiled at one another – easy but not ardent

– they didn't speak for a few moments while Sandra looked at the menu, put it aside, and wondered aloud why she bothered – she knew it by heart.

'It's a reflex, I suppose, illustrating the essential optimism of human nature. There just might be a fresh item.'

'There isn't, so I'll settle for a toasted sandwich as usual. You're looking more than usually pleased with yourself. What sort of morning?'

'Busy. You?'

'Successful. The Websters have bitten.'

'Well done!'

'I wasn't too surprised. The signs were there.'

The signs now being given out by Sandra Jordan were of a decisiveness and easy self-confidence that had not been in evidence in Peter's office, or when Phyllida had sat with her in the café. Was the change in her personality now down to the presence of her business partner, or simply to her confidence in her own business ability? Phyllida welcomed the old surge of adrenaline that flowed as she thought of Sunday night, and the likelihood of Mrs George Parker finding the answer to that question when she met Sandra Jordan as wife and stepmother.

Eight

'*J*ack. *It's absurd, but I don't even know the day you were born. Or the year.*'

'*I was born on the sixteenth of March, 1952.*'

'*Eleven years before me. On the seventh of July. Have you resigned?*'

'*I'm on extended leave.*'

'*So you haven't told them.*'

'*Not yet. It was only confirmed the day before you came to me.*'

'*Oh, Jack . . . You seemed so . . . so light-hearted. I think that was why it didn't occur to me at the time that where we met was significant.*'

'*I knew before I was told; I'd had time to prepare. Looking back, I think I'd known for some time.*'

'*Not when you met Fiona?*'

'*No. I was beginning to wonder when I applied for the job up here; there were a few signs . . . but at that stage I refused to read them. And I'd misread Fiona, so the chance to shake Seaminster off my shoes was attractive.*'

'*Was she that important?*'

'*Was I?*'

'*Yes, it was a silly question. The night I sent you away I stood outside the Golden Lion and was glad for the first time that the Agency windows were dark so I didn't have to talk to Peter. To anyone. Jack . . . Oh my God, Jack, I don't want to do that again!*'

'Send me away?'
'Stand there again without you!'
'Dearest Phyllida, you never will.'

Sandra Jordan answered the front door bell when Merle
Parker rang it in the frosty dark of Sunday evening. Phyllida
could see from her first glance that it was the wary Sandra
Jordan of her visit to the Agency and her solitary lunch
in the Outlook Café, but was aware again of the hint of
defiance she had caught a glimpse of when Sandra had
issued Merle her invitation,

'It is tonight, Sandra? You're expecting me?'

'Yes, yes of course. Come in. Goodness, I can feel the
cold on you.'

'It is cold, but kind of nice after so much bone-piercing
damp. The sky's moved upwards and you can see the
stars.'

'I go out to look at them sometimes, we have such big
skies here . . . I'll put your coat on this chair. Come and
meet my husband. And his daughter. And my mother.'

So Hugh Jordan's second wife didn't look on the girl
she had inherited as *our daughter*. Because she couldn't,
or didn't want to? Or because the girl had repulsed her? One
visit should yield the answer to that question, if no other.

'Lovely house,' Mrs Parker murmured as she crossed
the handsome, berugged hall at her hostess's side. She was
ushered into a large and elegant room in which the seated
man rose instantly from an armchair and crossed to meet
them in the doorway with hands outstretched.

'Mrs Parker. Merle, I believe. It's good to meet you!'

The smile at its maximum dazzle, but mercifully brief as
Hugh Jordan turned to indicate a frail-looking elderly lady
sitting close to a living-flame fire, and a girl flung back in
a small armchair a little removed from the circle formed by
the other chairs and a long sofa, her chin sunk on her chest.

76

'Etta! Susan! This is Mrs Merle Parker, a new friend of Sandra's!'

Sarcasm in the words 'new friend'? There was no way of knowing, the rich voice was as invariable as the smile; but Phyllida's sense of frustration eased as her host's eyes left hers and the smile faded slightly as Hugh Jordan's gaze moved from his mother-in-law to his daughter.

'Susan! Did you hear me?' The voice had sharpened.

Slowly the girl's head came up. 'I heard you, Daddy.' A slight coming to attention as the sullen glance reached Mrs Parker, a slight dawning of interest that amused Phyllida as well as encouraging her. 'Hullo,' the girl muttered.

'Hello, Susan. Mrs . . . ?'

Sandra Jordan's mother gave a gracious smile and slightly inclined her head.

'Andrews. Mrs Andrews. Come and sit down!'

Hugh Jordan was escorting Phyllida to one end of the sofa, a hand at her back. 'What will you drink? Gin? Whisky? Wine?'

'I would just love a dry Martini. Not too dry, I'm afraid, as I'm driving.'

'But not for a while, and I know Sandra has some rather nice bitties. Haven't you, darling?'

Sandra received the public smile, too, so it was impossible to know what was really behind the husband's gaze as it rested for a few moments on his wife's face.

'I've a few things in the kitchen. I won't be a moment.'

'You're usual, darling?'

'Please.'

Hugh Jordan strolled across the room to a corner cupboard, talking easily about the weather, and then the Golden Lion, as he poured drinks.

'Best hotel in Seaminster, if not the showiest. Always reliable.'

'I'm happy there.'

'Sandra tells me you'll not be there for long, though?'

So they did talk, and he did listen. Unless it was simply his sense of a host's obligation that had forced him to ask his wife for something to break the ice with her new friend. 'Not long-term, but for a few more weeks, I guess. I'm on a bit of a sentimental journey, as Sandra may have told you.'

'Yes.' The smile again, and no way of knowing whether he was telling the truth. At least, so far, there was nothing in the smile to suggest he saw Mrs Parker as more appealing than the other people he met and smiled at. The daughter, though, was now sitting up fairly straight and paying open attention.

'She didn't tell *me*. Why's it a sentimental journey, Mrs Parker?'

'Susan!'

The mother-in-law's first word, as she swivelled round to look disapprovingly at the now animated girl.

'It's all right, Etta.'

Hugh Jordan, sounding momentarily weary, and looking in a mixture of sorrow and perplexity – it seemed to Phyllida – at his daughter as the animation died away and the girl's full lips tightened.

'Of course it's all right,' Mrs Parker said hastily. 'My husband was over here briefly as a young man, Susan, and actually came to Seaminster. I didn't know him then, but there's a faint old photograph of him leaning over the rail on The Parade and smiling at whoever was taking it. Perhaps an early girlfriend – I never asked.'

'You should!'

'Too late now; he died, honey.'

'Oh. Sorry. Well, I bet you carry that photo about in your bag!'

One of these days Phyllida's imagination would get her into real trouble. 'No, honey; it's so frail it would

78

drop to pieces if I carried it around, so it stays safely back home.'

'You can get photos copied like new now, you know. Faded bits restored and so on.'

'That's an idea, Susan, a really good one. I'll see to it when I get home.'

'And then you can carry the new one round and not worry—'

'Here we are. Sorry for being so long.'

Even before Sandra Jordan had begun speaking the girl had broken off what she was saying and flopped back in her chair, the sulky look returned to her face. Sandra was carrying a tray of attractive-looking miniature vol-au-vents and tiny spirals of bread veined with smoked salmon and avocado.

'You've gone to so much trouble, Sandra! How very kind! It looks delicious.'

'She's a perfectionist, my daughter.' The sudden proud voice made Phyllida jump, and Susan Jordan cast a sneering glance in the direction of the fire. Hugh Jordan continued to smile, with the comparative moderation he showed when his beam was undirected.

'Nonsense, Mother. They're M and S, and all I had to do was pop them in the oven or put them straight on to a plate. Merle . . .'

Phyllida and the old lady both took something from the offered plates, but the girl shook her head impatiently, and Hugh Jordan declined with an intensifying of his smile as he distributed the drinks. Low tables were already within reach of all seats.

'So,' Mrs Parker began, when Phyllida had taken an approving sip of her well-made Martini. 'You both have interesting, high-powered jobs. What sort of architecture do you practise, Mr Jordan? D'you work for individual clients, or for companies? Are you modern or traditional?'

'Hugh, please.' The smile, still impersonal. 'I've been called maverick, which I think means that I don't go in for run-of-the-mill. I'll design for business or pleasure, provided my client really cares what I do and wants something original.'

'You've seen the round house on the way to Billing?' Susan had regained her animation, and was sitting upright. 'That's Daddy's. It's fab inside – rooms like big slices of cake.'

'I must go have a look. Is it a private home?'

'Yes! I wanted Daddy to buy it, but Sandra said no.'

'The client wouldn't sell, darling.' Hugh Jordan, weary again, and Phyllida saw a tic appear in Sandra Jordan's pale cheek as she, in turn, tightened her lips. 'You know that. And why would he want to, having paid me such a lot of money to design his dream?'

'All right, I know. But you could have designed another.'

'It was in the contract that I didn't.'

'And we all like it here, Susan.' Sandra, so diffident Phyllida for a moment could hardly believe her memories of the woman at the lunch table in crisp dialogue with her business partner.

'Yeah, yeah. Mind if I go now, Daddy? I've still got homework.'

'All right, Susan.'

'Nice to meet you, Mrs Parker. See you later.'

Susan Jordan pulled herself to her feet and left the room without a glance at either the older woman or her stepmother. Her pale face expressionless, Sandra Jordan settled herself back into the chair on the edge of which she had been perched, showing Phyllida as clearly as if she had put it into words that her stepdaughter was a source of the tension that gripped her – Phyllida now knew – when she was at home, and to some extent when she was alone with the opportunity to brood. Perhaps the behaviour of her stepdaughter towards her, allied with any as yet undiscovered difficulties between her and her husband, had sapped the self-confidence that now survived only in her work environment, where she had power and was respected.

Phyllida suggested this later to Peter, over a drink in which she asked for more water than usual. Because of the abundance of Sandra Jordan's canapés she had succumbed to a second dry Martini, and then had too little appetite to be able to accompany her large pot of coffee in her room at the Golden Lion with more than a sandwich.

'I've written my report on my laptop,' Phyllida said, as she handed the few sheets of paper across the desk. 'There seemed to be so many nuances I knew I'd lose some of them if I didn't set things down right away. There weren't any surprises – except perhaps that the parties gave themselves away in textbook fashion. With the exception of Hugh Jordan, of course. But he did show his impatience when at first his daughter was less than sociable. I'm pretty sure that was on my account, though – not his wife's. There were a few *darling*s thrown about, but no special looks in her direction, and she was nervous as a kitten until the daughter flounced out. After that she eased up a bit, but nothing like to the extent of how she was in the café with Joe Hardman; she never stopped being the slightly apologetic wife. I think Merle was a good choice, at least so far as the daughter's concerned – she came to life for a few moments before leaving us. Sandra's mother is rather *grande dame*, which I suppose could be part of the reason for her daughter's domestic demeanour – everything revolves around the Man of the House. What puzzles me is that Sandra should have developed so strongly outside the home, but still shrinks back into the dutiful wife when she gets back there.'

'It does seem strange. Love of her husband, perhaps?'

'Or fear of him? Love certainly didn't show. Any more than from him to her. I've a feeling, Peter, that I've got as far as I'll get in my invasion of the Jordan hearth. Not that I shan't have another chance. Hugh was as politely insistent I come again as Sandra was. Quite impersonally, let me hasten to add, and he seemed happy to let Sandra see Merle out. She invited them unspecifically for a drink with her at the Golden Lion, by the way, so I'll set that up in a few days if I don't hear from Sandra again. And Merle will go back to the Outlook Café and hope—'

The telephone rang.

'That's the first time in all our time,' Peter said, 'that we've had an evening interruption.'

'We're a lot earlier than usual; I was back at the hotel by eight and I couldn't wait till the customary time. Aren't you going to answer it?'

'Reluctantly.'

Phyllida felt reluctant too, and stupidly apprehensive, so that it was a relief to see the relaxation of Peter's face as he listened.

'Yes, she is,' he said, smiling at Phyllida. 'But that's all right; you'd better come in. Yes, now. No, it's all right; it's not late and we'll make an exception. See you in a moment.' Peter rang off, his smile turning into a grin. 'Did you hear that?'

'*No*! All I heard was a sort of squawking. I wish you wouldn't dangle me when you have something—'

'Sorry, sorry, it was Steve. He followed Sandra Jordan and Joe Hardman home last night and he wants to tell us what he thinks he saw.'

'He's had all day.'

'He may have done, but I haven't. I realised this morning that I haven't had a Sunday off in yonks, and decided I'd have this one. I'd only been back here an hour when you arrived.' Peter didn't add that he wouldn't have come back at all that night without hopes of his business partner looking for the light in the window.

'I came in the back way and didn't see there wasn't a light.' Peter had flushed slightly, and Phyllida wondered idly what his day off had entailed. She wouldn't inquire: before Jack they had neither of them ever exchanged information about their private lives and she hoped Peter shared her feeling that it was better to keep things that way. 'Steve sounded excited?'

'Does he ever? He sounded sort of portentous, as if he had Something To Impart. But reminding ourselves of his sense of the dramatic, let's not hold our breath.'

'Will you give him a drink?'

'A small one, if I don't already smell it on him.'

Steve was with them in ten minutes, dispensing cold air as he whipped off his scarf and overcoat.

'Scotch, Steve?'

'Would you have a beer, guv?'

'Surely.'

As Peter bent down, Phyllida found herself reflecting that the cupboard whose interior she had never seen was as mysteriously capacious as Mary Poppin's carpet bag. Peter produced a bottle of ale and a suitable glass from it, handed them across to Steve to pour, and asked him what it was all about. 'Have a drink first. No hurry.'

'Thanks, guv.' Steve took a long swallow, followed by a deep breath. 'I followed them to those new flats in Argyll Road, where they met a couple of clients and stayed inside until my toes were ready to drop off. They separated from the couple outside the block, and I followed them to Antonio's. They settled in there and took ages with the menu, so I reckoned I could settle in too and risk one good course. The chips are magic.'

'And you could hear what they were saying?'

There was a pause, in which both Phyllida and Peter could feel Steve's struggle between drama and truth.

'Only the odd few words,' he admitted ruefully at last. 'I was pretty near, but the acoustics were shocking . . .'

'Meaning excellent for the privacy of the clients,' Peter interpreted with another grin. 'OK, go on.'

'But I could see them pretty well, and they both looked cheerful and . . . well . . . sparky. You know.'

'Romantic? Gazing into each other's eyes? Holding hands?'

'Nah,' Steve confessed reluctantly. 'Nothing like that. But they wouldn't, would they, in public? They did look happy, though. I swear, guv, Phyllida, there wasn't a dull moment.'

'Mrs Jordan didn't look . . . uneasy, uncertain?' Peter asked, glancing at Phyllida.

'What? Haven't you been listening? Oops, sorry, guv, but if ever there was a woman on top of life, it was Mrs Sandra Jordan yesterday evening.'

'And Mr Hardman?'

'The same.' Steve looked from Peter to Phyllida. 'Why so hard to believe me?'

Peter nodded to Phyllida, and she told him.

'It's like the two of you are talking about two different women,' Peter said when she had finished; 'and we don't have the key to explain either of them. Is it her husband? Her stepdaughter? Or a combination of them both?'

'Or her business partner,' Steve suggested. 'Boosts her confidence because he's in love with her.'

'When I was watching them,' Phyllida said, 'I got the impression she didn't need any boosting, that she was confident in her own right as a successful businesswoman. She responded to Joe Hardman, but I didn't get the impression at all that she needed him to make her feel the way she looked. And they were quite abrasive. Not the faintest suggestion of lovey-dovey.'

'You didn't ring up because you wanted to tell us about the magic chips,' Peter suggested. 'So what happened when you all left the restaurant?'

'Ah.' Steve took another long swallow, and settled back in his chair. 'It was sleeting when we came out – not like tonight – and they put their heads down and ran to Hardman's car. It, and my car, were in the café car park, so I was able to leave pretty close behind them, and stayed that way back into town. Then some dirty great night-travelling lorry shot out of a side road immediately behind Hardman's car – probably going to park illegally for the night outside his house – and I'd lost him, hadn't I? I just had to hope he was on the way back to the office for Mrs Jordan to pick up her car – I'd made sure it was in the office park earlier. Sure enough, they'd driven into their own park, and were out of his car, standing beside it, when I eased past the entrance. I'd realised, o'course, that the hard part of things was not being able to take my car into a private park, but the road outside's derestricted and I stopped just past the park and edged my way in on foot, flat against the wall on the side where they couldn't't've seen me, the way I do.'

'We know,' Phyllida and Peter responded in chorus. Steve could be as shape-shifting as a black cat when the need arose.

'They were drawing back out of a clinch. No space between them when I first saw them, but the next second – I'm being dead honest here, guv – they were apart, and they stood still that way for a few minutes, talking I think, before she swung round and made for her own car. He looked after her for a moment or two before getting into his. I ran back to mine, and I'd only been inside a few seconds when his car passed it and I saw hers in my mirror going off the other way. That's it, guv, but I swear she was in his arms when I saw them first.'

'Well done, Steve. You're a master.'

'You've been brilliant,' Phyllida said. 'But it could just have been friendship, affection.'

Steve shrugged. 'Could have been. They didn't get back together for more, and there'd been no time for any funny business inside the car; but if they did want more they must have plenty of opportunity in the office when everyone else has gone home. Like now . . .'

Steve's face flooded crimson as his voice died away, and he looked so wretched Phyllida had to come to his rescue.

'It's a good illustration, Steve, and we know you were only talking about the setting and the opportunity; you weren't suggesting that Peter and I are up to anything.' He might think they were, of course – perhaps he did – but he would have to be put on the rack before he would ever admit to the ownership of such a thought, which made it all the more terrible for him that he might inadvertently have given the impression that he was making a total comparison with a possible Jordan–Hardman set-up. So Phyllida made herself laugh as she finished speaking, Peter joined in, and Steve looked relieved as his colour ebbed to its normal pallor.

'Thanks, guv, Phyllida. I wouldn't in a million years. But Jordan and Hardman . . .'

'Absolutely,' Peter finished for him. 'We take your very good point.'

'So what next, guv?' Steve had got to his feet, still looking tense and uncertain, as if his bosses might think, despite their protestations of understanding, that he was leaving them to snog. He was in a bit of a quandary, Phyllida reflected, with an almost maternal sense of pity for Steve's vulnerability, because he was probably afraid

86

that if he went on sitting, his bosses might think he was making too much of his one-off invasion of their private time. So he couldn't win.

Being Steve, though, he would make the best of it, and by the time Peter had told them he thought it was time to put his signature to the reports and deliver them to their clients, the junior field worker was almost his old swaggering self.

'There's more we can do, of course,' Peter said. 'There always is. But I've been thinking today that we've done enough to tell both of them something. So far as the report for Mrs Jordan's concerned, negative information is still information, and let's hope it satisfies her. Hugh Jordan shouldn't be too upset by what Steve's seen – at least his wife and Hardman spent their evening in public. What he'll make of our report on the difference in his wife's demeanour at home and abroad I've no idea, but he's asked for every last nuance, so we shall have to give it to him. We'll get both reports off tomorrow. Then call it a day unless both or either of them ask for more.'

'OK, guv.' But both Peter and Phyllida saw Steve's disappointment in the way he looked down at the carpet as he scuffed a shoe around it. 'I'll be off now. Thanks for the beer. Goodnight, Phyllida.'

As his footsteps clomped out of hearing, Phyllida and Peter looked at one another and said, 'Poor Steve!' in unison.

Nine

'*I can see for the first time that you're tired.*'
   '*A little.*'
   '*Shall I get something to eat?*'
   '*I'm still up to cooking the meal I promised us.*'
   '*Good. You're so much better a cook than I am, and you like cooking. Are you hungry?*' Please be hungry.
   '*I'll eat something. Come and be my dogsbody.*'
   '*Of course. First, though . . .*'
   '*What is it, my darling?*'
   '*I should wait till after dinner, when we're lingering over coffee and brandy.*'
   '*But you can't.*'
   '*No. Jack Pusey, will you marry me?*'

At the beginning of the following week, a bug invaded Seaminster and its environs. Not full-blown gastro-enteritis, just a two- or three-day involuntary purging that left its victims cleansed but weak. And not of epidemic proportions: Phyllida and Steve escaped it; Peter and Jenny succumbed during Tuesday, the day after Peter had despatched reports to the Jordans – to their respective work places, as requested. When Merle Parker telephoned Sandra Jordan that evening to thank her for an enjoyable visit, her husband answered her call and told her Sandra was in bed.

   'Some sort of gastric bug; it must be going round: a couple of girls in my office went home early today.'

'Gee, I'm sorry. I hope she'll pick up soon. I don't suppose she was able to go to work today.'

'Oh, yes, she went in this morning; she seemed to be all right then. Came home late afternoon. In the nick of time – it seems to be that sort of bug.'

The voice a bit quicker? Less warm and rounded? It could have been Phyllida's fertile imagination, but Hugh Jordan must have read Peter's report; and Sandra must have read hers, and should be easier in her mind that evening than in her body. Easier than her husband?

'Well, I hope she's gotten over it.'

'I think so. Short and sharp.'

'But it leaves you wrung out. Give her my best, will you, Hugh, and tell her I'll call again soon. Unless there's anything I can do right now; you know I've plenty of time on my hands.'

'That's very kind of you, er . . . Merle, but we're all right. I can boil an egg, plus, and Sandra's mother . . . Very kind of you, though.'

Still utterly impersonal. Merle Parker had not done to him what she did, under a variety of names and wigs, to so many of the men she met, including poor Steve. Whether because she was not Hugh Jordan's type, or he didn't have a roving eye, or that eye was fixed on Marjorie Turnbull or – it had to be possible despite appearances – on his wife, Phyllida would probably never know: Peter had decreed they leave it there unless asked to go further, and she must swallow her sense of frustration.

'Not at all. I'll see you.'

She wouldn't, of course: Mrs Parker's final call – or response to Sandra's – would be to announce her imminent return to the United States.

Anyway, there wasn't much time to think about the Jordans: Jenny's two-day absence had Miss Bowden busy at the computer, in the intervals of parrying a couple

89

of Peter's fortunately routine cases. Steve hadn't much pressing business, and proved a surprisingly willing, and winning, front-of-house manager to clients and other visitors, appearing with coffee for himself and Phyllida at short and regular intervals. The two of them also exchanged regular bulletins on their states of health, which to their mutual relief held up, so that they were both there to welcome Peter and Jenny back when they reappeared, pale but smiling, on Thursday, Jenny at her usual nine o'clock, and Peter in time for afternoon tea.

The usual routine not yet having been re-established, the four of them had tea together in Peter's office.

'Any response from the Jordans?' he asked Phyllida, at the end of a line of questions.

'Nothing from Sandra, but when Mrs Parker rang to thank her for Sunday night her husband said she had the bug, too. From him, payment with a non-committal note.'

'Um. Time for Mrs Parker to ring Sandra, I think, and tell her she's been called back to the States.'

'Right. I was only waiting for your OK.' And, Phyllida admitted to herself, for the chance of a final clue from Sandra. Well, she might just get it in this last telephone call, if she angled . . . 'I'll try her this morning. Home first, and if she's better, at work.'

But when Phyllida went into the general office, after Steve – as his personal concession to Jenny's convalescence – had cleared the tea mugs, it was an unknown man's voice that answered the telephone, and asked sharply who was speaking.

'It's Mrs Merle Parker, a friend of Mrs Jordan's. May I speak to her, please?'

'I'm sorry, that's not possible.' A pause, and a confused mêlée of male voices in the background. 'Mrs – Merle – Parker. A friend of Mrs Jordan's, you said?'

'That's right. Is there anything wrong?'

'I'm sorry, Mrs Parker, I can't say at the moment.' Another pause, some uninterpretable muttering not far from the other telephone. 'This is the police. Can you please let me have your address and a telephone number?'

'Oh, my God.' Phyllida just managed to retain the twang. 'Has there been an accident?'

She heard more muttering, the words 'on the news' in another male voice, and then the first voice came back to her. 'I'm afraid so. Mrs Jordan is dead. Will you please give me your address?'

'My God. That has to mean she's been murdered, doesn't it?' Because Merle Parker didn't exist it didn't matter what she said, or how *au fait* it might make her appear with what had happened to Sandra. In a very short time, if Phyllida was right, she or Miss Bowden would be talking to Chief Superintendent Kendrick.

'I can't say at this juncture, Mrs Parker.'

This juncture. Policemanese, Phyllida had long since learned, for the time not being ripe. 'No, of course not. I'm staying at the Golden Lion if you need to contact me.' The girls in Reception would say they were sorry, but Mrs Parker didn't appear to be in the hotel. 'Is Chief Superintendent Kendrick with you?'

'I . . . I don't . . . As a matter of fact yes, madam, he's just arrived. But how—'

'May I speak to him?'

'I'm sorry, madam, I can't bring the Chief Superintendent to the telephone.'

'No. Of course not. Thank you, officer.'

'I expect you will be hearing from us, madam. Particularly in view—'

'I don't doubt it. Goodbye.'

Phyllida charged into Peter's office at her own rather than Miss Bowden's pace and, after they had exchanged a few words, made her second call to the Jordan house on his telephone.

'I'm told Chief Superintendent Kendrick is at this number. This is his wife.' They'd decided during their short, urgent dialogue that the policeman who answered the telephone would be unlikely to be familiar with Miriam Kendrick's voice, and that even if she was away she might need to get in touch with her husband. 'May I speak to him?'

'I . . . Of course, Mrs Kendrick.'

'For God's sake, Miriam!' No more than a few seconds had gone by. 'What's happened, what's wrong?'

'I'm sorry, Chief Superintendent. This is Mary Bowden – Phyllida Moon. Please forgive the subterfuge, but we felt time was vital. I know what's happened because I just rang in one of my characters to speak to Mrs Jordan. The Peter Piper Agency has her and her husband as clients; each asked us independently to investigate the other without knowing—'

'I'll be with you as soon as possible, Miss Moon.'

An unnaturally pallid and shaken Chief Superintendent reflected, as he drove across Seaminster, on the extraordinary contrast between his state of mind now – exquisite relief – and what it had once been when a murder had been committed on his patch and he had discovered that the Peter Piper Agency (in the person of Miss Phyllida Moon in one of her many manifestations) was already *au fait* with the trappings of it, having been hired to investigate a situation that had escalated into an unlawful killing . . .

Once – and until quite recently – the discovery of the Agency involvement had evoked in him a terrible mingling of anger, frustration, wounded *amour propre*, and a painfully grudging admission that the involvement was likely to be beneficial to his inquiry. It always had been, but it had taken a couple of years, and the unmasking of Phyllida Moon through all her aliases, for him to have come not merely to accept but to welcome the help that her insider status gave him. In each past case he had managed – he could never quite understand how – to keep the Agency's involvement from the knowledge of the officers under him, and contrived intermittently to keep from himself the fact that his inability quite to believe Peter Piper's assurance that he had only one female member of staff in the field was a source of irritation that bordered on the paranoid. He could admit it now, Kendrick reflected as he forced himself to keep the speedometer at thirty, because he knew now that Dr Piper had been telling him the truth; but in the early days the succession of cleaning ladies, husky American sophisticates and button-mouthed frumps had had him tossing in the night as in his dreams they had melted into one another and then slid back into their separate identities as the single image refused to gel. An additional annoyance had been the dreams that had featured the husky American sophisticate alone, reminding him in the morning of his waking disapproval of himself for finding her attractive . . .

He had had his revenge, in a way. He had been admitted to the antechamber, as it were, which was Miss Bowden, the chief frump, who could be seen in Piper's office and who was the spokeswoman for the whole bunch of Miss Moon's creations. He would probably never have been permitted beyond her, but a piece of pure luck had brought him face to face with the unadorned centre of the disparate women, Miss Phyllida Moon. She had had the chance to bluff him, but she had been in hospital and less than vigilant, and she had given herself away, the only weakness he had yet discovered in her.

He had dealt with her mercifully, which was to say that he believed they had got on rather well. This was the first time since his unmasking of Miss Moon that he had found himself about to sanction the Peter Piper Agency to continue unofficially to help his investigation – how he had hated doing this in the past, and how anxious he was now to ensure that co-operation yet again! – and his sensations were all of relief and anticipation as he parked behind the Golden Lion, strode down the narrow lane that led beside it to Dawlish Square, crossed the Square and entered the building opposite. He couldn't wait for the stately, gilded lift to descend for him, and chopped up the curving staircase two steps at a time.

The Agency factotum Miss Timmis rose from behind the Reception counter and came smiling towards him. Kendrick noted absently that she appeared less rosy-cheeked than he remembered her, and was reminded of the now waning pestilence that had hit the town and was still depriving him of some of his best men . . .

'Chief Superintendent! Please come through.'

Inside Piper's office were Piper and Miss Bowden, Kendrick's foolish disappointment making him realise he had been looking forward to the ascetic beauty of Miss Moon's face, if not the more noticeable charms of her husky-voiced American. For God's sake, he had to take on board that it was unlikely he would ever see Miss Phyllida Moon as herself again.

Both his hosts had risen, and Miss Bowden was indicating the one armchair.

'Thank you.' Kendrick sank into the chair and spread his long legs out in front of him. 'So. You'd better tell me what's been happening.'

'Of course,' Peter said promptly, then looked at Phyllida. 'But Miss Moon's got to know Mrs Jordan and if you could perhaps tell us first something about—'

'It's bad, isn't it, Mr Kendrick?' Phyllida had never seen the Chief Superintendent look like he was looking now.

'I'm afraid so. I've grown pretty hardened, but I don't think I've ever seen a killing that's disturbed me more. I'm sorry, Miss Moon' – Miss Bowden's make-up couldn't give much away, but it was impossible to disguise the widening of the eyes and the sudden trembling of the hands – 'but it will be in the papers and on the news and I think you'd prefer to hear it from me.'

'Of course, Chief Superintendent.' The hands folded now, and motionless on the severely tailored skirt.

'Mrs Jordan was lying on the floor in her drawing room. A wound on the side of her head is consonant with blood found on the sharp corner of the fire surround she was close to. That blow could have knocked her unconscious, or it could have killed her. We may never know which, because after she'd fallen someone took the ornamental brass poker out of the set by the fire – a gas fire, so the poker and the brass-backed brush and shovel it was hanging with were probably there to create the illusion of a real fire . . .' Kendrick drew a deep breath and passed his tongue over his dry lips as the scene came back to him. 'Someone took this poker and brought it down on the back of Sandra Jordan's head. At least twice. Even the post-mortem may not tell us whether one of the blows killed her, or whether she died when she fell; but thank God we can assume she was unconscious when the blows were struck – she took them passively. Which means, though, that as she didn't defend herself we won't find any skin under her nails or any alien threads anywhere on her body.'

'And you'll never know whether or not it was murder,' Peter said slowly, while Phyllida thought of Sandra's slender body and delicate face and coughed to try to subdue the nausea rising in her throat.

'Perhaps not, in the strict sense; but in the circumstances I can't see a jury being influenced by what they will see as an academic point of law. But we've got to catch the devil first. Which will be all the harder because the killer won't have had to worry about blood any more than about leaving DNA – the blows were struck into the hair, which was thick enough to absorb it. So no blood on carpet or walls or the murderer's clothing – only on the fire surround.' Kendrick's deep-set dark eyes had been haunted as he spoke, and Phyllida, mastering her own reactions, saw the vision pass from them and the old single-minded intensity return as he leaned forward in his chair. 'No sign of either of your reports in the house. Am I right in assuming neither knew the other was setting up an investigation, and that they asked for the reports to be sent to their respective places of business?'

'You're right, Chief Superintendent.' Peter leaned into a desk drawer. 'Here are copies. I'm afraid . . . We haven't discovered any evidence of the husband's infidelity, but nor have we ascertained that there's been none. God forbid I should be directing your attention to the innocent, but Mrs Jordan had just one suspect in her line of vision: her husband's secretary, Marjorie Turnbull, with whom he also goes singing with the Seaminster Choral Society. Hugh Jordan had a chief suspect: his wife's business partner, Joe Hardman. My field worker Steve Riley appeared to see Mrs Jordan and Mr Hardman emerging from an embrace in the dark, and that sighting has, of course, gone into the report I prepared for her husband.'

There was silence for a few moments as the three of them looked at one another. Then Phyllida asked the Chief Superintendent who had found the body.

'I'm sorry, I should have told you everything we do know before starting the speculations. I'm afraid Mrs Jordan was discovered by her young stepdaughter soon after twelve noon. We can't be more precise until we've had the post-mortem results, of course, but the doctor thought death had occurred a very short time before the girl raised the alarm. She's gone into clinical shock, but managed to tell us she'd been upstairs in her bedroom recovering from this bug that's been going around.'

'That was why Mrs Jordan was at home,' Phyllida said. Since Kendrick's announcement she had been speaking in her own voice; his news was too much of the real world to be met with play-acting. 'She was convalescent, too. And . . . and, perhaps not as strong as usual.'

'That is a possibility, Miss Moon.' Kendrick couldn't annoy himself by being attracted to the sophisticated American, but he was briefly self-critical as he tried to repress his sense of pleasure at being reminded of the pleasant sound of Phyllida Moon's own voice. 'That could be why she fell in the first place. If she was pushed, and was too frail . . .' There were tears now in Miss Bowden's unadorned eyes, and he didn't finish the sentence that had to be finishing itself in the minds of all three of them. 'The girl picked up the poker, she didn't deny it, so the one set of fingerprints will be hers, indicating that if she didn't kill her stepmother, the person who did had wiped the poker clean. The only other thing Susan Jordan managed to tell us before going into shock was that she'd come downstairs to get something to eat, so we can't tell what her gut reaction was to her terrible discovery. If, again, she hadn't . . .' Kendrick paused, allowing another sentence to finish silently. 'There's something more. Mrs Jordan's mother must have come into the room, either during the assault or after the assailant had gone. She was found on the floor by the door that leads into a conservatory. A heated place with easy chairs, where she was probably sitting when the attack took place. She's alive, but she's had a massive stroke. Brought on, it seems likely, by what she saw when she entered the drawing room. But we may never know that either; she's in a bad way and the doctor's first comment was that it would be a miracle if she could ever tell us anything.' No frustration could be as bad as the frustration of the two dead women found the previous year on a wooded roundabout – no hope of any clue beyond the limited circular confines of the traffic island – but this was pretty near to it, and Kendrick had to make a savage effort to contain and diffuse his sense of helpless fury.

'It's hard to believe,' Phyllida said slowly. 'Not, Mr Kendrick, that I can tell you that everything on my Sunday visit appeared to be domestically happy. You'll see from our report how sullen the daughter was and how on edge Mrs Jordan. The most striking result of my investigation – which you'll read in the report as well – is the different woman she appeared to be when she was with her business partner. I observed them once at close quarters, and Steve Riley spent the evening prior to the embrace he noted near to them too and confirms my reactions. What neither of us could tell was whether her confidence then was caused by her self-belief in her business abilities, the presence of her business partner, or the absence of her husband.'

'And that is something else we may never discover.' To the relief of both Phyllida and Peter, the rage died quickly from the dark eyes, and Maurice Kendrick leaned back in his chair with a sigh. 'So much background knowledge – thanks entirely to your Agency – and so little certainty about its interpretation.'

'When you've read the reports,' Peter said gloomily, 'I think you'll decide that there are rather more than two suspects.'

'I expect I shall.' In each mind, as for a few silent seconds the three of them dropped their gaze, was the terrifying thought of Hugh Jordan's daughter. 'Well . . .' Kendrick leaned forward again and this time got to his feet. 'We must put our hopes of narrowing the field into watertight alibis,' he said bracingly. 'And no one else with any possibility of involvement being ostensibly at home on his or her own, recovering like Mrs Jordan from the local bug.'

If those hopes were fulfilled, the thought of Susan Jordan would terrify them even more . . .

The Chief Superintendent had paused, and was looking from Peter to Phyllida. 'In the meantime . . . there's a rather remarkable coincidence that could—'

'Would you like Mrs Parker – that's the American woman who scraped an acquaintance with Mrs Jordan in the Outlook Café – would you like her to call at the house, ignorant of what's happened? That would only be useful, I suppose, though, if Mr Jordan and his daughter are staying there, which I can hardly imagine . . .'

'I'd certainly be grateful for your further help, Miss Moon, Dr Piper.' How it had cost Kendrick once, to say that, and how grateful he was today that Miss Moon had suggested it! 'There will be no necessity, though, for you to contact the Jordan house. Hugh Jordan told me before I left it just now that he and his daughter would be staying in a hotel for the foreseeable future.' Kendrick paused again, his searching gaze going slowly from Peter to Phyllida 'They will be moving this afternoon. To the Golden Lion.'

Ten

'*My dearest girl . . . beyond a few months as a husband, all I can offer you is widowhood.*'

'*Is that the only reason you haven't asked me to marry you?*'

'*Of course. It's reason enough.*'

'*Knowing you, I see that. Which is why I asked you. That makes it an entirely different proposition. It tells you what I want.*'

'*To be a widow?*'

'*Stop it, Jack. To live a lifetime of months as your wife. To be Phyllida Pusey until I die, too.*'

'*You're certain?*'

'*I've never been more so.*'

'*In that case, my darling, if you bring me the telephone book I shall ring the office of the Registrar of Births, Marriages and—*'

A fingertip against the beloved lips. '*Not yet, Jack. Not yet.*'

'Did you leave your office at any point yesterday morning, Mr Jordan?'

'If I tell you I did, will you arrest me for the murder of my wife? If so, I should like to telephone my solicitor.'

'There is no question of an arrest, sir. Of anyone. At this juncture. It's merely for elimination purposes, as I am sure you know, that we have to ask all . . . all family members and close friends and associates of the deceased to tell us their whereabouts at the time of a murder.'

'I don't think you'll get much satisfaction out of asking my daughter.'

'The detective sergeant is asking *you*, Mr Jordan.' Detective Chief Superintendent Kendrick's famous – notorious, some of his junior officers would have called it – preference for personal hands-on policing had brought him to the other side of the table from Hugh Jordan, next to DS Philip Wright and listening attentively to the DS's dialogue with Jordan. 'Do you have a problem in answering him?'

'Of course not, Chief Superintendent. I left home at half past eight and was in my office until half past ten, when I went out to keep an appointment at eleven. It was over by twelve and I drove down to The Parade for a breath of fresh air before returning to the fray.'

'I see, sir.' DS Wright shifted in his seat as Kendrick felt his heart sink and wondered how Jordan's was feeling. The man gave nothing away, and the smokescreen smile Phyllida Moon had spoken of before he left the Peter Piper Agency was still just in evidence. *That one can smile and smile, and be a villain.* Hamlet's words came unbidden into Kendrick's mind as he watched Hugh Jordan's face. Miss Moon had described the smile as a mask, and that was how he was seeing it too, particularly in circumstances where a smile was the last facial expression to be indicated. A mask indeed, deliberately assumed? Politeness carried to the point of paranoia? A quirk of nature, whereby what in response for the majority would be a slight seriousness was for Jordan, involuntarily, a smile? There was no way of knowing, and it was taking an effort for Kendrick to make himself see the smile without seeing a deviousness of mind behind it, a double view that could well do the man a serious injustice . . .

DS Wright was asking Jordan if he had seen anyone on The Parade he knew, spoken to anyone.

'Not a soul, I'm afraid, Sergeant. I can only tell you that when I'd parked behind the Golden Lion I walked through to The Parade, walked eastwards out of town for twenty minutes or so with pauses now and then to lean on the rail and look at the sea, then walked back to my car. That had me back in the office car park just short of a quarter to one – I know because I looked at my watch before getting out of the car – and my secretary brought me coffee and sandwiches at my desk while I made some preparations for a meeting in my office at two. The meeting interrupted by your telephone call . . .' Hugh Jordan broke off, and to Kendrick's intense interest his face abruptly crumpled and reddened for the few seconds it was visible before Jordan dropped it into a large handkerchief and started to sob. The two men opposite him sat still and silent as they watched his shaking shoulders, Kendrick at least wondering if he was witnessing a piece of play-acting, or the onset of genuine, irresistible, grief.

'All right, Mr Jordan,' he said with comparative gentleness, as Hugh Jordan lifted his head and blew his nose. 'This must be very distressing for you, particularly in view of the involvement of close members of your family—'

'Involvement of my family!' A look of outrage now, banishing the imminent return of the smile. 'Are you suggesting my *daughter* is involved in the murder of her stepmother?'

'I'm suggesting that for her to have discovered her stepmother's body in such horrific circumstances and to have been sent into shock must be an additional cause of distress to you as her father, Mr Jordan. However' – as the outrage receded – 'I'm afraid you must face the fact that your daughter's youth does not preclude her from a place among those, including yourself, who could have murdered your wife.'

Hugh Jordan bowed his head. In acquiescence, or to conceal a suddenly ungovernable moment in his face, Kendrick had no way of knowing. 'Anyone in Seaminster could have killed Sandra,' Jordan said calmly, as he looked up, 'if she opened the door to them. That's the only way I can see it, Chief Superintendent. A stranger. But if you insist on looking at the family . . . my mother-in-law was in the house. Are you including her among your suspects?'

'No. The way she fell indicates that she was entering the drawing room, not leaving it. And we doubt she would have had the strength.'

'But you believe my daughter would. When she was able to speak, Mr Kendrick, Susan didn't deny that she picked up the poker.'

'That, I think, Mr Jordan, could point to either innocence or guilt in equal measure.'

Now the face opposite Kendrick was ashen, and the smile had not returned. 'You're talking about my daughter, for God's sake! My thirteen-year-old daughter. It's obscene!'

'We have to consider every possibility, however unpalatable and unlikely, until we reach the truth.'

'Ah. The truth.' Hugh Jordan offered no further response, staring ahead of him yet giving Kendrick the strange impression that he was staring inwards, and after according a short respectful pause to the noble concept of the truth, DS Wright asked him if, so far as he knew, his wife had had any enemies.

'How easily you put her into the past, Sergeant. Sandra? Enemies? What a ridiculous idea!'

'To do with her working life? Would you know?'

'Of course I'd know! Sandra didn't talk a lot about her work, but it was obvious she was happy in it. She was with Hardman and Andrews when we got married just over two years ago – well, she *is* Andrews; it's her maiden name. Joe Hardman, her partner, comes from time to time to have dinner with us'

'He and your wife got on all right? Personally as well as businesswise?'

With the Peter Piper Agency report in his desk drawer, and his knowledge that it was there because Hugh Jordan had suspected his wife of having an affair with her business partner, Kendrick had to admire the way Jordan took the question: no reaction beyond another reflective gaze. But mingled with his admiration there came a renewed sense of frustration: if Jordan could so brilliantly dissemble his suspicions of a liaison between his wife and Hardman, what else couldn't he hide? Yet fate, Kendrick encouraged himself by thinking, in the shape of the covert co-operation between the Agency and the senior policeman now study- ing Jordan's face, had not dealt the man a good hand, whether he was innocent or guilty.

'So far as I know,' Jordan said judicially, his brow wrin- kling slightly to indicate a mental survey of the innocent little he knew about Joe Hardman *vis-à-vis* his wife. 'They both enjoyed their work and were good at it; when Joe came to dinner I could feel their enthusiasm, although they did their best not to talk shop the whole of the time.' Yes, Jordan was clever; and yet he must know (innocent or guilty, again) that his cleverness could backfire on him if Peter Piper decided, when he heard about the murder, that he had a civic duty to tell the police about the report Jordan had commissioned. It must at least have crossed Jordan's mind, Kendrick reasoned, that he might be better advised to let himself be the one to inform the police of the existence of the report. It could work for him, too, by offering a possible motive for Joe Hardman to be the one to have done Sandra Jordan to death.

So there was the possibility that Hugh Jordan could be

too clever for his own good. Too sure of himself. Or too much the gambler. There was even, in the light of his performance now, the possibility that he might be considering an approach to Piper to suggest an accommodation . . .

'Is Mr Hardman married, Mr Jordan?'

'I believe he was. Divorced, Sandra told me, a few years back. No children.'

'Girlfriend?'

'That I wouldn't know.' The full smile. In deeper and deeper, he must be aware, if Piper felt it his duty to turn the report over to the police. Not cleverness, Kendrick decided. Foolhardiness.

'Thank you, Mr Jordan,' he said, getting to his feet. 'That will be all for now, but of course you will realise we shall want to talk to you again. Interview terminated at – what is it? – 10.50 a.m.' Kendrick turned to the sergeant. 'When you've shown Mr Jordan out, Sergeant, I want you to take me to the hospital.' Kendrick's eyes were on Jordan as he spoke, and the smile he received in response triggered his biggest frustration of the morning. Thus far.

Gazing half an hour later into the staring eyes of Etta Andrews, he thought wistfully of the ancient superstition that the eyes of the done-to-death hold the picture of their killer. Mrs Andrews wasn't dead, of course, and whoever had murdered her daughter hadn't touched her; but he or she had driven her into the catatonic state from which she was not expected to emerge as surely as if they had brought the poker down on her head, too. And Kendrick, to his annoyance, found himself looking closely into those accusing eyes and searching for an image he didn't find.

'Does she ever close them?'

'When she sleeps.'

'So she's awake now? Can she hear me?'

The hovering sister shrugged. 'It's possible, but there's no way of telling.'

'If I ask her to press my hand if she *can* hear me?'

'You can try.'

Kendrick took hold of the nearer hand lying motionless on the sheet. A pretty hand, he noted, as he noted its chill, the nails well shaped and carefully polished, and the shaft of sorrow that was always waiting to pierce him in a murder case, and was often triggered by something comparatively trivial, shot through him so that for a moment he had to struggle for breath.

'Are you all right, Chief Superintendent?'

'Certainly, Sister.' He had always, in these moments, managed to preserve his carapace of invulnerability, although he sometimes wondered why it was so important to him that he should. 'Mrs Andrews.' He encircled the hand gently with his. 'Mrs Andrews. If you can hear me, press my hand. Can you hear me?'

There was no response. Nor when he tried again, then tried a third time with the other hand.

'I didn't think we'd get anywhere,' the sister said, 'but it's always worth a try.'

'How long will she live?'

'It's hard to say, Chief Superintendent. She could die at any moment, but it could just be that she could . . . continue breathing for quite a long time. It's too early yet to say.'

'Brain death. So there could be an ethical decision to be made.'

'Eventually, perhaps.' The nurse passed her hand across the still neatly curled grey hair in a gesture of professional compassion.

'Thank you.' Kendrick moved away from the bed after a last look at a face in which he must have been imagining there was still outrage. 'The girl. When will she recover?' He felt fear clutch him. 'She *will* recover? In her mind?'

'The doctors seem confident she'll recover entirely quite

soon, Chief Superintendent. I'm sure your constable will let you know as soon as this happens.'

'I'm sure he will, Sister. But I think I'll go along and have a word with him now. And a look at Miss Jordan.'

'Of course.'

'Her eyelids flickered half an hour ago,' PC Watson whispered, getting hastily to his feet as the Chief Superintendent and DS Wright, led by the sister, entered the other side ward a stone's throw from the one they had just left. 'And she's been threshing about a bit.'

'Let's hope it's the prelude to coming back.' Kendrick went up to the bed and gazed down on the pale, solemn face that looked small and pinched in its tousled surround of long blonde hair.

'Poor girl,' DS Wright ventured, as Kendrick joined the other two policemen by the door. 'I shouldn't think her subconscious wants to come back. I should think—'

'Hold on.' The Sister had remained by the bed. 'She's coming round.'

She was suddenly bolt upright, big blue eyes wide and a terrified gaze moving from one intent face to another.

'No questions now!' the sister said sternly. 'I want you all out of here. Talking to her will be a lot more valuable later on,' she conceded, when she had almost shooed them to the door. Kendrick noted with sardonic amusement that the two junior policemen were avoiding his eye as if to reassure him that they hadn't really been aware of his part in their triple routing. What wasn't amusing was the morning's second wave of frustration.

He had only been back in his office for a few pacing moments when his private phone rang.

'Chief Superintendent, this is Peter Piper. I'm concerned because—'

'Hugh Jordan has approached you about your report on his wife.'

'Yes. How did you—'

'I should have thought of it when I was with you. If he didn't confess to the police that he'd commissioned the report, he was bound to have decided to try and square you over it. He didn't confess, which told me he would be likely to contact you. Tell me exactly what he said.'

'He rang early – nine or so – from his office, he told me. I'd spent the night in my office, which I sometimes do if I've been working late – there's an enormous sofa – so I was here to take the call. As soon as I heard who it was I started recording, so I can let you have the tape.'

'That was a good decision, Dr Piper. But give me a résumé now, if you will.'

'Of course. Jordan asked me if I knew his wife had been murdered, and when I said I did, he said that of course he had had nothing to do with it, but that the existence of the report on her he had commissioned from the Agency could make things awkward for him, and he hoped I wouldn't feel I had a duty to hand it to the police. As you'll hear, I advised him as an innocent man to hand it to them himself. He said then that he would prefer the existence of the report to remain unknown, which would be a simple matter if I was prepared to destroy it. When I repeated the words *destroy it* with an exclamation mark in my voice, he amended it rather hastily to "bury it in your files until the murderer is brought to justice, when it will no longer be of any significance", or something like that.'

'And what did you say then?'

'I told him I couldn't say yea or nay just like that. I would have said nay if I had been the only one involved,' Peter went on hastily. 'I wouldn't have hesitated. But it just occurred to me that you might want me to string Jordan along, pretend to suppress the report . . . Anyway, he's asked me to call on him at the Golden Lion late this afternoon to tell him my decision. He indicated in a roundabout way that there might be an inducement. I was very angry, Mr Kendrick. If I'd been on my own, again, I'd have let him see it. But as things are . . .'

'You did very well, Dr Piper. You couldn't have done better.' Kendrick examined his reactions as he spoke, to see if there was any of his old resentment left at accepting yet again the help of a private detective, and accepting it with openly expressed gratitude, and was unable to decide whether he was glad or sorry that there was not. 'I think, though, that the police will get further with Hugh Jordan by letting him know we've seen your report rather than by carrying on as if we haven't. So, I'd like you to tell him that you handed it over to me this afternoon. Not until this afternoon, I want you to stress: if he thinks I knew about it during his interview this morning, and suppressed that knowledge, he'll no longer trust me – assuming he trusts me now – and it could hamper co-operation between us.' Kendrick hesitated. 'I don't want to sound melodramatic, Dr Piper, but as there isn't going to be a discussion over this and you're merely going to inform Jordan of a *fait accompli*, I suggest you tell him over the telephone. If he isn't a murderer, which we must assume for the moment he isn't, there would obviously be no risk in your visiting him in a hotel room; but as things stand I think the telephone will suffice. Oh, and before I go. Susan Jordan is out of shock, but I don't know yet when she'll be leaving hospital.'

'That's great news! Thank you for telling me. And for your advice re Jordan. I must say I'm pretty relieved to have it.'

He *was* relieved, Peter told himself truthfully as he hung up. It was just that the particular passion in him that had earned him a doctorate in Crime Fiction had already created a black-and-white mental scenario in which he and Hugh Jordan skirmished laconically across an anonymous hotel bedroom, before . . . But that was as far as the scenario went, and he had no taste for what would have been the other part of a potential deal with Jordan: the temporary image of himself, even though false, as a private eye who was venal.

It was just after twelve noon, and Kendrick decided to contact Joe Hardman. He wanted to talk to Jordan's secretary too, of course, in the light of the report prepared by the Peter Piper Agency for Jordan's wife, but he didn't as yet want Jordan, ignorant of that second report, to know he had an interest in Marjorie Turnbull. She, therefore, would have to wait until evening, when he would attempt to get in touch with her at home – if she wasn't out comforting her boss. The morning's third wave of frustration was averted by the realisation that, if Sandra Jordan's suspicions were justified, boss and secretary would hardly risk coming together except telephonically for some time to come, and, if they weren't, were unlikely to be together anyway outside working hours apart from their joint visits to the Aeolian Hall. As he recalled Jordan's reckless gamble over the existence of the report on his wife, Kendrick had a sudden mental picture of the man loping, crouched, up Miss Turnbull's garden path in the darkness of evening, and was vouchsafed a few moments of near-cheer: if he discovered the lady comforting her boss that evening in the privacy of her home, it could take weeks off the inquiry . . .

At least there would be no one interested in suppressing the wife's report, Kendrick reflected sourly as he climbed into the passenger seat beside his favourite and longest-serving detective sergeant, DS Fred Wetherhead, one of nature's philosophers whose occasional gnomic comments on human behaviour Kendrick took note of and respected – and who was the only man in his force who knew about the Peter Piper Agency's recent role in his policing.

It was an ugly day, The Parade drained of colour: low, featureless grey sky, darker grey sea, the horizon an HB pencil-line. Even on a day like this, being on the edge of the land exhilarated Kendrick, and he found himself remembering an occasion at the start of his career when he had turned down what sounded like a good career move because he would have had to live as far from the sea as it was possible to get in Britain.

Here he was, still on the coast, and at the top of his profession; and running a murder inquiry with the covert co-operation of a private eye . . . Sometimes, since he had admitted that the Peter Piper Agency had proved its worth to him, he tried to take himself unawares and get back the sense of shocked reluctance with which he had for so long accepted their help, but it would no longer come. Which was just as well, Kendrick told himself with a grim inward smile, in the current circumstances: Miss Moon and two of his chief suspects under the same roof and her partner the source of his knowledge that there was more – or less – to the marital relations of the Jordans than met the outside eye . . .

'Let's hope Hardman will be there, sir. With not ringing, we could be disappointed.'

DS Wetherhead knew what his boss's disappointment could be like.

'I'll bear with it, Fred.'

He could, of course, have summoned Joe Hardman to an interview at the station, or at least, as Fred had just suggested, ascertained whether or not he would find him in his office; but Kendrick was interested in seeing something of Sandra Jordan's work set-up as well as meeting the man who had brought her husband to the Peter Piper Agency. He had a reputation for fairness as well as severity that he believed was deserved, and the police would be expected at some point to visit the offices of Hardman and Andrews in connection with the murder of a partner, so that his visit would generate no embarrassment to Joe Hardman to compound his . . . shock? Grief? Guilt? At least they shouldn't have a smokescreen of a smile to contend with.

He should have been prepared for the main premises to be closed, Kendrick told himself with annoyance as he watched DS Wetherhead back away from the door and turn to the car, shaking his head. He was already on his mobile as the DS got back into the car, and within seconds it was answered.

'Thank you for your call, but I'm afraid we're closed until further—'

'This is the police. We appreciate why you're closed, but we're outside your premises and we'd like to come in. I'm Detective Chief Superintendent Kendrick and I have Detective Sergeant Wetherhead with me. If you come to the door you'll see the car.'

'Of course, er . . . Chief Superintendent. Right away.'

The door opened before they reached it, holding out their IDs.

'Come in, both of you.' The girl had red and watery eyes, and the other girl, sitting behind the reception desk, was blowing her nose. 'We're carrying on in here, but Mr Hardman didn't want the public at the moment . . .'

'Understandable, Miss . . . ?' DS Wetherhead responded.

'Barlow. Jill Barlow. This is Lyn Crawley.'

'We'd like to talk to you both. When we've talked to Mr Hardman, if he's here.'

'Oh, yes.' Lynn Crawley got to her feet and came round the desk. As she approached him, Kendrick saw that she was older than the other woman, and her manner gave him the impression she was in charge of the outer office. 'Mr Hardman said he couldn't cope with not having something to do, even though it meant being in the place where he and Mrs Jordan had . . . had . . .'

'Yes, Miss Crawley?'

'Had worked together for so long.' Was that what she had been going to say from the start, or had she decided it would be wiser to be bland? There was no way of knowing, and Kendrick was visited by yet another wave of frustration.

'Of course. Understandable,' he managed to repeat. 'Perhaps you'll take us to him.'

'Oh, yes. Of course. Jill?'

Still sniffing, the younger woman led them through a door behind the reception counter and across a small, square inner hall. She paused for a moment outside a door marked *Mr Hardman*, then tentatively knocked.

'Yes!' Kendrick heard both weariness and impatience in the monosyllable. 'Come!'

Looking unhappy, Jill Barlow opened the door and stood diffidently in the doorway.

'Well, Jill?'

'It's . . . it's the police, Mr Hardman. Very senior,' she went on hurriedly, as he stared at her. 'Chief Superintendent Kendrick and Detective Sergeant Wetherhead.'

Ah! thought Kendrick wistfully, as he led his sergeant into the room, one's memory when young! 'Good morning, Mr Hardman,' he said aloud, as Jill Barlow closed the door on them. 'I'm sorry to be calling on you for so distressing a reason, but you'll appreciate the necessity of examining every aspect of Mrs Jordan's life and talking to her—'

'You haven't found her killer, then?'

'We have not,' Kendrick responded, less amiably. He wasn't often interrupted, and did not like it.

'Please sit down,' Hardman suggested, after a few seconds looking into Kendrick's face. 'Both of you.' He came round his desk to move the second of the two wooden chairs closer to its farther side. 'What can I tell you? That I'm very upset and bewildered I'll tell you without

113

being asked. Sandra was a good friend as well as a valued partner.'

A bit of a cocky beggar, Kendrick decided, with his bright, dark eyes, glistening dark hair as curly as his own, and quizzical expression betokening a taking of this senior police visit in his stride; but – as he continued to look into Hardman's face – a man who could not quite hide the fact that he was reeling from a blow.

'Close friend?'

'Yes. For three years or so, I suppose. Before that – well, I'd be a fool to try to keep the fact from you, Chief Superintendent – before that, for a short time, we were an item.'

'You and Mrs Jordan had an affair?' DS Wetherhead stolidly interpreted.

'That's right. Oh, way before she met Hugh Jordan.'

'So what brought the affair to a close, Mr Hardman?' Fred asked.

Joe Hardman shrugged. 'It was never anything very much on either side, really just a temporary extension of our friendship. It had pretty well fizzled when Sandra met her Hugh, and that gave it the *coup de grâce*.'

'Did she tell Mr Jordan of the affair, do you know?' Kendrick asked. Beyond the window behind Hardman's head he became aware of a small courtyard garden with a rustic seat and a few tubs containing winter stalks, and marvelled absently at the hidden corners of this old seaside town – absently, because he was so intent on both hearing and seeing Hardman's reaction to his question.

There was no change in the voice, however, and nothing to see beyond a slight intensifying of the man's aura of confidential openness. 'I don't think she did, Chief Superintendent. I wanted her to – I thought she ought to and I told her so – but I don't think she could bring

herself to, even though what there had been between us
was so totally over.'

'Was she afraid of her husband, Mr Hardman?'

This was Fred, and not for the first time Kendrick was
reminded of the value of the man

'No, no. But . . .' *Let me put it man to man.* Kendrick
could almost hear the words, although they hadn't actually
been spoken. 'She loved him very much, and she was . . .
well, I think a little in awe of him. I don't think she'd ever
been in awe of anyone before and . . . well, it changed
her. Perhaps she'd never been really in love before, I don't
know.' Hardman closed his bright eyes for a moment, and
Kendrick wondered if the end of the affair had been as
painless a process for him as he had just made out. 'But
whenever I visited them for a drink or a meal, I found her
a very different woman from the woman I knew here at
work. I suppose the fact that Hugh's daughter didn't take
to her didn't help.'

'They didn't get on?' DS Wetherhead asked.

Joe Hardman shrugged. 'Hugh's wife had died, and an
only child . . . Perhaps it would have got better. I hope so.
But it's all academic now, isn't it?'

'Not our search for Mrs Jordan's killer,' Kendrick said,
watching the tic newly at work in Joe Hardman's cheek. 'I
hope my men didn't cause you too much disturbance when
they went through her office last evening.'

The third shrug. 'They shut themselves in. They were
carrying a few bags when they left, but when we looked
in after they'd gone we wouldn't have known they'd
been there.'

'I'm glad to hear it.' His men had brought back Sandra
Jordan's desk diary and her copy of Dr Piper's thin file
on her husband, but at this stage of the investigation there
was no way of discovering if the file had Joe Hardman's
fingerprints on it short of asking him if he knew of its

existence, and Kendrick was not ready to inform him of it if he didn't already know. 'Thank you, Mr Hardman.' Kendrick got to his feet.

As DS Wetherhead got to his feet, he asked Joe Hardman casually if he'd been a victim of the recent lurgy.

'No, I was lucky, I escaped. It seems to have been quite random; one of the girls went down but not the other.'

'It's been the same story at the station.' Fred Wetherhead beamed fellow feeling at Hardman before composing his features into comparative gravity. 'You'll appreciate, sir, that we shall probably require to speak to you again.'

'Of course, Sergeant.' But the twinkling-eyed gypsy was looking no more put out by the warning than had the man with the overriding smile. On his way out to the car Kendrick tried to cheer himself up with the thought that Hugh Jordan, at least, was about to pay for his hubris.

Eleven

'*Witnesses?*'
　　'*I hardly know my colleagues well enough. But if I resign and invite a couple of them at the same time . . .*'
　　'*Oh, Jack . . . But they'll be all we'll need.*'
　　'*Are you sure?*'
　　'*Absolutely. I don't have any friends in or near the city.*'
　　'*And don't want to ask any to come up from elsewhere? Bridesmaid, or whatever?*'
　　'*No.*'
　　'*Relations?*'
　　'*There are only my father, and a cousin. My father married again after my mother died, and he's happier with his second wife than I am. He and I are still close, Jack, but it's a long time since we've needed one another. I'm fond of Jane, but having her here for our wedding isn't important enough to summon her from Devon. I'd love you and my father to meet, but . . .*'
　　'*As things are, you'll tell him after—*'
　　'*I'll tell him eventually. Your family?*'
　　'*My son's in South America; I heard from him just before you arrived that he'll be there for another three months or so, and as you know, his mother's dead. There's no one else. So let's settle for a couple of my Edinburgh colleagues.*'
　　'*Let's. Jack . . . have you told your son? About me? About . . . yourself?*'

117

'Not yet. There'll be a letter. Phyllida, if you'd like to stay at a hotel the night before . . .'

'That's sweetly conventional of you, but I'd rather stay here.'

'Good. I won't ask you what you're going to wear, and I promise to keep out of the way while you're getting ready.'

'Oh, Jack! Jack . . . Jack . . .'

Miss Bowden was in Peter's office when the chief superintendent rang again in the late afternoon.

'You did another good job, Dr Piper. Hugh Jordan brought himself unbidden to the station, all contrition. How did he appear to take the news of your decision to hand over the report on his wife?'

'Calmly. I felt the shrug down the wire. I even got the idea he might have been relieved.'

'I think he was. He said how foolish he felt he'd been to attempt to suppress a document that contained no real evidence that his wife was having an affair, and kept stressing that he'd done so only because he loved her very much and didn't want her memory besmirched – yes, he used that very word – by so much as a suggestion that she hadn't been – and I quote again – "the best wife in the world".'

'The man's either too good to be true, or a consummate liar. How did you rate his performance, Mr Kendrick?'

'I don't know.' I don't know anything in this case, Kendrick continued sourly in his head. 'It was plausible. Dr Piper . . . Hugh Jordan said he'd just been to the hospital and told his daughter she could stay overnight or join him at the Golden Lion. She opted to join him.' Kendrick paused. 'Is Miss Moon with you?' Kendrick realised only as he heard himself speaking the name that the multi-faceted figure of Dr Piper's new business partner had, to his relief,

118

coalesced in his consciousness into the person that it truly was. 'I apologise, I should say "Miss Bowden".'

'Miss Bowden is here. Would you like to speak to her?'

'In a moment, when I've spoken further to you, Dr Piper. I'm wondering . . .' Peter winked at Phyllida across his desk and she nodded, smiling. 'Miss Bowden said in her report of her visit – Mrs Parker's visit – to the Jordan house that the daughter had appeared to show some interest in the American. The girl believes Mrs Parker to be staying at the Golden Lion, and if they meet there's bound to be some reaction, which might extend to her telling Mrs Parker something of use to the investigation, even if it isn't in words. And Hugh Jordan himself . . . he'll have to stand and listen to Mrs Parker's condolences and make some sort of response . . .'

'I belive Miss Bowden is about to cross the square and bring Mrs Parker to life. I'll hand you over to her.'

'I might have known, Miss Bowden,' Kendrick responded to the brief, severe greeting. He *had* known, of course, but as a policeman for more than three decades he had had to make sure; and to point out the crux. 'I'm very grateful. Particularly if . . . It would be of maximum assistance if you could be seen – regularly – in the public parts of the hotel as Mrs Parker, until you're confident that the character' – the effect of whose perfume, to his annoyance, Kendrick found himself attempting to recreate in an olfactory section of his mind as he spoke – 'has milked the situation as dry as you feel she can. Then, if the Jordans show no sign of leaving the hotel, Mrs Parker will, of course, leave Seaminster.'

'And Miss Bowden continue a covert surveillance.'

'That, of course, would be of assistance. But up till then – for maximum effectiveness it would have to be a pretty well full-time job.'

'I understand, Chief Superintendent, and I'm on my way.'

'Thank you, Miss Bowden.' Kendrick hesitated. 'I may . . . I think I should warn you that I may appear at some point in the Golden Lion, so that you don't betray your surprise if you see me.'

'Oh, I shan't do that, Chief Superintendent.'

It was the voice of Phyllida Moon, slightly mischievous, and Kendrick's chagrin at having questioned her skills aloud was eased by his amusement at her riposte.

'Of course not, Miss Moon. I'm sorry for having suggested it.'

'Not at all, Chief Superintendent.' Miss Bowden was back. 'It is always better to know what to expect.'

Kendrick replaced his receiver, feeling slightly shocked by his reluctant realisation that he and Miss Moon appeared to have reached a stage of familiarity that permitted of verbal sparring, plus the possibility that there might be two reasons why he was thinking of visiting the Golden Lion, and Phyllida smiled inwardly as the po-faced Miss Bowden marched briskly across Dawlish Square. She was feeling almost cheerful anyway, and realised as she reached her room and began rounding up the externals of Merle Parker that the feeling was engendered by the prospect of slipping into her most charismatic role. Was she feeding her own ego, Phyllida wondered idly as she slipped into the American's coffee-coloured satin underwear, by enjoying the attention always accorded to her favourite carapace?

Probably, she decided, and why the hell not? But her spirits abruptly descended at the sudden yearning for Jack's reaction, and when she was ready and sitting at her dressing-table mirror, she had to work to summon Mrs Parker's lazy smile.

Phyllida would have said, if asked, that she had experienced every possible permutation of her working life *vis-à-vis* two sides of Dawlish Square, but as she settled herself on to one of the stools beside the bar that stretched the length of the Golden Lion's spacious lobby, she realised this was the first time that the maintenance of a character in the public areas of the hotel was a possibly vital part of an investigation. Realised too, as with a rueful smile she surveyed her current persona in the gilt mirror that marched the length of the bar, that a solitary woman as eye-catching as Merle Parker could all too easily become associated in the public mind with the bar stool on which she might be destined to do a lot of sitting.

'Good evening, Mick.'

'Ah! If it isn't . . .'

'Mrs Parker.'

'Of course. Mrs Parker. Why not the small bar?' Mick inquired, when he had expressed his delight at the renewed patronage of Phyllida's American manifestation. 'I thought you preferred it. I prefer the paler hair, by the way, but you still look great.'

'Thank you, Mick. I have to stay out here, I'm afraid, because one of the contacts I hope to make is very young and unlikely to be taken into your inner sanctum by her father; and because her father will be around her all the time, she won't be able to make herself look older and chance it there on her own. I'd rather be in there, so that the whole world didn't have to witness Mrs Parker's addiction to the bar. So let's hope I make contact before I'm seen as a hopeless lush. A pity there's no drink that proclaims itself to be non-alcoholic.'

'So you'd rather not have one of my dry Martinis?'

'I'd rather have two. But I'll spin them out. And then have dinner in the restaurant and hope my subjects do that same thing.' John Bright had assured her and Peter that the murmur of the name *Moon* would always secure her a strategically placed table. 'D'you know, Mick, I've never had dinner in the Golden Lion restaurant.'

'Just you? Or all your ladies?'

'All of them. If I'm here at mealtimes, I eat in my room. Sandwiches.'

'I'm shocked, Mrs Parker' – and Mick looked shocked, pausing in his polishing of some glasses. 'With the hotel's gourmet reputation! Have you no culinary curiosity?'

'Not much,' Phyllida confessed, 'but I'm feeling kind of curious tonight. About the food, I mean, as well as about my subjects.'

In the mirror Phyllida saw a man and a woman squirming on to a couple of stools a little way along from where she was sitting, and Mick gave her a valedictory smile. 'Talk to you later, Mrs Parker.'

Phyllida nodded, blessing, not for the first time, the comprehensive view afforded by the enormous mirror in its neo-classic surround of husks, ram's heads and wine-red damask. Even to reach the images at the far end of the bar she had scarcely to turn her head and she had an excellent view of people crossing the lobby behind her, which was a piece of luck, she forced herself to realise, because as things were with the surviving Jordans, and the publicity both national and local that had begun its inevitably expanding progress the previous evening, they were unlikely to have much taste for public places. At least they would have to cross the lobby on their way to either lift or staircase, so that all the surveillance needed was a reflective gaze into the glass. Both glasses, Phyllida mentally amended, as she saw that she had finished her first Martini and hoped Mick would take some time to return and pour her her second . . .

Hugh Jordan would surely collect his daughter from the hospital in person, so that she would be able to identify the couple from no more than a quick glance, which should give her time to turn round and hail them. Not quite so simple as it had at first seemed, Phyllida realised further as she watched the gold hands of the clock in the central pediment of the mirror move steadily on. There was no way Mrs Parker could know that the Jordans had moved to the Golden Lion and she'd met them only once, so a rushing forward on a glance in a mirror could seem surprising as well as, in the circumstances, crudely intrusive. She would have to leave the bar the moment she saw them and, lost in thought, bump into them . . .

So she was pleased, after all, to see Mick on his way towards her glass. 'I may have to depart in a hurry,' she told him as she speared her second olive. 'If I see certain people.'

'Of course.' Mick's eyes were sparkling and his face was flushed. He probably got as much fun out of her chameleon presence in the hotel as the girls in Reception.

'And thanks for staying out here.' By seven o'clock Mick had always moved into the small bar at the back of the lobby and left his two minions in charge outside, but tonight he had dispatched the senior of them into his sanctum and remained within sight and sound of his favourite client.

Three quarters of an hour later she had finished her second Martini, withstood Mick's coaxing towards a third, and was reluctantly abandoning her hitherto comforting thought that the back door was too discreet and uninviting for the Jordans to use it and climb the back stairs to their rooms. However discreet, it gave on to the car park, and although Hugh Jordan would be confident that the media were so far ignorant of his move to the Golden Lion, photographs of him and his daughter had been shown on the national and local lunchtime news and would appear again that evening, so that they must already be going in fear of being recognised. So Hugh could well decide to smuggle his daughter up to the room he had already checked into and ring down to request a member of staff to bring up the key to her room and the wherewithal to enable her to check in, too . . .

'I'm going to have dinner,' Phyllida told Mick, before slipping from her stool and looking casually around her. The same man had walked behind her three times, each time more slowly, but wasn't at that moment in the lobby. It was time to move on. 'The Agency account as usual.' But something for Mick himself, from her.

'Cheers, Mrs Parker,' he said as he took it. 'Good to have you back. You're my favourite customer among your ladies, though I do like Miss Moon.' Mick cocked his head and looked a question, and Phyllida laughed. She had suspected that Mick didn't know who she really was. 'Then you like me,' she murmured, as Mrs Parker strolled away.

The acoustics of the Golden Lion dining room were so subdued it took Phyllida a few moments to realise that its hushed lamplit space was largely occupied; but not, Mrs Parker's lazy gaze told her, by the Jordans. John Bright was near the door, talking to the maître d', and turned to look at her with smiling admiration.

'Good evening, madam. For one?'

'Please. Phyllida Moon.' It was a whisper. 'So if you could manage back to the wall and facing the door.'

'Of course, Mrs Parker!' Phyllida heard the exclamation mark she heard in the voice of every member of John Bright's staff in the know, when they realised who stood in front of them. John had, of course, been informed earlier in the day that Mrs Parker would be checking in, but this was the first time he had met her. 'Philip, will you show Mrs Parker to table eleven?'

Although Phyllida had little culinary imagination, she had a healthy but discriminating appetite and savoured the outcome of the culinary skills of other people, so for a time the deliciousness of the meal she had ordered helped to assuage her disappointment at the non-appearance of the Jordans in the restaurant doorway. By the time her coffee tray arrived, however, her disappointment had swamped her enjoyment of the gourmet food and the two glasses of fine claret and a depression was settling over her that made her dread her return to the spartan office with its one small window on to an inner well, which tonight and perhaps for nights to come was to be her bedroom too, with the loss of Jack's comforting arms around her even more bleak than when she lay in her own bed and could look across the bay to Great Hill, feeling the richness of a world that would always encompass them both.

'Sorry I haven't managed it till now. We're rather busy, with the race meeting at Billing.' It was a pleasure out of all proportion to see that John Bright had dropped into the chair opposite. 'Have you enjoyed your dinner, Mrs Parker?'

'I don't think I've ever enjoyed a dinner more.'

'That's good. Particularly as you don't seem to have enjoyed anything else since you came in, and I can't believe you came in merely for the gourmet experience.'

'No "merely" about it, Mr Bright.'

'Thank you. Phyllida . . .' John Bright had dropped his voice. 'I don't know why you're here and I'm not asking you, but I hear the news and I thought you might like to know that Mr and Miss Jordan have checked into the hotel and are upstairs. They came in the back way to avoid any possibility of being recognised.'

'Thank you, John. That's very useful. And it means I can go to bed.'

'I thought it might. Sleep well, Mrs Parker.' John Bright raised his voice as he got to his feet.

'Thank you,' Phyllida repeated, her voice still low.

'For so much. Including not asking questions.' He never had done.

'All part of our service. Goodnight.'

She couldn't even cross the square, Phyllida thought gloomily, as she watched his retreating back; Peter had told her he wouldn't be there. Well, she had nothing to tell him and she'd had enough to drink; in her current mood more might make her maudlin. She hoped he was on a date, one that might be more successful than his usual amorous sorties. Not that he told her in words when things didn't work out – they neither of them discussed their personal lives – but the repetitive morning-after impression he gave her of an inner disarray was information enough.

It was ten o'clock, and there was no point in sitting on display any longer; she'd been lucky that the man who had eyed her in the lobby hadn't come in for dinner. She should get up the back stairs and not push her luck.

For the first time she could remember, Phyllida had to force herself to assume the American's easy strolling gait, and when she reached the back stairs she let it go and toiled up them, leaning on the rail and dismissing a ridiculously optimistic scenario of colliding with Hugh Jordan as he raced down them to retrieve something from his car.

There was a smell of cabbage in her room, and she went straight across to the small sash window and pulled it shut, then wafted some of Mrs Parker's perfume spray around the small space. Usually she began to dismantle her character the moment the door was locked behind her, but tonight Phyllida sank down into the one small armchair, too weary and disappointed to make a start.

The shrill of the telephone had her leaping to her feet and over to the bed.

'Hello!'

'Miss Moon?'

'What is it, Gail?'

'There's been a call for Mrs Parker from room 113. We said we thought you were in the hotel but you weren't in your room. Was that all right? Are you officially in your room now?'

'Yes . . . Who's in room 113, Gail?' The adrenaline was running so strongly she wondered she couldn't see it rippling the veins in the back of her hands.

'Miss Susan Jordan. Just a moment, please . . . Mr Bright would like a word.'

'Phyllida!' John Bright's voice was excited. 'Miss Jordan hasn't of course been given the number of your room, but I assume that in the light of her phone call there's the possibility that she's going to ask to come and see you. So I feel we should move you pro tem to a setting more in keeping with Mrs Parker. If you agree, Sam will be up in a moment to take your things to room 98 on the first floor. Near the Jordans – their rooms connect – but not too near. Would that be in order?'

'It would be wonderful. Thank you, John.'

'You'll want to ring her back. As she's so near her father, I have a feeling she may not want you to visit her, so perhaps you can ask her to give you half an hour, say, while you make some phone calls? If I meet you in ten minutes at room 98?'

'I'll be there.'

'Don't carry any clothes or cases, you could just bump into a Jordan. Sam will be up any moment.'

'He's knocking now. And point taken, I'll just bring my bag. Will you hold on a moment?' Phyllida let Sam in, waved her arms round the room and towards the bathroom with a grin. 'Can the girls put me through to room 113?' she asked John, as Sam got to work.

The ringing tone cut out as it began. 'Yes?' The voice a breathy whisper. 'Mrs Parker?'

'It is, honey. Oh, Susan, I'm so very sorry to hear what's

127

happened; but so glad you felt you could call me. What can I do for you?'

'I'd like to speak to you. Face to face. Can I come to your room?'

'Of course. But you'd rather that than I come to yours?'

'Yes! Daddy's next door.'

'And you can't talk to *him*?'

'Of course I can, but I want some . . . some impartial advice, and he wouldn't like the idea of that. So I have to come to you.'

Have to. On a sudden picture of Susan Jordan's sullen, uncompromising face Phyllida recalled the Chief Superintendent's warning to Peter not to enter a hotel bedroom where a possible murderer awaited him, didn't know whether she felt apprehensive or amused, and realised she felt both.

'All right, honey, you come to me; but give me half an hour or so, if you will, I've a couple of long-distance phone calls I have to make before ten o'clock. Say if I call you when I'm through with them?'

'All right. What's your room number?'

'Ninety-eight. Just round the corner from you.'

Phyllida was glad there was a corner between the rooms as fifteen minutes later she opened the door of room 98 to Sam, heavily arrayed with the contents of her office. Her personal belongings were negligible, but there had been no time to pack all the outward appearances of her cast of characters and the arms holding the loaded bags were crooked to take the contents of the coat hangers.

'No more secrets, Miss Moon!' he said cheerily, as he deftly transferred the hangers to the rail in room 98's large and elegant mahogany wardrobe. 'Everything else is in the bags. I tried not to look.'

'I've nothing to hide from the people who know why I'm here.' Phyllida looked round the handsome, impersonal room. 'Though it's a pity I haven't anything that looks personal.' Except Jack's photograph, which she had carried against her heart and which was now on top of the Gideon Bible in one of the little drawers beside the king-size bed.

'The room's fussy enough. No one would want to live the year round with this décor.'

'Lots do, Sam. As you very well know.'

'Yep. Well, see you later, Miss Moon.'

'Thank you again, Sam.' Cash changed hands, and Phyllida sank into her second armchair of the evening – larger and more importantly upholstered – as Sam closed the door behind him.

She still had ten minutes of the half-hour she had requested, but Susan Jordan must not be allowed to go off the boil, and within seconds Phyllida had left the armchair and was sitting on the bed with the telephone in her hand.

'Susan, honey? I've gotten my calls over; they didn't take so long because there were a couple of no replies. So would you like to come over?'

'Yes. Thanks.'

The knock on the door came before she had counted twenty. Susan Jordan was wearing jeans and a loose, cowl-necked sweater, and looked desperately thin.

'Honey, you look starving cold! My kettle's boiled, and I'm going to have coffee. It isn't up to much, of course – it never is in hotel bedrooms – but will you join me?'

'OK. Thanks.' The girl huddled herself, uninvited, into the armchair Phyllida had vacated, and when Phyllida had prepared them each a cup of coffee, she took the smaller chair after placing the usual spartan hotel biscuit offering on the small table between them.

The girl uncoiled as she drank, leaning back in the chair and spreading out her legs.

'Feeling better, honey?'

129

'Yeah. What d'you think, Mrs Parker?'

'What do I . . . Ah!'

Susan Jordan had set her coffee cup down and pulled her sweater slightly up and her jeans slightly down to reveal her navel. A tiny circle of gold protruded from it.

'Susan! Does your father know?'

'Of course not; he'd kill me. Sandra didn't know, either. Like it?'

The gold ring could have been a snake, the way it held Phyllida's eye. It appeared to have a small jewel in it, but she didn't want to look any closer. 'It's very . . . It's a bit unnerving, frankly, for someone as old-fashioned as me. But it's certainly . . . eye-catching.'

'That's right.' To Phyllida's relief the girl adjusted her clothes to cover her middle, then patted it with a contented smile.

'And I'm flattered that you felt you could share it with me. Well now, honey . . . what is it?'

'It's . . .' The sudden direct gaze was disconcerting, and Phyllida felt herself blink. 'Would you always tell the truth, Mrs Parker?'

'Ah.' Phyllida thought, and was relieved to discover that she and Merle Parker shared the same ethical stance. 'In big issues, I think I would. In small ones – where a white lie would save someone's feelings and do no harm – I might not.'

'This is a big issue.'

'Go ahead, then.'

'I said . . . I said that when I went downstairs my stepmother was alone, and dead.'

'Yes?'

'That's true. But what I didn't say was that before I went down I stopped at the top of the stairs that come down into the corner of the drawing room. It's not the main staircase; it's a little stair that leads down from the half-landing where my bedroom is, and I was about to come down it when I saw . . .'

'Yes, Susan. What – who – did you see?'

'I saw Sandra sort of fighting with this person. Then she fell and hit her head. And when this person had looked at her, they went and picked up the poker and . . .'

'Yes, Susan, I know what they did. But who was it?'

'Oh, Mrs Parker . . . d'you think I ought to tell the police?'

'Yes, honey, I do.'

'OK, then. But I'll tell you first. It was Daddy's big fat secretary. It was Marjorie Turnbull.'

Twelve

'*Jack . . . That new TV crime series starts in a moment on ITV.* A Policeman's Lot.'

'*I've read about it. You'd like to watch it?*'

'*You wouldn't?*'

'*If you would, I'm happy to. I didn't know you liked fictional crime. Oh, Phyllida, how much we haven't learnt!*'

'*You've more to learn tonight than you can imagine. Watch closely.*'

'*I'm watching closely.*'

'*The private eye, Jack. That's why I looked for a job as a PI, to get some hands-on experience.*'

'*Oh, my God . . . Phyllida Moon, who are you?*'

'*I sometimes wonder, but I know for sure at this moment that I'm the woman holding your hand.*'

'*But . . . where's the publicity? The opening of supermarkets? The interviews on breakfast TV?*'

'*You won't see my name in the credits. And I hope you wouldn't have recognised me if I hadn't prompted you.*'

'*I don't know . . . My darling, even you can't be* that *modest!*'

'*I might be. But it's academic. I know I went to work for Peter because I wanted my role in the series to look as authentic as possible, but what happened was that I found my real work vocation. Oh, it was a thrill to be cast in such a prestigious series, and to do the part as well as I could, and it got me out of my rep rut.*

But since I joined the Agency, that's been my working life.'

'And if you'd found me ι . . . a well man?'

'I'd have found an agency in Edinburgh. Which wouldn't have been so difficult, Jack; I'd have had Peter's reference to help me. Darling, what is it?'

'It's a hatred of all these conditional tenses. "Would have". "Could have". "Might have". Oh, Phyllida, I'm so sorry.'

'Don't be. We could so easily never have found one another again.'

'So you're prepared to sign a statement, Susan, that you saw your father's secretary, Marjorie Turnbull, hit your step-mother with the poker from your drawing-room hearth?'

'Yes.'

'Why didn't you tell us at the time?'

'Or as soon as you came out of shock,' DS Wetherhead added, with a wary glance at his superior officer.

'I . . . I didn't know what to do. And she frightens me. She's a big lump of ego and she was after Daddy, you could see it a mile off. Not that he was interested.'

'So you kept quiet. What made you change your mind? Decide to put Miss Turnbull in the frame? Your fear that the report your father commissioned on your stepmother would put *him* there? That you might find *yourself* there?'

Kendrick saw to his annoyance that the social services woman sitting beside Susan – a drab, Miss Bowden type – had pursed her lips and shifted in her seat, but to his relief she remained silent.

'No! Yes . . . Miss Turnbull was always in the frame because I saw her hit Sandra. But I had to think . . . Daddy told me about the report before he told you' – Kendrick heard DS Wetherhead's strangled snort – 'but once you knew . . . Daddy doesn't have an alibi and I got frightened then that if I didn't tell you what I'd seen you might arrest him. All right, or me. Because you knew for sure that I was there in the house when . . . when it happened. Miss Turnbull can't get herself an alibi, of course. The best she could do was to say she was out buying sandwiches for Daddy's lunch. Yuk.'

'Your accusation against Miss Turnbull, Susan, could be interpreted another way: as a story made up to protect both your father and yourself.'

'No! I saw her!' Susan's strident response almost drowned out the social services bleat, and to Kendrick's further relief the girl continued robustly. 'She beat my stepmother to death! I'll write it down and sign it!' The brief blaze of fear in the wide blue eyes at Kendrick's last words was now a blaze of conviction.

'All right, Susan. Let's go through it step by step.'

'All right, Mrs Anderson?' DS Wetherhead echoed. During their introductions Kendrick hadn't troubled to catch the woman's name. Not, he now assured himself, out of indifference, but simply because of his total reliance on his sergeant in such matters of detail.

Mrs Anderson nodded, telling Susan not to be afraid and to go ahead.

'I heard the front doorbell,' Susan began promptly, with a contemptuous glance at her official protector, 'and then I heard Sandra answering it. She was downstairs and I think she was sitting in the drawing room reading or something; she'd said she didn't feel better enough to go back to work. I suppose like I felt I wasn't ready to go back to school. I decided I could do with a Coke, and when I got up – I was sitting at my desk – I heard her and Miss Turnbull's voices and then, when I got out on to the landing, the voices went louder and sounded angry, and when I got to the top of my stair I saw Miss Turnbull sort of shake Sandra and Sandra fall and hit her head on the corner of the brass fender round the fireplace. There was blood right away, coming from under her head; it sort of shone in the light from the conservatory door. Sandra . . . didn't move. She was lying almost on her face.'

'She didn't move,' DS Wetherhead repeated. 'But you didn't run downstairs to help her.'

Colour flooded the intense white face, and quickly ebbed. 'I . . . I couldn't seem to move. It was like I was watching a film. Miss Turnbull didn't move either, for what seemed like ages; then she suddenly sort of marched across to the fireplace – she was standing by Sandra's feet and it was only a few steps – grabbed the poker and . . . and hit Sandra's head with it. Twice. I heard . . . I heard a sort of crack . . .' Susan Jordan's face crumpled, and for the first time, in Kendrick's view, she looked like a terrified child.

'Shall we have a little break here?' DS Wetherhead asked, with an unfortunate choice of words, as he leaned across the table to place his hand on the girl's. She let it lie there until it was withdrawn, but shook off the arm Mrs Anderson had ventured round her shoulders.

'No! I'd rather get it finished. I heard Miss Turnbull draw a sort of big breath; then she looked at the poker as if she didn't know how it had got into her hand, took out a handkerchief and wiped the handle very thoroughly and carefully, then put it down by Sandra. As she was straightening up, Sandra's mother came into the room from the conservatory; I heard her before I saw her because the conservatory door's on the same side of the room as my stair. I heard her sort of shriek, and then I saw her head and shoulders as she fell forward. I remember being scared when La Turnbull crossed the room towards her, and I backed off so that if she'd looked up there was no way she could've seen me. I didn't hear anything for what felt like hours – I suppose she was making sure old Granny

Andrews wouldn't be able to tell you anything – and then she went quite quickly – for her – to the door and out into the hall and then for ages again I didn't hear anything; I suppose she was wiping both sides of the front door. Then I heard it slam shut and her car starting. Then . . . then . . . I made myself go downstairs and the next moment I was holding the poker. La Turnbull was lucky: she wouldn't have had any blood on her. The only place it was was on the carpet by Sandra's head and in her hair and on the end of the poker . . .'

Susan Jordan leaned forward, retching, and Mrs Anderson said sternly that enough was enough.

'I'm all right.' The girl flashed another scornful look at the woman beside her as she straightened up, then turned to the policemen. 'Is that what you wanted to know?'

'Thank you, Susan,' Kendrick said, shaken by an unbidden comparison between this girl and his own young daughter, and the sudden query in his mind as to what it would have done to her if he and Miriam hadn't got back together and one of them had taken a new partner. 'I know that was an ordeal for you, but it was very helpful. Now, we'll arrange for you to be taken back to the Golden Lion.'

'The Golden Lion? I want to go back to school.'

'Susan! Surely . . .'

Another contemptuous glance silenced Mrs Anderson.

'You're sure about that, Susan?' Kendrick asked.

'Of course I'm sure. There's nothing wrong with me.'

And you couldn't bear to pass up your day of fame. The interpretation of Susan's apparent fortitude passed between Kendrick and Wetherhead as they glanced at one another.

'All right, Susan,' the DS said, 'we'll take you back to school.' He smiled placatingly at Mrs Anderson, who opened her mouth to speak, then shook her head and led the way out of the interview room.

When DS Wetherhead joined Kendrick in his office after handing Susan Jordan over to a driver and thanking a grim-faced Mrs Anderson for her assistance, he sat heavily down and looked across the huge desk at his chief. Kendrick stared stonily back, and it was Fred Wetherhead who eventually broke the silence.

'That sounded like the view from a ringside seat, sir.'

'It did, Fred.'

'How will you tackle her, sir? Miss Turnbull, I mean. Bring her in for questioning, or carry on with the softly softly?'

'The girl could get on to the media – I'd say it would be in keeping – or her father could if she's shared her – what is it, Fred, truth or fiction? – with him. We'll have to drop my idea of questioning Marjorie Turnbull discreetly at home and do it here; and for the other reason: that we'll want her out of the way when we search her house.' The mere prospect made Kendrick feel weary, and he wasn't going to be doing the job. 'We don't want to waste any more time, so we'll have to bring her in from her office.'

'At least we needn't ask for her house keys until we're back here and can hand them over to the uniforms,' DS Wetherhead said anxiously, and was relieved as the Chief Superintendent nodded. 'And if there's nothing found in the house, we can't hold her.'

'No. I'm just wondering . . .' Kendrick found himself shocked at the eagerness with which he now turned to thoughts of the Peter Piper Agency and what it might do for him, but not profoundly enough to be deflected from the idea that had just come into his head. At least he could share it with Fred, who had never, yet, given any indication of how he viewed what had become his senior's regular bizarre deviation from the straight path of duty. 'If Marjorie Turnbull really did do it, there might be some collusion between her and Jordan and they might just risk a meeting somewhere, if not at the Golden Lion. If she did the deed on her own, the girl might be in danger – there's no way we can withhold the identity of our informer. So I'm thinking about asking Dr Piper if he could put his chameleon boy on to following her. The Agency was on the case before we were,' Kendrick added, in mitigation.

'So it would be merely an ongoing piece of Agency enterprise,' Fred supplied, and a ghost of a smile flickered fleetingly from face to face.

'Just so, Fred. I'll get on to Piper before we approach the lady, so that the lad can be standing by when we let her go.'

Kendrick found it a relief, when he arrived in person at Hugh Jordan's office and asked for the boss, to learn that he was out. He suspected Jordan's daughter of not having informed her father of what she was going to tell the police at her interview – as much because of his reading of her as because a bewildered (or angry) Jordan hadn't been on the blower to him – and had decided, if he was there, to fill him in before confronting Miss Turnbull. In his absence, a request to speak to his secretary would cause little or no adverse speculation about Miss Turnbull *vis-à-vis* the murder of her employer's wife. Kendrick felt a little smug: it was not always easy for him to remember that even the most obvious culprit was technically innocent unless and until he or she was proved guilty.

Hugh Jordan's secretary received them graciously in an office as large and as handsomely upholstered as she was herself.

'Thank you,' she said, as she glanced at their proffered IDs. 'I'm sorry Mr Jordan isn't here at the moment to receive you. What can I do for you in his absence? Please sit down.'

'It's you, in fact, that we're here to see, Miss Turnbull,' DS Wetherhead said gravely, following his superior's lead and ignoring the more spartan of the two offered chairs.

'Yes, Miss Turnbull,' Kendrick continued. 'A very serious allegation has been made against you. That you were seen to strike Mrs Sandra Jordan with a poker and possibly kill her.'

'What? I . . . ?'

Observed closely by both policemen, the bewilderment appeared convincing; as did the outrage that quickly succeeded it.

'That's a wicked lie, Chief Superintendent! I was nowhere near the Jordan house . . . that morning. Oh, God . . .' Miss Turnbull felt behind her for her desk chair, and sank into it. 'This is a nightmare. I have to be dreaming.'

'I'm afraid not,' DS Wetherhead said gently, before crossing to a table against the wall and pouring her a glass of water. 'Drink this.'

Kendrick reflected, on another wave of frustration, that shock could have been expected whether the lady was innocent or guilty: if guilty, the shock of unforeseen discovery.

'Who has accused me?' Marjorie Turnbull demanded, when she had drunk from the glass, set it down on her desk and risen to her feet.

'Mrs Jordan's stepdaughter, Miss Susan Jordan, has signed a statement to the effect that she observed you,' DS Wetherhead responded reluctantly. He and the DCS had agreed that there would be no advantage, merely a gratuitous cruelty, in withholding information that could soon be in the public domain.

'The wicked girl! I had no quarrel with Mrs Jordan. And even if I had . . .' Briefly Miss Turnbull closed her fine eyes. '. . . I would never, ever, have taken any sort of violent action against her. Of *any* kind, against *anyone*, let alone murder . . .' Miss Turnbull sank back on to her chair, her face suddenly bloodless, and Fred Wetherhead crossed the room again, this time swiftly, and pushed her head down towards her knees. Then waited beside her until she lifted it, and guided the glass of water back into her hand. 'Take your time,' he said soothingly. 'You must appreciate, Miss Turnbull, that we have to act on information received in . . . in such grave circumstances.'

'Yes. Of course.' A little colour had come back into Miss Turnbull's face. 'Unfortunately for myself, I was out of my office between about eleven o'clock and one on the morning Mrs Jordan was . . . killed, but I made a number of contacts and you can check—'

'We shall, Miss Turnbull,' the DCS interrupted. 'And you will appreciate that even before this . . . accusation . . . we were preparing to interview you in the light of your business and leisure connections with Mrs Jordan's husband. I think you'll share our preference for the interview to take place at the station rather than in your office, so if you'll come with us now.'

'Not in handcuffs I trust, Inspector.'

'Chief Superintendent,' the DS murmured on a reflex.

'Chief Superintendent,' Marjorie Turnbull repeated impatiently. Both policemen could see that anger was now her dominating emotion, and that it had restored much of her strength.

'Of course no handcuffs,' Kendrick said. 'Just three people leaving the office amicably together. That's up to you, Miss Turnbull. We didn't identify ourselves at your reception desk.'

'You probably didn't have to.' Miss Turnbull's eyes encompassed Kendrick's six foot five inches from feet to curly dark head, then locked, in proud outrage, on his. 'Most people these days watch television.'

'I'm sorry, Miss Turnbull.' There was nothing else they could do to make it easier. 'Shall we go?'

By tacit agreement both policemen allowed Miss Turnbull to precede them out of the building, when with restored aplomb she had informed Reception that she would probably be out of the office for the next hour or so, and that they should inform Mr Jordan accordingly if he was back before her; but sitting beside her in the back of the unmarked car, Kendrick asked her for her house keys.

'And what do you expect to find, Chief Superintendent?' Close to, Kendrick found her physical presence disconcertingly strong. 'Bloodstained clothing? A diary entry, confessing all?'

An innocent Marjorie Turnbull could have assumed there would be blood. A guilty one could have pretended the assumption, secure in her knowledge that bloodstained clothing would not be among the items the police would be looking for. There was no way of knowing which one they were facing, and Kendrick had to withstand another wave of frustration as he decided he was on one of the most disagreeable investigations he had ever had to lead.

There was one small light beyond the predictably drawn-out denial that occupied the next three-quarters of an hour. When he had arranged for Miss Turnbull to be taken back to her office in an unmarked car, and despatched a couple of uniforms to follow up her story of her movements on the morning Sandra Jordan had died, Kendrick rang Dr Piper again.

This time Susan Jordan's late evening call was put through to room 98, where Phyllida was pacing in comparative splendour, wondering whether to venture a call to room 113 or abandon Mrs Parker for the night, descend as herself to the front of the hotel and look across the square for a light in the Agency windows. Underneath her professional

141

dilemma a sense of personal bleakness made the thought of Peter's cheering company especially enticing, and she had almost decided to call Merle Parker a day when Susan's call came.

'Mrs Parker . . . I'd like to come and see you!'

'And I'd like to see you, honey! I've been wondering . . . did you—'

'I'll come, then?' It was barely a question.

'Why, yes. Of course. If you feel you can.'

'Oh, I can. I've just said goodnight to Daddy. He's in bed.'

Jordan would hardly risk sneaking out of the hotel from a room the other side of a door that connected with his daughter. That night, at least, there was no need to speculate that he might be with Marjorie Turnbull – where he would hardly want to be, anyway, if his daughter had told him what she had told Merle Parker. Hugh Jordan's smile had been weakly and intermittently in evidence when she had met father and daughter by chance in the lobby bar earlier, and it had been impossible to read if he was suffering from a further blow.

The girl was there within minutes, in dressing gown and bare feet, her long fair hair tumbled about her face. She made her way immediately to the larger of the two armchairs, and curled up in it.

'Coffee, honey?'

'Yes. Please. No biscuits, I've eaten my own.'

'That's fine. Susan, have you told your father what you told me?'

'No. But I've told the police.'

'Who will tell your father.'

Susan shrugged. 'That's OK.' The relief briefly relaxing the tense face showed Phyllida how much harder it would have been for the girl to tell her father what she'd seen than it had been to tell Kendrick and Co. 'I was with the police anyway; they called me for an interview. They asked me what I knew, and I told them. I told them what I saw. She'll deny it, of course.'

'Of course. Anyone would, if they thought they could get away with it.'

'I know.' The girl made a nestling movement in her chair. 'But I've got something . . .'

'What's that, honey?' Phyllida put the two coffee cups down on the table between the chairs.

'Just something . . . if she tries to get away with it and put the blame on me.'

'Well, Susan, all I can say is that I hope justice will be done.'

'Oh, it will be.' The girl yawned. 'I'm tired.'

'You must be. I was surprised to learn when we met in the lobby bar that you'd decided to go back to school; I thought you'd want to wait a while.'

'Why? I'm not ill.'

'Of course not. But . . . with what's been on the news and all . . . you must have felt a bit . . . well . . . uncomfortable.'

'No.' Susan paused, wriggled her feet, then said in a rush, 'Everyone wanted to talk to me. Or just stand close to me when I was talking to other people. It was exciting. It made me feel good.'

'Well, that's fine, honey. If you felt like that.' Looking into the suddenly flushed face, Phyllida felt a pang at the sheer youthfulness of the enthusiasm the girl, for all her attempts at sophistication, had been unable to suppress.

'Oh, I did.' Pinched and white again. Wary and watchful. Not of Merle Parker, which was a minor miracle, but of the rest of the world she was confronting. 'Thanks, by the way, for not letting on to Daddy that we'd had a chat.'

'You knew I wouldn't, or you wouldn't have asked me for one.'

'You're right. What will the police do about Miss Fatty?'

'I beg your pardon?'

'Miss Turnbull. Will they arrest her?'

'On your say-so? I doubt it, honey, but she'll be their front runner and I should think they'll turn her house over.'

'Good.' Another nestling movement. *And one person who came between me and my daddy will be cancelled out by the other.* Phyllida could almost hear the words behind the expression of satisfaction as Susan Jordan finally relaxed into her chair and closed her eyes.

When Phyllida turned round from pouring herself another coffee, the girl was fast asleep, her face childlike and innocent, one hand dangling over the arm of the chair and her bare feet drawn up underneath her. Looking down on her before wakening her and sending her off to bed, Phyllida shivered as she found herself afraid there might be two front runners for the role of murderer of Sandra Jordan.

Thirteen

'*I, John James Pusey . . .*'
    '*I, Phyllida Jane Moon . . .*'
    '*. . . husband and wife.*'
    '*It's a funny honeymoon, my darling, an afternoon in a botanical garden.*'
    '*It's beautiful. I just hope it isn't hurting, to have come back . . . as a visitor.*'
    '*Nothing hurts now. The season's right, isn't it? Golden autumn.*'
    '*Yes. Don't be cross because I'm crying; just put your arms round me . . . I want to live forever in this moment, Jack. How can I do it?*'
    '*Tell yourself this is happening* now, *and – in the future – you'll always be able to reach back for it.*'

When Susan Jordan had trailed off to bed, Phyllida rang the Agency with noisily beating heart. Whether it was her chilling thoughts about the girl, or her big-dipper spirits taking one of the nosedives that since Jack's death were always lurking to plunge her downwards when she came out of character, she could do with a couple of drinks in Peter's company.

    'Yes?'

    The relief was enormous; but the voice had been drowsy and reluctant. 'You were asleep?'

    'Yes, but I'm always glad when it's you that wakes

145

me.' Peter regretted his choice of words the moment they'd come out, but he'd been too sleepy to put his guard up. 'What news?' he continued quickly. 'Have you seen a Jordan this evening?'

'Hugh joined me about half past six at a table in the lobby bar for a drink. Unplanned. I – Merle – said to talk if he wanted to, or be silent, and he was mostly silent. As was his daughter, scowling over her Coke. Susan hasn't told him, by the way, what she told the police – I'll explain in a moment how I know. I could tell Hugh was straining to be polite when he suggested Merle join them for dinner, too, and I said I was going out. Then went upstairs and had coffee and sandwiches amid the splendours of room 98. You'll smile when I say I can't wait to get back to my business address.'

'I expected it. You're awfully spartan with yourself; I've always thought so.'

'I had my reward tonight. Susan rang half an hour ago: could she come and see me again? She—'

'Why not cross the square and tell me in person?'

'Oh, I'd be glad to!' But Phyllida hesitated. 'If I go out the back and come down the passage to the square, all right to come as myself? Merle's too showy, and I haven't the energy to assume La Bowden.'

'Of course. I haven't seen you in ages. In fact I'd begun to wonder if I'd ever see you again. How long?'

'Fifteen to twenty minutes.'

The first drink was waiting at her place across the desk from Peter's chair, and they smiled companionably at one another as they raised their glasses. 'It's good to see you, Phyllida,' Peter said, his smile becoming a grin before a more serious look claimed the expressive face. 'Not that you look all that well. Altogether too fragile for the stuff you're doing.'

'So it's just as well I'm doing it in disguise. Nothing was

said about the murder when we were in the bar earlier, but Susan's just told Merle she accused Marjorie Turnbull to the police when they interviewed her this afternoon. She didn't tell her father, which Kendrick will remedy in the morning. Did Steve get anything beyond cold feet?'

'Not yet. To elaborate on Kendrick's latest call to me, he said that, when confronted with Susan's accusation, Miss Turnbull was all outrage and disbelief. No sign of fear.'

'From what I've seen of her I'd hardly have expected otherwise. Where did she go when she left the station?'

'Back to her office. From her own inclination, Kendrick thought, but also guided by him in that direction because of the possibility that the police wouldn't have finished their search of her house. They didn't find anything incriminating, which I don't think really surprised anyone. Kendrick's asked Jordan to call on him in the morning, when he'll tell him about Susan's accusation. He told me there'll be nothing fed to the media unless something's found to back up the girl's accusation.'

'Unless the girl feeds the media herself. Marjorie Turnbull must be well aware that Kendrick's promise to keep temporary shtum is pretty valueless with the girl at large. Innocent or guilty, the woman must be living a nightmare. Oh Peter, I do wish I'd managed to find out if there's more to her relationship with her boss than meets the eye. Their faces certainly touched outside her front door the night I followed them, but neither I nor the camera could tell whether they met at lips or cheek.'

'You know, I'm not sure that that's so important. If Miss Turnbull's obsessed with Jordan, she could take action to get his wife out of the way whether or not he was reciprocating. It'd just indicate a higher grade of criminal insanity. By the way, now you're my partner – my business partner – you ought to have your own office.'

'I have. Across the square. I don't need a room to myself

147

over here. Jenny's almost always in Reception and when Steve's in he tends to favour the restroom over the general office. It's all I need, Peter.'

'If you say so. Though I'll go on thinking.'

'No need. But yes' – in answer to the gesture and the smile – 'I will have another drink.'

Steve's reward took a couple of eventless cold spells to arrive, but when it came it was spectacular. He'd set out in pursuit of Marjorie Turnbull's car when at half past five it left the car park near her office, cursing what in Seaminster was the equivalent of rush-hour traffic as he almost immediately lost it, withheld (contrary to instructions) the news from his mobile in the desperate hope that he'd find her car in her own carport – for Steve, every professional task was an assault on his competence – and shouted his relief aloud when he saw it there. The relief helped him through the next couple of hours, at the end of which he ate his sandwiches and drank some of his coffee, then rang Peter.

'Nothing, guv. Except the onset of frostbite. She came straight home' – it wasn't a lie; he'd caught up with her so quickly there was nothing she could have done on the way beyond posting a letter – 'left her car in her bit of a drive, and just now came out and put it away. Appeared to go straight back inside, but I can't see her front door from where I am – this is a hell of an open place; I'm expecting a bang on the window any minute from a suspicious neighbour. I've started to have fantasies about the first-floor window opposite; if I was police I'd be warm and comfortable behind there, with endless householder snacks and mugs of tea and a zoom lens focused on her front door, I'd—'

'As she's put the car away, Steve, I think you can knock off for the night; but I'd like you back in position

148

to follow her in the morning – I'm told she gets into the office promptly at nine. If that's where she ends up, you can knock off again and resume your watch, say, mid-afternoon, in case she leaves early. If she does go to her office, come in to yours and we'll have a chat. I'm sorry it's such a cold night.'

'So am I, guv.'

Ten hours later, refreshed by eight hours of the dreamless sleep into which he always sank the moment his light was out unless his long-suffering girlfriend Marilyn – or, occasionally, some other girl less well known – was beside him, Steve resumed his vigil in the second of the two spots he had decided were the least prominent in the baldly neat piece of suburb where Miss Turnbull lived. This time he managed to keep her in sight all the way to the car park near her office, and when he went into the Agency he was accorded, for his long, cold devotion to duty, an invitation to take his mid-morning coffee with his two bosses in Dr Piper's office, plus an update on the progress of the murder investigation.

'It doesn't amount to much,' Peter said wistfully. 'The girl's at school, your subject's at work as usual, and Kendrick's informed us that when Hugh Jordan left the station he went back to his office, armed with the news of his daughter's accusation of Miss Turnbull. It's surrealist to try to imagine the reunion of boss and secretary.'

'I should've been hiding there. Did the DCS say how he took the news?'

'Initial disbelief. Then a look of hurt. The smile went and didn't come back. Kendrick said he got the feeling Jordan was more shocked by the idea of his daughter telling her story – fact or fantasy – to the police rather than to her father, than by the possibility that his secretary murdered his wife.'

149

'Which he would be,' Steve interposed, 'if he murdered her himself.'

'We know, we know. Whatever, a refusal to believe in his secretary's guilt persisted through the interview, which could indicate how highly he rates her. Which doesn't, of course, have to mean sexually.'

'So, being so sure of his secretary's innocence,' Phyllida said, 'what can he be making of his daughter's accusation?'

'He told Kendrick he didn't believe she'd seen anything, and had made up her story because of being traumatised by the loss of her mother, then the terrible shock of finding her stepmother's body. He'd have to invent a motive he could live with or he'd be torn in two.'

'But why Turnbull?' Steve asked.

'That bit's easy,' Phyllida said reluctantly. 'Jealousy. One woman who came between father and daughter had disappeared, so she decided to try to dispose of the other.'

'Hugh Jordan didn't say *that* to Kendrick,' Peter said, 'but I suppose it makes sense, and it's certainly a motive for the girl herself to have carried out the killing. I cringe at each news bulletin I hear.' Peter indicated the small radio, moved from its usual place on a shelf to the edge of his desk. 'I've such a vivid picture of that girl going to the school loos, say, making a quick phone call to a branch of the media, and putting Marjorie Turnbull in the stocks for the whole nation to shy at. And there's nothing I, or the Chief Superintendent of the Seaminster police force, can do about it if that's what she decides on. Oh, yes, the DCS also told me they've completed their fine-tooth-combing of the Jordan home and it's confirmed there's nothing in the way of alien fingerprints or DNA in significant places. Or anything else untoward apart, bizarrely, from traces of plasticine in the folds of one of the girl's nightdresses.'

'Perhaps she was sticking pins into a model of her

stepmother,' Steve suggested. 'Well' – as Phyllida and Peter turned sceptical looks on him – 'you come up with a better idea.'

'We can't,' Peter said. 'Any more than Mr Kendrick can, so maybe you're right.'

'It could be in character,' Phyllida said. 'She's the oldest and the unhappiest thirteen-year-old I've ever encountered.'

'Nothing on doorhandles, even?' Steve persisted.

'Nothing. Front door inside and out without any fingerprints, so obviously wiped, which bears out the girl's story that the murderer came and went that way. The poker was clean except for the girl's prints, so that was wiped too – if it wasn't used by the girl herself. If it was someone from outside who used it, he or she doesn't appear to have panicked.'

'Why didn't you say Marjorie Turnbull?' Steve asked Peter with interest.

'Because we don't know who it was,' Peter responded with slight severity. 'On forensic findings – or lack of them – I'd say with the DCS that the girl saw what she says she saw, but there seems no way of knowing if she saw the person she says she saw, or . . .' Peter paused, and Steve finished his sentence with relish.

'Or was describing what she did herself.'

He thanked his lucky stars that he'd obeyed Peter to the letter, when at just before four o'clock, twenty minutes after he had tucked himself into his chosen vantage point, Miss Turnbull entered the car park near her office. His reward began with the comparative mid-afternoon ease of following her, and continued with her setting off in the opposite direction to her way home. When she reached a suburb a lot leafier, to Steve's relief, than her own she began to slow down, moving more and more slowly and then sliding to a halt. Short of some imposing gates through which a few teenage girls were beginning to trickle.

Ten minutes later Susan Jordan emerged as the centre of a small group, hopping and skipping around her as they reached the wide pavement, and in that moment Steve realised that Miss Turnbull, whatever the current state of play between her and her boss, would know the movements of his daughter.

Steve knew his Seaminster as well as any local taxi-driver, and that Claire College was in the hinterland of the town almost directly in line with Dawlish Square. Miss Turnbull would know that too, and would also have learned – or hoped – that Susan Jordan would walk back to the Golden Lion, shedding school fellows as she went.

Even for the practised Steve it was a tricky ride. He had to trim his pace to Miss Turnbull's, who in turn had to make frequent pauses to allow for the series of partings that Miss Jordan's friends were clearly so loth to undertake. Several times he was afraid he'd been spotted, if only because, if he had been Miss Turnbull, he would have been alert to the possibility of being officially followed, and decided it had to be the strength of her desire to confront Susan Jordan that was making her less than vigilant.

At last, and on the loneliest stretch of road they had traversed – had Miss Turnbull worked this out, too? – Susan Jordan was alone, still hoppng and skipping along in the euphoria of her popularity. The road was suddenly downhill as if acknowledging its descent to the sea ahead, and Steve had a good enough view to enable him to stop and still be able to see Miss Turnbull's car edge up to the girl. When she was just short of her, Miss Turnbull stopped too, leapt with unexpected nimbleness out of her car, and seized the startled girl by the arm, pushing her in through the driver's door.

It was an irony that Susan should shout in the direction of

Steve's car – he saw her open mouth and her pleading gaze fixed on his bonnet – but Miss Turnbull didn't even glance in his direction as she manhandled the thin, slight figure – no match for her – across to the passenger seat and got back behind the wheel. As she drove rapidly away, Steve could see the girl, in silhouette, struggling, and failing, to open the passenger door.

His luck had been phenomenal, but within minutes it had dramatically changed. Not only did a lorry – for the second time that week – emerge into the road between him and Miss Turnbull's swiftly moving car; it made a clumsy turn to the right, grazing his front offside lights as it attempted to get past.

For the first time in his life Steve found himself praying to be the victim of a hit-and-run; but his car had stalled, and the lorry-driver's mate was at his window before he could get it going again, making conciliatory signs and turning the window down in dumbshow.

It was all very fair and square, but Steve was glad to see the number of witnesses – most of them still standing around in the hope of further action – and, noting the gleam in the eyes of the two men from the lorry as they assured him in chorus that the damage to his car was minimal, he asked for, and obtained, a couple of signed statements. This procedure noticeably soured the mood of the lorry-driver and his mate, but Steve's experience at the Agency had taught him that two signatures in the hand were worth any amount of goodwill in the bush, and he accepted their final whining words with equanimity.

By the time the witnesses had responded to his request, and the addresses of the drivers and their insurers had been exchanged, Miss Turnbull and her prisoner were, of course, far beyond Steve's ken. As he looked wearily at his watch, he realised with a sinking of the heart that Miss Turnbull had had time to take her prisoner somewhere he now had no possibility of finding; and – here his heart turned cold – of arriving home alone.

Despite its wounds his car performed as usual, and he had difficulty sticking to the speed limit as he made his way to Miss Turnbull's house. As he drove slowly past it he saw that her car was in the carport and her front door closed. A point of light behind an uncurtained downstairs window, just visible in the waning winter light, was the only sign of life within.

Steve went straight on to the office, where he cast himself despairingly into Peter's smallest and least prestigious chair before beginning to recount the shifting fortunes of his afternoon.

'God's honour, guv,' he concluded, 'it wasn't my fault. You've only got to ask the driver or his mate; and even if they change their story, the facts are there. I got two signed witness statements.'

'Well done. Not that I'd have disbelieved you; but the drivers of big, bullying vehicles are very wily. I remember having an innocent contretemps once with a post office van that was already covered in small old wounds and the driver's eyes just dared me to try to make something of it . . . I'll get on to Kendrick.'

Chief Superintendent Kendrick was well aware of his tendency to carry hands-on policing farther than befitted a very senior officer, and when he had received Dr Piper's call it was against all his instincts not to accompany the immediately despatched team of uniforms to Miss Turnbull's house. He instructed them to inform him at once by telephone if they found Susan Jordan there, alive or dead, and awaited the call with an impatience so ill-concealed that DS Wetherhead elected to keep out of his way.

Dr Piper had also relayed the frustrating news of Steve's accident, and Kendrick instructed half the team that, whether or not Miss Turnbull was found to be playing host to Susan Jordan, they were to bring her in, while the other half remained to carry out a more detailed search – unlikely though it was, had the girl been brought to the house, that Miss Turnbull could have killed her and disposed of her body in the short time that had elapsed since Steve had watched the car carrying woman and girl out of sight. So he could hardly hope for results from a routine prising up of floorboards and a search for freshly turned garden soil, although these exercises would, of course, have to be undertaken.

The team reported, after one of the longest half-hours of Kendrick's life, that there was no sign of Susan Jordan on Miss Turnbull's premises.

So had she managed, he asked himself as he paced his office, to escape and get back to the Golden Lion? There'd been no frantic phone call from Hugh Jordan.

Contact, Kendrick realised reluctantly, as he paused beside his sea view and failed to draw comfort from it, would have to be made by him, but only after he'd discovered if Miss Turnbull was prepared to tell them what had happened after she had manhandled Susan Jordan into her car.

She stood up when he entered the interview room behind DS Wetherhead, as strong and dignified a presence as she had been the first time they had met, and Kendrick found himself admiring her courage, whatever it had led her to.

'Miss Turnbull.' He indicated her chair, and reluctantly she sat down.

'You know why you're here,' he said, now indicating the empty chair beside her as he and Fred took the seats opposite. 'Would you like us to call your solicitor?'

'I have no need of a solicitor, Chief Superintendent. I am not intending to deny that I took Susan Jordan into my car when she was on her way home from school this afternoon.

I wanted to talk to her, try to find out why she made that wicked accusation against me.'

'And did she tell you?' DS Wetherhead inquired.

'She told me nothing; it was a waste of my time and energy. Particularly as I already knew that what she said came out of her jealousy, her intense love for her father.'

'So why did you go to such lengths to talk to her, Miss Turnbull?' Kendrick asked. 'Were you perhaps hoping to . . . persuade her . . . to withdraw her accusation?'

Miss Turnbull appeared to consider. 'Perhaps I was,' she said slowly. 'I'm not sure. What motivated me to get her alone was to break through the feeling that I was up against a monster, to try to get at the human child and bring her back to a sense of justice, to reach the kindness and compassion there has to be in the daughter of Hugh Jordan—' Miss Turnbull stopped abruptly, biting her lip and dropping her gaze to the table, and Kendrick thought, *Another intense love.* 'But I was wasting my time,' she said after a few seconds, looking up. 'I realised that very quickly, and after driving round for a few minutes – I can tell you my exact route, Chief Superintendent – I stopped and told the girl to get out. Which she did, without a word.'

'So I don't suppose she told you of any plans she had for the rest of the day?' Kendrick inquired, offering a lifeline.

Miss Turnbull didn't take it. 'She told me nothing; she scarcely opened her mouth. Once she'd decided it was no good struggling, she just sat there looking sullen. She's a girl in a very bad way.'

'Who hasn't been seen since you picked her up, Miss Turnbull. Who didn't come home from school.'

Please God he was lying. Watching the look of horror dawn in the hitherto composed face, Kendrick knew he must find out, asked the hovering WPC Jardine to take his place, and went quickly back to his office.

His hand was out towards his telephone when it rang, and he snatched it up.

'Yes?'

'Mr Hugh Jordan is on the line, sir. He particularly asked to speak to you.'

'Put him on . . . Mr Jordan?'

'Mr Kendrick . . . Susan hasn't come home from school!'

The sinking of Kendrick's heart was no metaphor; he felt it drop in his chest. 'You were expecting her at her normal time?'

'Yes . . . but I didn't worry at first when she was late; she sometimes calls in at a friend's house. But I've just rung her best friend, and she didn't go home with her, and it's a couple of hours beyond her usual time . . .'

'I'd like to talk to you, Mr Jordan. May I come over now to the Golden Lion?'

'Oh, God. Something's happened, hasn't it? Or you wouldn't . . . Tell me now, I beg of you!'

He must, but until they were face to face, a bowdlerised version. 'Very well. Your daughter was seen by . . . by a surveillance officer getting into Miss Turnbull's car.'

'Miss Turnbull's . . . I don't understand.'

'That's why I want to come and talk to you, Mr Jordan. Were you in the office this afternoon?'

'I can't think . . . Oh, yes, but only until about three o'clock.'

'Did your secretary tell you she was going to leave work early?'

'She told me she had a headache and that she might go home . . . Mr Kendrick, you can't believe Marjorie Turnbull would harm my daughter!'

'You know your daughter claims that she killed your wife.'

'It's all . . . crazy. Susan, Marjorie . . . all the things you say . . . Susan's found life . . . difficult . . . since her mother died, and perhaps she . . . Oh my God, I don't know. But not *Marjorie*!'

Disbelief more desperate, it seemed, over secretary than over daughter. Because he loved Marjorie Turnbull? Because he had hitherto respected a Good Woman? Because he and she together had colluded in the murder of his wife and the disbelief was an act? Frustration rolled over Kendrick again, as he realised there was no way of knowing. And that Hugh Jordan might still be smiling.

Fourteen

'*No walk today, my darling, I'm afraid.*'
    '*Jack . . .*'
    '*It's all right.*' *The encircling arms, still warm and strong. 'You know I have to be losing strength. Phyllida, believe me – and you must – it's so much worse for you than it is for me. Unless we're raging egotists we never feel . . . poignant . . . about ourselves. The people who . . . go away . . . are always less bereft than the people who stay behind.*'
    '*That's what I want. I want it to be worse for me.*'
    '*On my honour, it is. And will be. Think how blessed I am; I shall have you with me for the rest of my life.*'

'She was kind of . . . excited.' The boy spoke reluctantly, perhaps with distaste, and DS Wetherhead mentally rejoiced to recognise a classmate he could see right away had elected not to join the Susan Jordan fan club. Perhaps that was why her form-master John Taylor, who had struck Fred as a sensible sort of a chap, had singled out this boy as the first of her fellow students to be questioned by him and DC Watson.
    'By the murder, you mean, Colin?' DC Watson asked. The interviews were being conducted in the small but quite comfortable room where pupils were directed, the form-master had told them unnecessarily – to help diffuse his sense of unease, Fred Wetherhead suspected – either

when they were feeling unwell (but not seriously enough to be sent home), or had committed some misdemeanour on which a member of staff deemed it fit that they should ponder awhile in solitude.

When the morning had dawned with no sign of Susan, and no forensic indication so far that she had ever been in Marjorie Turnbull's house or garden, Kendrick, with the fervent backing of Susan's father, had decreed that one or two boys and girls from her own form, to be selected by their form-master, should be asked how they thought Susan had reacted to the murder of her stepmother.

'Well, yes, by the murder, I suppose. She was always . . . well, a bit over the top, saying and doing things for effect. Making a drama out of everything and seeing herself as God's gift.'

'You don't like her, Colin. Is there any particular reason for that?'

'I've just given you it.' But the boy, a redhead with freckles, had coloured. 'I hardly knew her. I just don't like people like that.'

'And there's nothing else?' Fred asked, with mild persistence.

'No . . . Oh, I suppose I'd better tell you in case one of Susan's cronies does, although it's more a reason for Susan to dislike me than for me to dislike her: she tried to make up to me a day or two ago. Said she'd had it off with the other boys and it was my turn. I didn't know whether or not to believe her, and anyway I wasn't bothered what she'd done, or not done. I told her I wasn't interested, and she . . . well, she sort of hinted that if I said anything to anyone about her asking me to . . . to do it and me turning her down . . . she'd tell the police I'd killed her stepmother because she'd told me she wished her father had never got married again. I was off school with the tummy bug when . . . when Mrs Jordan was killed, and Susan remembered.'

'You weren't frightened?'

'No! I was at home in bed that morning, and I just thought she was crazy, and that I wanted to keep out of her way anyway.'

Susan's best friend, a brunette styled in Susan's image but open-faced and smiling, told them Susan made things 'come alive'.

'Wherever Susan was, something seemed to be happening. Something exciting.' That word again. The DS and the DC exchanged glances. 'She had so many ideas.'

'Good ideas? Bad ones?'

Another young face suddenly suffused red. 'She did get us into scrapes sometimes; she liked to upset some of the staff, the ones who aren't too sure of themselves. She could be a bit unkind, I suppose, but she was so *funny!*'

'At other people's expense?'

'Well, sometimes . . . Oh, no, you're not suggesting . . . Susan would never *kill* anyone! You mustn't think I was saying . . . Oh, please!'

'It's all right, Lorraine; of course we don't think you're suggesting Susan killed her stepmother. We're just trying to find out what kind of person she is. And if she's in any danger, how she'll cope with it.'

'Danger? What d'you mean?'

'Well . . . if she's been abducted, say.' The news of Susan's disappearance hadn't been given to the media, but the DCS had decreed that if she hadn't turned up by late afternoon, twenty-four hours after she'd gone missing, the police would see that the news of it was on the evening bulletins; but not, at least for the time being, the news of Miss Turnbull's possible involvement.

'That's ridiculous! Susan'd never go willingly with anyone she didn't know!'

'People can be in danger from those they know as well as from those they don't know, Lorraine. Tell us, did Susan have any plans for last evening? Something that would involve her not going back to the hotel? She would have told you, wouldn't she, if she had?'

'Of course she'd have told me! We never have secrets from each other. She wasn't planning anything. A group of us left school together and she and I were the last; my home's the nearest to the Golden Lion. Oh . . .'

'What is it?' DC Watson asked.

'I've just remembered, she pulled a face when we said goodbye and said she wasn't looking forward to another evening among Seaminster's boring oldies. So you see. She *was* going back to the hotel.' Lorraine stared from one policeman to the other, her eyes widening with fear, and then to the consternation of both of them burst into tears. It was Fred who got to his feet, went round the table, and put an arm across her shaking shoulders.

'I'm sorry we've upset you, Lorraine,' he said soothingly; 'but we have to do all we can to find Susan, even if it means facing possibilities we'd rather not think about.'

DS Wetherhead was discovering that the economy with the truth decreed by Chief Superintendent Kendrick – that Miss Turnbull's possible involvement in Susan Jordan's disappearance should be kept under wraps – was something of a relief to him in that it saved him from having to describe the work of Dr Piper's field agent as the public-spirited action of yet another anonymous good citizen phoning in to report something possibly significant that he or she had seen. Fred (and, he suspected, his Chief) had begun to fear the day when a group of junior policemen, idly discussing recent business in the canteen, would comment on the unusual number of recent phone calls from members of the public who had inadvertently witnessed events about which the police wanted information and discover, when they pooled their experience, that none of them had been involved in the subsequent interviews . . . So DS Wetherhead found himself thankful not to have to report the latest findings of the Peter Piper Agency as the action of yet another good citizen doing his or her civic duty, and to know that Miss Turnbull now had an official police tail. 'D'you think there's any chance, Lorraine, that Susan's playing one of her tricks? That she could be hiding somewhere from choice, having a good laugh or a good cry?'

'No! She would have told me, and she didn't even hint . . . She's dead. I know she's dead . . .' and the weeping began again.

This time DS Wetherhead remained in his seat. 'Lorraine,' he said softly, leaning over the table (and finding it strange, in these familiar circumstances, to have a tablecloth under the hand he slid towards her rather than heavily scored and inked wood), 'tell us one thing, if you can. And think very carefully before you answer. Is there any chance that Susan could be . . . not quite herself? As you know, she went into shock after she'd discovered her stepmother's body, and from all accounts she seems since to have been . . .'

'On a high,' DC Watson supplied, as Fred Wetherhead turned slightly towards him, a question in his eyes. 'D'you think she might be in a state, at the moment, in which she could be acting strangely, doing things she wouldn't normally do? Like running away?'

Lorraine sat upright and blew her nose, pondering. 'I suppose she just could,' she said eventually. 'But . . . she was, well, she was *enjoying* being the centre of attention so much I can't see her choosing to give it up. I mean, just before we said goodbye yesterday afternoon she was laughing about the way some people in the form who didn't usually have anything to do with her had started hanging about the edge of our group. I just can't see her going off somewhere by herself when there'd have been more of it today, and tomorrow. Something has to have happened to her.' The tear-sparkling eyes widened accusingly as they captured Fred's.

'We're doing all we can to find Susan, Lorraine.'

'It doesn't seem to be enough. Can I go now, please?'

What the other boy and girl the policemen talked to told them amounted to much the same thing. Of this pair, the boy was the Susan Jordan fan and the girl had obviously stood back, noting the excitement surrounding Susan without sharing it, or apparently wanting to. 'I thought it was all a bit sick,' she said earnestly, blinking from one policeman to the other through thick-lensed spectacles. Obviously not, in Susan Jordan's eyes, a Beautiful Person, and perhaps having been boomed off by her. 'I mean, her father's wife had been murdered, and she was . . . she was *excited*!'

That word for the third time. When the girl left the room, DC Watson followed her, found the form-master and asked if he would be good enough to join him and the Detective Sergeant for a moment.

DC Watson pulled the chairs away from the table, to indicate that the formal interviewing was over. 'The word *exciting* kept cropping up,' DS Wetherhead said as the three of them sat down. 'It seems Susan was something of a focus of peer attention. Has that always been the case?'

'Up to a point, I'd say. But until – this tragedy – it was rather Susan's group, and then the rest of the form. People were . . .'

The form-master paused, and DC Watson suggested, 'For her or against her?'

'Thank you; that's precisely it. In the last few days Susan's group has grown rather large. I gather from what I and other members of staff have seen and overheard that she hasn't been exactly reticent about the crime she discovered. My feeling is – very reluctantly – that she's actually enjoyed being the centre of attention for such a terrible reason.'

164

'Susan has obviously always had some influence over her fellow students,' DS Wetherhead observed. 'Would you say, Mr Taylor, that it's been a good influence on the whole? Or . . .'

The form-master sighed as he looked from one policeman to the other. 'I'd have to say, Sergeant, that on the whole I feel it hasn't.'

That evening, news bulletins on radio and a couple of TV channels would proclaim Susan Jordan's disappearance and remind the public of the girl's recent discovery of her stepmother's murdered body. No mention would be made – and no information had been given to the media – of her accusation of murder against a named individual, nor would it be reported that just over twenty-four hours earlier Miss Turnbull had dragged the girl into her car.

'For the time being,' Kendrick informed Miss Turnbull sternly, when the fruitless search of her house and garden was concluded and he had told her before sending her home that she would not be charged with abduction. He did not tell her that her movements would be monitored because, if she had imprisoned a live Susan Jordan somewhere, that information would prevent her renewing the girl's supplies of food and water. Not, Kendrick supposed wearily, that the woman would thereby conclude she really was a free agent: she would suspect surveillance even if she hadn't been officially informed she was to receive it, and it could be that her assumption of police vigilance would cost Susan Jordan her life.

Thinking again of his own beloved Jenny, and of what her disappearance would do to him, the Chief Superintendent, to his surprise and slight sense of shock, found himself inclined to feel sorry for Hugh Jordan, so that he tried to preserve his sense of proportion by frequent reminders to himself that both father and daughter were high on his list of suspects.

Hugh Jordan's frantic grief had struck him as genuine, and Kendrick was confident there was no bias in favour of the man in his decision, if the evening's media announcement of Susan's disappearance yielded no reports of any sighting of her, to mount an appeal next day on the lunchtime bulletins, which (again, if it bore no fruit) would be repeated in the evening.

He had just given orders for the media to be informed of his wishes when his private telephone rang.

'Chief Superintendent? This is Miss Bowden.' Speaking in Miss Bowden's voice, and Kendrick irritably dismissed his pang of aesthetic disappointment.

'Miss Bowden. What can I do for you?'

'I have what I think might be a useful suggestion to make in connection with our current concerns. Rather than talk on the telephone, we wonder if you would consider—'

'I'll be straight over.'

Although it was very cold, it was windless and sunny, and Kendrick decided to walk to Dawlish Square. He could be so much more unobtrusive arriving on foot (he smiled ruefully at the idea of a chief superintendent of police needing to be unobtrusive), and the thought of the short walk was attractive as he realised how long it was since he had done more with the outdoors than stride from house to garage and from car park to office and regard his sleeping winter garden through his windows. Police headquarters were at the other side of town from the Peter Piper Agency, but Seaminster was compact and the HQ was on a lateral line with the square, which meant a short walk down a couple of lanes to reach the sea, the main part of the walk along the central stretch of The Parade, and then just one lane up to his destination.

He wanted his walking image to look purposeful, but

was unable to resist a steadily mounting desire to pause for a moment by the long blue railing and lean on it, looking from side to side at its unbroken line shooting straight out of sight, and then turning to the gently heaving sea, mockingly blue under the sharp blue sky and cold sun, the horizon a soft smudge of grey.

A horizon, Kendrick realised as he gazed across the water, no longer blocked by the murder of Sandra Jordan. He had been amazed before by the way a few moments, consciously wrested from a greyly busy day, could transform his mood, and berated himself as a fool for not setting them up more often. He completed his walk without further pause, but as he crossed Dawlish Square he found himself gratefully aware of the improvement in his spirits and his renewed awareness that there was more in his life than his current investigation.

Peter and Phyllida were aware, too, the moment he came into Peter's office, of the comparative lightness of the Chief Superintendent's mood.

'You've some good news?' Peter suggested, as he returned Kendrick's smile.

Kendrick shrugged as he took his usual armchair. 'Not so as you'd notice. We've been talking to some of the girl's schoolmates, and I think we have to accept that she's off-line, if only temporarily, and that her disappearance could be voluntary. Which I suppose is reassuring. Now . . .'

The intent gaze was back as Kendrick leaned forward and looked into Miss Bowden's face, managing to give no outward sign that part of the intensity was his failed attempt to discover any trace of the delicately featured Phyllida Moon. 'You have something to suggest, Miss Bowden?'

'Yes.' At least Miss Moon was using her own voice. 'The second time Susan visited Mrs Parker in her room at the hotel . . . she said she'd got "something", and when I

167

asked her what, she said "something" again, and then, "if she tries to put the blame on me". I may not have got her words exactly right, because of course I could hardly write them down, though I did write down what I remembered as soon as she'd gone. She looked at me with a sort of self-conscious significance when she mentioned this "something", but I did get the feeling it was more than bluff, especially as she said it twice. So I thought . . . if she's chosen to disappear she'll have taken whatever it is with her, I suppose, if it's portable. But if she didn't choose . . .'

The three of them sat in silence for a moment. Kendrick broke it, after another intense look from Phyllida to Peter. 'If she didn't choose to disappear, it should still be there. In her room at the Golden Lion, I would have thought, rather than at home. All her possessions were gone through before she and her father packed to leave, but it wasn't a situation where we could search her person and depending on what "it" is she could either have been carrying it on her or had hidden it somewhere about the house or even in the car . . . You're suggesting her room at the hotel should be searched with what she said in mind, Miss Bowden?'

'Yes.'

'And that you'd be the best person to carry the search out?'

'I wasn't suggesting that, Mr Kendrick; I haven't had police training. I *have* had some success with lateral thinking, and I suppose I just might see significance in something that on the surface doesn't look important, but I don't—'

'I think you and a couple of my men would make the best team, Miss Bowden,' the Chief Superintendent interrupted. 'If you agree.'

'I agree,' Phyllida said, as Peter nodded. 'Thank you. Susan's room – is it sealed? Does her father have a key?'

'As from lunchtime today her father does not have a

key,' Kendrick said. 'And Mr Bright is in sole charge of all keys. So the room is sealed, in effect, which means there's no possibility of your being disturbed and you can take your time.'

'Even do a spot of clairvoyancing,' Peter suggested, 'if nothing immediately hits you as being of significance.'

'Just so, Dr Piper,' Kendrick agreed drily; but the picture conjured up in his mind by the conversation in which he was taking part made him suddenly and vividly aware of the surrealist nature of his relationship with the Peter Piper Agency, so that he felt briefly dizzy and decided to postpone getting to his feet for another minute or two.

'Forgive me,' Miss Bowden went on. She could only look severe, but there was a sympathetic note in Miss Moon's charming voice. 'You look a little weary, Chief Superintendent. Let me make you a cup of coffee before I cross the square and assume Mrs Parker.'

'Thank you. I *am* a little weary,' Kendrick responded, and knew as he spoke that the confession marked the most bizarrely surrealistic moment of their association. He was doubly glad, now, that he had walked to Dawlish Square, and would have a second opportunity to contemplate the long view afforded by the sea.

Phyllida was surprised, when Merle Parker came downstairs just before seven and peeped into the Caprice Bar, to see Hugh Jordan hunched behind a corner table. Surprised, too, that when he saw in the dim light who it was standing before him, his initial cringe was replaced by a leaning forward.

'Mrs Parker! Do please join me. I thought for a moment . . . Members of the fourth estate come and go.'

'The lobby seems clear of them at the moment. How are you?' Phyllida sat down. 'And Susan?' It was one of those rare moments in which she hated her occupation.

The light died out. 'Susan. You didn't see the news, then.'

'Pardon me, I don't—'

'Susan's disappeared, Mrs Parker. She didn't come home from school yesterday.'

'Yesterday . . . Oh, my God, you must be . . . Mr Jordan, I'm so terribly sorry.'

'It's a nightmare. I'm only sitting here because I'm expecting my . . . my wife's business partner to arrive at any moment. He rang me when he heard the news and very kindly suggested coming over to see me, and although quite frankly I don't feel very much like talking to anyone at the moment, it was a kind gesture and I said I'd be delighted to see him.' More delighted still, Phyllida interpreted, to see someone else as well, at least for the difficult moment of meeting. 'And I think I was ready for a break from my room; it's been getting smaller and smaller.'

Mick was promptly at their table, with no more than a raised eyebrow. Hugh Jordan had started to tell him they were waiting for a friend when Joe Hardman came smiling sadly into the bar, holding both hands out to Hugh as he reached the table. After a second's hesitation Hugh held his out in response and the two men made brief clasping contact.

'Hugh! There's nothing I can say.'

'No. Joe . . . this is Merle Parker; she's living at the hotel at the moment. She and Sandra were friends. And Susan likes her.'

It was a pathetically moving moment. Phyllida saw Joe Hardman's Adam's apple do a noticeable bob as he swallowed hard, and she herself had to look away from Hugh's yearning face. Whatever he had or hadn't done, each moment that passed increased the possibility that he had lost his only daughter.

She asked for a dry Martini from the hovering Mick;

Hugh ordered a first Scotch for Joe and another for himself, and they awaited the drinks in a painful silence punctuated by attempts at reassuring smiles. Phyllida was beginning to think they might have done better without Mrs Parker, when Hugh announced that the police had promised to contact him the moment there was news of Susan.

'They know I'm here. I'll be here until I have her back. Except when I do the TV appeal tomorrow.'

'TV appeal . . . That's a good move, Hugh, but she'll be back before it happens, you'll see. She'll just have gone to ground somewhere with the shock of . . . of what she saw.'

The first reference, obliquely, to the woman they were certain was dead. Susan Jordan's disappearance had given them the option of not speaking of her stepmother, and Phyllida interpreted the frown on Hugh Jordan's handsome brow as a wish that they could have gone on that way; but he still had the option of not taking the reference up.

'Gone to ground where, for God's sake, Joe? The police have combed our house and garden – not that I believed she'd go back there; she never liked the place – she's not with her best friend, and I'm her only family.' So Hugh Jordan hadn't told Joe Hardman about Miss Turnbull's role in his daughter's disappearance, and was continuing to protect her . . . Phyllida was shaken by a sudden rage against herself for her failure to discover the nature of his now openly demonstrated regard for his secretary. 'I'd rather we didn't speculate; it gets us nowhere.'

'You're right,' Joe Hardman came back. 'I'm sorry, Hugh.'

Phyllida saw the first sparkle of the evening in the eyes that had sparkled the whole time she had watched them looking at Sandra Jordan; and the first smile it elicited in Hugh Jordan's pale, anguished face.

'No, no,' Hugh said. 'It's for you to forgive *me*. I'm

afraid I'm not quite myself. You'll stay for dinner, won't you, Joe? I'll be glad if you will.'

'Of course I will. Thanks.'

Phyllida had noted the expressionless looks the men exchanged as they spoke. 'The restaurant's excellent,' she told Joe. 'I'm always a bit wistful when I have to go out in the evening, and miss a gourmet treat. Like tonight.' The relief was politely concealed, but as she glanced at her watch, Phyllida was aware of the infinitesimal relaxation of both male bodies.

Merle Parker got to her feet. 'I've been forgetting the time. Thank you very much for my drink, Hugh. I must leave you now so as not to be late for my appointment.' With coffee and sandwiches in room 98, and then with PCs Whitson and Lacey in room 113.

Fifteen

'*I*'m glad your work's waiting for you, Phyllida. It will help.'

'*I suppose so. Just now it's on another planet.*'

'*In my letter to James I've asked him to contact you as soon as he gets home. I've given him your Seaminster address.*'

'*Jack, stay . . . a bit longer . . . in the present. Don't think or talk . . . ahead. Not just yet.*'

'*Ahead is coming closer. Which I think you know. But you're right, my darling: we must live the present while we have it. When I've asked you . . . Phyllida, what do you think there will be? Afterwards?*'

'*I don't know; I'm the archetypal agnostic. I can only see the orthodox religions of the world as manmade. But it's so miraculous that we're here, that we know we're here, and can say – what is it,* Cogito, ergo sum *– it gives me hope there'll be other miracles. What do you believe we're facing, Jack?*'

'*I believe that when we die – and we all will, Phyllida; the only difference between your fate and mine is time – I believe that we'll either know nothing – the eternal sleep – or we'll know everything. Like you, I've never had comfort from orthodox religions. From the people who say they know* now.'

'*I did for a time, at school in my early teens. Looking back, it was a sort of infatuation, like first love. All that's left of it, like in Pandora's box, is hope. And now I'm going to cry, Jack, so put your arms round me . . .'*

It was Tracy from Reception who knocked at Phyllida's door an hour later, and told her the coast was clear. 'Mr Jordan's still in the restaurant, still on his main course; he and Mr Hardman are both looking glum and hardly talking or eating. The wine glasses are up and down more than the knives and forks. Even a couple of press men went off after looking at them for a few minutes from the doorway . . . It's great having the chance to talk to you face to face, Miss Moon.'

'I'm sorry it can't be for longer, Tracy, and that it isn't quite my face your talking to. Let's go.'

The two young PCs were standing with their backs to one another near the centre of Susan Jordan's room, giving Phyllida the impression they had stopped in their tracks while pacing about and making sure they didn't come into contact with any furniture.

'Good evening, boys,' Merle Parker greeted them, as Tracy withdrew. 'I guess you don't have to worry about spreading your DNA around; it isn't forensic evidence we're here to look for. Now, Detective Sergeant Wetherhead has told you what this is all about?'

Chief Superintendent Kendrick had thought wistfully about appointing himself the overseer of Mrs Parker's search, but another rabbit out of yet another hat would be a piece of magic too far for one investigation, and reluctantly he placed the matter in the hands of his trusty DS. Fred Wetherhead, if the PCs he chose for the job had the temerity to question the genesis of this probable cul-de-sac on the road to the apprehension of Sandra Jordan's killer, was to tell them – truthfully, this time – that an American friend of the Jordan family had broached it with his chief, who had thought the idea worth a try.

'The sergeant said you'd fill us in with the details,' the smaller and slightly older-looking of the PCs told Phyllida. He was plump and pale with shiny dark hair, in slightly humorous contrast to the tall, thin, close-cropped redhead now at attention beside him. 'Oh, I'm PC Bill Whitson, and this is PC Alan Lacey.' Two IDs shot out with precision timing.

'That's OK. Well, now. I've gotten kind of friendly with Miss Jordan.' Mrs Parker perched on the edge of the bed, waving the PCs to the two armchairs, which they gingerly took. 'Since she and her father moved to the hotel she's visited me in my room of her own wish a couple of evenings, and the last time she spoke about having "something" – she used the word twice – that would point a finger at the person who murdered her stepmother.' Phyllida's careful avoidance of the name *Marjorie Turnbull* reminded her of an earlier tricky session she and Peter had had with the DCS. 'Now, I've no idea what that something might be, and I know you-all combed through her belongings before she left home, but having got to know the girl I contacted your chief superintendent and told him it just might be worthwhile for me to have a look through what she brought here with her and maybe be able to interpret something which on the face of it doesn't seem to have any significance. You know . . . ?' Merle Parker let her lazy drawl fade away as she smiled at the two young men, and Phyllida was gratified to see them lean eagerly forward, their self-consciousness forgotten.

'Great idea!' the redhead said. 'Where will you start?'

'I thought the closet. Pockets . . . though if whatever it is is small enough to fit a pocket, I guess she may have taken it with her. But let's look.' Mrs Parker rose languidly and swayed across the room. 'All right if I help?'

'Of course!' came in chorus as the young men scrambled to their feet.

175

There wasn't much in the wardrobe: three dressy dresses, a couple of pairs of trousers, two blouses, a leather jacket and a dressing gown. The PCs looked in glum silence at Phyllida when it had been ascertained that all pockets were empty of anything beyond tissues and fluff.

'So let's try the drawers!' Mrs Parker said, comparatively bracing. 'Is there a police formula? Top or bottom?'

'Let's try bottom.' PC Whitson bent down to the lowest and deepest of the drawers and pulled it out with a flourish.

It was empty, and with a more restrained gesture he pulled out the third of the four. In here were some underwear, several pairs of socks, and a packet of Tampax, which he handed without comment to Mrs Parker before he and PC Lacey turned with a brief excess of assiduity to dismantling the pairs of socks and shaking out the underwear.

More blanks, and the men stood back, sighing, as Mrs Parker replaced the Tampax in the drawer.

'If I'm anyone to go by, it gets more individual the higher you go,' she observed, and this time Phyllida was bracing herself as well as the disappointed young men.

She was correct in that the second drawer, containing scarves, belts and hair bands, gave the first clues since the wardrobe of Susan's personal tastes, but Phyllida could make nothing significant out of any of the items she handled, and felt as deflated as the young men looked by the time PC Whitson pulled out the top drawer.

Here there were a few cosmetics – a lipstick, some eye-liner, a bottle of pink nail varnish – plus a hair brush, a comb, some hair gel and a packet of tissues. Also a small linen bag, which when opened was found to contain handkerchiefs.

'Man-size,' Phyllida murmured, when PC Whitson had

handed the bag over and she began pulling the handkerchiefs out. 'And mostly unironed. She probably uses them
under her pillow at night; I used to get stick from my father
for pinching his. Hang on.' Phyllida crossed the room to the
bed, pulled back the top of the heavy brocade coverlet and
then the two pillows. 'There you are, you see.' Reposing on
the undersheet was a large, crumpled white handkerchief.

'Wow,' contributed PC Lacey, saucer-eyed. PC Whitson
said, 'That's very well reasoned, Mrs Parker,' with a severe
glance towards his colleague. 'They're specially comforting when you have a snuffle,' Merle said, restoring pillows
and bed cover and returning to the bag of handkerchiefs.
'All these are large; she probably uses tissues during the
day. Well, we found them, didn't we, in her pockets; but
there are a hell of a lot of these biggies. A hankie under
the pillow lasts for weeks unless you have a cold, which
Susan hadn't. So we'd better go through them; they're the
first thing we've seen that maybe doesn't quite add up . . .
Hey! Take a look at this!'

Although none of the handkerchiefs had been ironed,
they appeared to be clean. Until Phyllida reached the
centre of the stack and came upon one that was heavily
stained.

PC Whitson strode forward, took it, after a questing
look, from Phyllida's hands, and spread it carefully on
the bed. Then counted backwards and forwards from the
place where it had been.

'The exact centre,' he said in an awed voice, as his
colleague came forward to gaze down on the stained
square. 'And that's blood, I'll bet my life.'

'Two lots of blood,' PC Lacey contributed.

'And gotten on to the handkerchief in different ways,'
Mrs Parker said in her turn. 'See . . . there's this really
heavy patch; it must have been soaked, and there are gobby
bits – all sort of wavy at the edges. Then these two little

round spots on the other side. I guess you're going to have to take this to your superintendent, boys.'

'I guess so.' PC Whitson gave a deep sigh of satisfaction, produced a small plastic bag from a pocket, placed the handkerchief carefully inside it and sealed the top.

'Hadn't we better just look in the bathroom?' PC Lacey suggested, with a hopeful look. Phyllida suspected him of having such a good time he was loth to bring it to an end.

'Of course,' PC Whitson agreed. This time Phyllida interpreted his sigh as one of relief that his enthusiasm for the bloodstained handkerchief hadn't led him into a dereliction of duty he would have been unable to conceal.

The bathroom yielded nothing from its shelves beyond toothbrush, toothpaste, deodorant, facecloth, shower gel, bath cap and soap; and nothing at all from the curves of the piping or the lavatory cistern.

'I guess that's it, then,' Mrs Parker said, as she led the way back into the bedroom. 'I do so hope that handkerchief means something. D'you boys believe it could have been deliberately hidden among the others?'

DC Lacy said, 'Sure,' and DC Whitson said, 'Like hiding a pebble on a beach. It's a classic hiding place, putting like with like.'

'The police mustn't feel bad about not having found the hanky in the house,' Mrs Parker said. 'I guess Susan kept it on her when she'd picked it up. In a plastic bag it would have to be, still being wet and all, but she'd have had as much time as she wanted and there'd be no one to see what she did or didn't do before calling you-all. She'd feel safe here in the hotel – no more police searches – so she'd transfer the hanky to a drawer.' She'd better stop there, Phyllida decided, seeing the reverential look in the two young faces, or the detective constables' report would make the Chief Superintendent think, perhaps

178

rightly, that his hitherto cool assistant had gone over the top.

'You should be in the force, Mrs Parker,' PC Whitson said.

'I guess it's just that I've got plenty of time to think about things.'

'The girl'd only feel safe, though,' PC Lacey said, 'if she thought she was coming back to the hotel. If she knew she wasn't, you can bet she'd have taken the handkerchief with her. So . . . something or somebody kept her away against her will.'

There was a moment's gloomy silence before PC Whitson visibly pulled himself together and thanked Mrs Parker for her valuable assistance. 'I'm sure the Chief Superintendent will let you know the results of the forensic examination in due course.'

'I'm sure he will, Constable. Now, we'd better ring down for cover.'

Watching Hugh Jordan's white, unsmiling face as they took their seats behind the statutory long table and faced the TV cameras, Kendrick found himself with uncomfortably vivid memories of the apparently broken fathers, stepfathers and brothers whose faltering appeals for the return of their loved ones he had watched, moved, from the other side of the TV screen – the men who had turned out to be the killers. There was no doubt that Hugh Jordan would move viewers of that day's news bulletins, with his good looks and expressive voice, and the loss within so short a time of both his wife and his daughter. Without, in either case, so much as the ritual farewell of a funeral: it would be a while before Sandra Jordan's body could be released to him, and if he was what he claimed to be he would be crying to the heavens inwardly that no second funeral should be necessary.

At least Miss Moon's discovery was with Forensics, who'd promised to hurry their processes through. It was, of course, the isolated spots of blood he was interested in; he was already painfully sure of the source of the larger stain.

'. . . led by Chief Superintendent Maurice Kendrick.'

It was time for his part in the sad proceedings. Reading his self-written autocue, Kendrick went lightly over the death of Hugh Jordan's wife – the facts were more shocking, he had reasoned, without embellishment – then leaned towards the cameras.

'And now Hugh Jordan's daughter has disappeared after saying goodbye to schoolfriends in Bagehot Street at about 4.45 p.m. the day before yesterday. Her father expected her back at the Golden Lion Hotel, where they are both staying in the aftermath of their tragedy, but she didn't arrive, and there has been no word of, or from, her. A girl answering her description was seen getting into a car, apparently against her will, near the place where Susan Jordan had left her friend soon after 4.45 p.m. If anyone witnessed this abduction, or later witnessed a girl answering to Susan's description being forced out of a car, please come forward. It could quite literally mean the difference between life and death.' Kendrick felt sick as he spoke the words and thought of Jenny, but underneath his nausea a part of him was still free to reflect wryly on the latest surrealist twist to this most disconcerting of cases: usually he was frustrated at this point by a witness's failure to record the number of a suspect car. With this case he already knew the number by heart, but had decided not to reveal it. This time without frustration: if a member of the public had seen a woman drag a girl of Susan's description out of a car and into some unknown place, the car number plate would be irrelevant to the probable significance of the sight. 'And now Mr Hugh Jordan, husband of the murdered Sandra and father of the missing Susan, would like to appeal to you. Mr Jordan?'

Kendrick couldn't turn and study the man as he spoke, although he itched to do so. He'd see the video as soon as he got back to his office, and Jordan's voice was doing brilliantly, throbbing with controlled emotion as he begged the world beyond the cameras to help him find his daughter. Then begged his daughter, if she could, to come back to him.

'My dear sweet girl, I miss you more than I can say.'

Kendrick wondered how much cynicism would be engendered by Hugh Jordan's choice of adjectives – it would threaten to choke Marjorie Turnbull – and how Jordan would have chosen to describe his mother-in-law. Just before leaving for the TV studios he had received the news that she had died without regaining speech or movement, and had asked Jordan if he would like this mentioned as a further sad repercussion from one act of violence. Jordan had given a quick, sharp *No!* which he had immediately tried to moderate, but Kendrick suspected the man of being afraid that any mention of the old lady would harden the resolve of his daughter, if she was a free agent, not to return to the fold. Jordan had managed to pussyfoot to the police about how things were between his daughter and his mother-in-law, but Phyllida Moon had told Kendrick she was convinced the girl had no more affection for her step-grandmother than she had for her father's second wife.

Jordan broke down in tears as his plea came to an end. He really did – Kendrick saw one splash down on to his beseeching hands – but Miss Moon had so awesomely extended his respect for the power of good acting that he was still not entirely convinced of the genuineness of Jordan's performance.

'Brilliant! Absolutely brilliant!' The technical cast had no reservations.

'D'you want to go back to the hotel?' Kendrick asked Jordan as they emerged on to the street. The man appeared to be flagging so, it took him all his time not to take hold of his arm; but there were photographers everywhere and the gesture might put something into some inventive mind.

'Of course,' Jordan muttered. 'That's where she'll come. But now I really am media fodder I'll stay in my room to wait for her, Mr Kendrick, spare myself, and the hotel, a full lobby.'

Phyllida had watched the proceedings on her own television. As she had no immediate business, Peter had ordered her to take a break on call until her resumption of Merle Parker towards evening, and without a protest she had gone gratefully home. When she had switched off the television she stayed in her armchair, lazily reviewing the case in her mind as she enjoyed what felt like the rare luxury of being herself in her own surroundings.

She must have fallen asleep: the peal of her front-door bell had her gasping herself upright in a shock that was quickly followed by a sense of foreboding. She would not be called on at home unless something very serious had happened. Or unless, of course, she realised with relief, it was a parcel delivery, or a freebie newspaper – something from the everyday life of Phyllida Moon that had seemed so distant during the past few days.

On the step was a tall young man with curly dark hair, and wary eyes that she decided on the instant ought to be twinkling. Just as the grave face was made to be smiling. *Jack's eyes. Jack's face.*

'Oh dear God! Oh, come in! James! I'm so very glad to see you!'

'Phyllida . . . Pusey?' There was no response in the face, but James Pusey held out his hand. Phyllida took it and,

182

holding it, tried to draw him inside. Then stopped abruptly at the slight resistance, releasing him. How could he be other than wary?

'I'm sorry, I've been so looking forward . . . Yes, I married your father before he died. We had six months together. James, please come in.'

'Thank you.' She saw him cast an anxious glance over his shoulder at the long black car outside her front gate. 'I called earlier,' he said, as she led the way into her sitting room. 'I was thinking of leaving a note.'

'I'm sorry. I'm out so much. Your father said he would tell you what I do. Did he? Please sit down. I'll get tea or coffee in a moment. Or something stronger, if you feel you need it. Oh, James . . .'

'Dad told me you're an actress, and that you work for a detective agency. "Sleuthing in character", he called what you do.'

'That's right. And it must have sounded very unreassuring.' That was how it had sounded to Phyllida, out of James Pusey's reluctant mouth. (Not Jack's mouth, and Phyllida was aware of a rare pang of resentment at the thought of how much of Jack his first wife had had.) 'It isn't, though. We work quite closely with the police. Peter Piper Detective Agency in Dawlish Square, if you want to . . . Did your father tell you I was in character when I met him?' She was talking too much, but she couldn't stop. 'I had to make friends with him as part of my job – you might call it the more distasteful part – and then when my character had to disappear . . . well, I couldn't bear it and I went to look for him as myself. And found it had been hard for him to bear it, too. Did he tell you?'

'Yes.'

'I hope he also told you I made him promise his marriage to me wouldn't take a penny away from his legacy to you. My job's well paid, James, and I've just had a leading role in a prime-time television series.' Phyllida shuddered inwardly as she forced out the vainglorious words, but she had to sell herself now as never before. 'You won't see my name on the credits – and your father said he didn't think he would have recognised me – because my everyday job relies on my anonymity. All I do, in the public eye, is take far too long writing a book about women and the stage. Will it be a drink, or tea or coffee?'

'I'd like coffee, please.'

'Good. Come out to the kitchen with me while I make it. I'm busy on a murder case at the moment,' she said as she led the way, so longing to turn round and hug the tall figure behind her that she had consciously to keep her hands at her sides. 'Which includes a missing teenager, so this is the first day I've had in some time, being at home as myself. I'd even fallen asleep in my chair when you rang the bell. James' – now she turned to face him, giving herself the support of the units behind her – 'your father was the love of my life. I don't know if I was the love of his, because I know he loved your mother.'

'You didn't love your first husband?'

'I thought I did, when I married him as a very young woman. Perhaps I just wanted a centre, travelling from place to place in rep without a home . . . I don't know. But he was unfaithful to me for years and I got to know that he didn't love me. Catching him in the act was the trigger that let me walk away. I'd no idea until I met your father what love can be.'

Turning from the impassive, intent face Phyllida busied herself with the kettle, cafetière and cups, longing for Jack's son to speak. 'I hope your father gave you that assurance about his money,' she said into his silence without turning round. 'If he didn't, I will. Legally. Witnessed and signed.'

'He did give it.'

'Good.' Phyllida turned to face him. 'Then can we perhaps . . . be friends? There's not much more than ten years between us. Will you keep in touch with me? Let me get to know you?'

It was one of the big moments of her life, bigger than any debut on any stage, and she was unable to keep a tremor out of her voice or stop her hands and her lower lip fom trembling. At least he had met and was holding her eyes, and then, suddenly, there were the smile and the sparkling eyes, and Phyllida cried, 'Jack!' and began to cry.

He didn't touch her, but his voice when he spoke was no longer sharp. 'Go and sit down,' he said. 'I'll finish off the coffee.'

'There are biscuits in that blue-and-gold tin,' Phyllida sobbed. 'And plates—'

'That's all right. Go and sit down. I'll find what I need.'

With the lightening of James Pusey's face, it was nothing but glorious astonishment to have a piece of his father resurrected before her eyes, and when James carried the tray into the sitting room Phyllida had stopped crying and was sitting forward in her chair, her hands clasped between her trousered knees, making him think of an excited child.

'It's all right,' he said, as he put the tray carefully down. 'You're not at all what I expected.'

'Good,' she said, hearing her tremulous laugh. 'You could only have expected the worst. So far away and your father writing to you so uncharacteristically. You must have thought his illness had affected his brain.'

James laughed too. 'I did. I was frantic. That's why I came pretty well straight to see you when I got back to England. To get it over as soon as possible.'

'And now . . .' She got to her feet and turned her back on him again as she poured the coffee.

'Now it's all right,' he repeated.

'So we'll keep in touch.'

'If you want to.'

'Oh, I do, James, I do.' Phyllida turned round. 'Milk? Sugar?'

'Milk. No sugar. How do you manage your personal tastes when you're in character?'

'My characters *always* take a little milk, and no sugar. That's *de rigueur*. I can't always please myself over drinks, though. I don't have many characters who regularly drink gin and dry Martini.'

'There's a lot to learn, isn't there?' he said, grave again after a flash of smile. 'When Dad said you were eleven years his junior, I had visions of . . . of . . .'

'A mature Lolita? Someone looking for a sugar daddy?'

'Something like that. I'm sorry. I see now that you're . . .'

'A plain Jane. Except sometimes when I'm in character, and then you had better watch out.'

'A rather beautiful woman, actually. But not in the way I was afraid of.'

'Thank you.' It was the best moment of her widowhood. 'So if you've booked into a hotel, I hope you'll check out and stay here.'

'It's just a day trip this time. I wasn't expecting to want to stay. But I do, and I will. Phyllida, Dad's letter now I've met you . . . He did love you.'

'I know; and I loved him. James, I can be personally reticent to the point of idiocy, but when I found your father had left the Seaminster Gardens I went to Edinburgh to find him, I was so confident of us both. And I think . . . I think in those last few months I made him happy.'

'I think you did.' James's eyes were sparkling now with tears, and for a few moments they sat in silence. 'I like your house,' he said, when he had blown his nose and looked round the room. 'So light and . . . well, sort of calm. I look forward to staying here. Oh, you must have my card.'

They got to their feet to make the exchange, and James said regretfully that it was time he was on his way. 'I've only been back in England twenty-four hours and I'm seeing friends in Town tonight; I wasn't expecting to stay in Seaminster a moment longer than I had to. Now . . . I'll give you a ring, pretty soon. Once I've readjusted to an office desk. I suppose Dad told you I work for National Geographic?'

'He did.'

'This has been my first field trip. Wonderful, until . . . That's my flat number; use it any time.'

'I will. Oh, thank you! I do pretty well on the whole, James, because your father's always with me; but there are times . . . Now, I'll never feel totally bleak again.'

On the doorstep he turned to face her, looking for the first time uncertain.

'What is it?'

'Can I ask you . . . Was it a struggle? Did it hurt him? Did it take long?'

She put her hands on his shoulders. 'No, and no, and no. He went to sleep first; I saw and heard his regular breathing. Then realised it had stopped. Only because I couldn't hear it or see it any more; there was nothing else to mark his passing, not even a sigh. So he was unaware of the moment. The last thing he knew was the familiar sensation of falling asleep. I was so glad for him; it helped me to bear it.'

'It helps me too. Thank you.'

As he drove away he waved through his open window, and through her joy Phyllida felt a pang of sorrow for the family in Seaminster that had been blown apart by death and disappearance. The ringing of the telephone was the outward sign of her return to work, and she was expecting Peter's voice when she heard it.

'I'm on my way,' she said. 'I would have come sooner, but . . . Peter, I've just had a visit from Jack's son. He's so like his father. I think we've made friends . . . Sorry, you didn't ring me to hear this. What is it?'

'I'm so glad about Jack's son,' Peter said, swallowing on his jealousy. 'I've got some news, too. As you know, Kendrick and Co. already had Miss Turnbull's DNA, and they sent it to Forensics with the handkerchief. The big splash is Sandra Jordan's, and there are a couple of hairs, too, that confirm it as blood from the head wound. As Kendrick anticipated, the spots of blood aren't hers. But they aren't Miss Turnbull's, either.'

Sixteen

'*H*appy Christmas, darling.'
      '*Happy Christmas, Jack. Oh, it is! It's the happiest I've ever had.*'
   '*Truly?*'
   '*Truly. I don't have to think about it.*'
   '*Then it's as happy a Christmas as I've ever had.*'
   '*I'm glad you've had other happy Christmases, Jack. I want to think of you being happy.*'
   '*I'm happy by temperament, I think. And my life on the whole has let me be.*'
   '*When I met you as Fiona . . . the way you were smiling . . . I think I knew right away you were a happy man. Because you didn't keep it to yourself.*'
   '*So perhaps, eventually, you'll be happier than you used to be, Phyllida.*'
   '*Perhaps. Now, let me help you into the sitting room.*'
   '*Thank you, my darling. I need your arm today . . . Your tree's so beautiful. Did you enjoy doing it?*'
   '*Yes. It's the first tree I've dressed since I was a child.*'
   '*Promise me you'll dress a little one next year. Promise!*'
   '*I promise. Jack . . . what will we say when we lift our glasses in six days' time?*'
   '*What we've always said. What we've just been talking about and realised how much of it we have. Happy new*

year; here's to happiness. I want you to rejoice for me, Phyllida, when you weep for yourself. Because for the rest of my life – for the next very few weeks, my darling – it's the only sensation I'm going to feel. You will feel bleak, but I never shall; and when you do, I want you to remember what I've said.'

'We'll have to get the girl's DNA via her father,' Kendrick said wearily to DS Wetherhead.

'It'll be a handy way to get the father's too,' Fred encouraged. 'And the old "for the purposes of elimination" will oil the other wheels as usual. Turn your chair round, sir, and take a look at that sea.'

Reluctantly Kendrick swivelled. Every now and again he remembered the long view through the large window behind his desk, and took a few moments off to turn and contemplate it as the next best thing to being on The Parade, leaning on the rail. He had never failed to turn back without a renewed sense of proportion, however frail; yet he had felt so bogged down by this brutal case he hadn't once during it turned for solace to his view, while never needing it more.

Idiot, he shouted inwardly now, as he obeyed his sergeant. It was another sharp, dry day with a pastel sun spreading no warmth, only late-Turner light through a thin film of creamy cloud. The sea was a delicate dove-grey, its calm surface broken here and there by sudden darts of white that went as quickly as they came and reminded Kendrick of the mean little knife wind he had walked into on his way from car to police HQ. Roofs and chimneys obscured The Parade, and the only sign of human life was a pale ship moving diagonally away from the thin grey line of the horizon.

'Um.' After a long, silent moment Kendrick swivelled back to his desk. 'As you said, Fred,' was his only comment before reluctantly looking down at the forensic report in front of him. 'You also said "Other wheels". There'll be plenty of those. We'll have to include Mrs Jordan's business partner and the office staff. And the girl's classmates at school; she seems to have had such an influence over some of them, she could just have got one of the boys to carry out the murder for her, grim as the thought is. The presence of the handkerchief in her drawer is enough to tell us how cool she can be. Even if she's innocent of murder . . . Can you think of any other thirteen-year-old coming on a scene like that, and having the nerve to secure herself a lever against a killer before calling the police?' Kendrick thought of Jenny, and felt sick again.

'No, sir, I can't; and even this one went into shock. What about Miss Turnbull now?'

'I've never been more glad about anything in my life, Fred, than my decision to keep her name out of it. But we still haven't found the girl, so Miss Turnbull isn't off the hook. I've been lenient enough to give instructions for her to be officially informed that we haven't found any DNA evidence to link her to the murder, but Susan Jordan made a very grave accusation against her, and she can't prove her statement that she let the girl out of her car. Being innocent of the smaller of the bloodstains on the handkerchief doesn't necessarily make her innocent *vis-à-vis* the disappearance of Susan, and I'm still not convinced personally that she's had nothing to do with it, despite her boss's PR job. And there's another thing.'

'Yes, sir?'

'I think we have to consider the bizarre possibility that Susan Jordan purloined herself a handkerchief that already had the small blood spots on it – if not her father's, then a trophy perhaps from a boy she had her wicked way with.'

'And applied it to Mrs Jordan's wounds.' DS Wetherhead completed. 'Which I'm afraid could mean, sir—'

'That the handkerchief has no significance beyond confirming the dire state of Susan Jordan's psyche.'

'Just so, sir. But, if I may say so, that seems to me to be very unlikely.'

The Chief Superintendent sighed. 'Whatever, Fred, we've got to go through it. I want you to take charge of the school operation, with a DC of your choice. I suppose I'd better go myself to Sandra Jordan's office and pussyfoot around her partner and her staff. When I've seen Hugh Jordan.' Kendrick sighed again, and got to his feet. 'No way but the truth over this, although I think for the moment that we'll be economical with it again and limit description of the handkerchief to "an object". So far as Hugh Jordan's concerned – if he's innocent – "a man's handkerchief", with all its unique implications for him, could make him wonder if he'd learned up to now just how bad a nightmare can be, and "an object" should be enough to provoke a reaction of shock in any other owner of the handkerchief, which I trust whoever is witness to it will take note of.'

'You can rely on that, sir.'

'I'm sorry I can't suggest that you eliminate all class-mates who were in class at the time of the murder, Fred. If Susan Jordan was given – or filched – the handkerchief, we still need to know who it belongs to, because if it belongs to someone all present and correct in school when Sandra Jordan died, then we have to assume either that Susan was the killer, or that she had some reason for falsely involving a schoolmate.'

'Having already involved Marjorie Turnbull. D'you think she's off her rocker, sir?'

'If she's accusing two people, I suppose she could be. Or still in partial shock. The hell with it, if only we could find her!' *Alive or dead.*

'I suppose she could just have done away with herself, sir. Particularly if she was the killer.'

'Remorse?'

'I couldn't say, sir.'

No, of course you couldn't, Fred. Looking sideways at his sergeant's serious face, Kendrick was seized by a rare impulse to laugh at him. Fred could be so gnomically wise, but Kendrick suspected that he lacked a sense of humour. 'All right, Fred, I'd better get going; at least I can tackle Jordan tonight. The others will have to wait till the morning. Thank God it isn't a weekend.'

At the Golden Lion Reception desk, one of the girls asked the Chief Superintendent diffidently if he'd mind going upstairs to Mr Jordan's room. 'He's staying up there at the moment, sir, having his meals sent up. Very considerate of him – all the press people have given up and we're back to normal down here. And I expect Mr Jordan doesn't feel like being among people at the moment, with there being no news about his daughter.'

There was a question in Sharon's smile, but the DCS returned it with no more than a request for Hugh Jordan's room number and the suggestion that, while he was on his way up, she should ring the room and reassure Mr Jordan that his visitor really was the Chief Superintendent.

Jordan still asked who it was before opening up.

'It's Chief Superintendent Kendrick, Mr Jordan.'

Kendrick wasn't easily shocked, but he was appalled by the transformation of the tall, smiling, confident figure of Hugh Jordan. The man seemed to have shrunk within days, his colour had fled and his mouth was a thin straight line. Kendrick noticed that, as they sat down, his hands were trembling so violently he had to clasp them together and push them down between his knees.

'You have some news for me, Mr Kendrick?'

'Not about your daughter, I'm afraid, Mr Jordan. But . . .'

'No news is good news. Don't bother to say it. If her body hasn't been found, we can hope that she's still alive. So why have you come?'

'An object has come to light that just might help us to discover who killed your wife, Mr Jordan. The further investigation has, I'm afraid, to involve the taking of DNA from a wide group of people. Including her family. I'm sorry.'

'If it helps to name the murderer.' Jordan seemed to Kendrick to have shrunk even further, huddled in the large armchair. 'You can't take Susan's, Mr Kendrick, but you can get it from mine, can't you? The Duke of Edinburgh—'

'We can. Thank you for anticipating me.'

'Is there any chance . . . Can it be taken here?'

'Of course. Someone's on the way.'

'Can you wait? Let them in? I know I must sound paranoid, but I feel so . . . well, so *bewildered*.' Hugh Jordan lunged to his feet and started stamping about the room. 'I don't feel I know anyone or anything any more. It's a terrible feeling, as if I'm not in the real world; but it helps the pain of Susan's . . . of Susan's disappearance, in a way.'

'I'm so very sorry, Mr Jordan.' Kendrick had had to turn away from the agonised face, and it was a huge relief that the telephone rang. A questing look, and a nod from Jordan, and Kendrick answered it. 'Send them up,' he said.

The Forensics team had sent two of its young members, a man and a woman, both of whom Kendrick had come to know slightly. He stayed behind when the job was done and they had left.

'Is there anyone you would like sent for, Mr Jordan? Friend, or . . . relative?'

'There aren't any relatives any more, Mr Kendrick. And friends . . . Thinking about Sandra and Susan's bad enough, and whoever it was, there'd be no way we could talk about anything else. I'll just stay here by the phone and try to watch some television.'

'Very good, sir. You know that we'll be in touch the moment—'

'I know, Chief Superintendent. And thank you.'

'Try to rest now, Mr Jordan.'

'I'll try. I'll tell Reception again not to put any calls through until morning. Unless the police ring with news of Susan.'

'A good idea.'

Even an actor as incredible as Phyllida Moon couldn't fake bodily degeneration, Kendrick thought. Hugh Jordan had to be genuinely distraught. Though it could be with fear as much as – or more than? – with grief.

Phyllida Moon . . . Walking with unaccustomed slow steps along the wide corridor, feeling his feet sink slightly into the plushy carpet and scanning the numbers of the bedroom doors as he went, Kendrick realised that he had known since entering the hotel what he was going to do when he left Hugh Jordan. Well, in all the circumstances, not to do it would be churlish. Dr Piper had told him earlier that he had given her a rest day, but that she would be around as Mrs Parker towards evening, in the remote event that Hugh Jordan might descend to the public parts of the hotel, or approach her direct for some human contact. It could be that the husky-voiced American had already gone downstairs, in which case he would see her in the lobby and maybe suggest a drink – there could be no danger from the media in that. And if she was in process of transformation, she would inform him so through the door and he would go away . . .

Strange not to know who among a number of women might answer the door of a room let to only one. Kendrick smiled to himself as he approached room 98. But his face grew grave as he reached it and he hesitated for a moment, annoying himself by glancing to right and left to ensure that he had no witnesses, before raising his hand and knocking.

She was there; he heard immediate movement. And then the drawling voice.

'Who is it?'

'It's Maurice Kendrick. Are you decent?'

'I am, sir.'

The door opened, and Merle Parker stood there, smiling at him. 'You've timed it well. Please come in.'

'Thank you.' He was astonished, as he followed her through the small lobby, to find himself disappointed not to have been received by Phyllida Moon.

'This really is an unexpected pleasure,' Mrs Parker said, and then Phyllida said, in her own voice, 'Since inventing my American I've decided that clichés sound a lot less cliché-like when uttered in an American voice. Would you agree, Chief Superintendent?'

'I haven't thought about it until this moment, but yes, I think I would.' They wouldn't sound too bad, either, in Phyllida Moon's own soft tones. 'How are you, Miss Moon? You haven't had much time as yourself, lately.'

'I've been glad of that, Mr Kendrick.'

'For a particular reason?'

She'd asked for the question, but Phyllida still hesitated before answering it. 'I was recently widowed.'

The shock took his breath, and then he was shocked by his own unwarranted assumption. 'I'm so very sorry,' he managed. 'I hadn't realised . . . I didn't know you were married.'

'You yourself have called me professional, Mr Kendrick.' There was no temptation to tell him any more. 'Now, may I offer you a drink?'

'The lobby's empty of the media, and I don't think Hugh

196

Jordan has any intention of leaving his room tonight. So, thank you.'

'Think nothing of it,' the American sophisticate drawled with a smile, then sashayed across the room to its statutory stocked fridge.

Kendrick's restored marriage was proof against even mental infidelity, but he found Phyllida Moon likeable and intelligent, and left her half an hour later feeling he had secured a friend. They had even moved to *Maurice* and *Phyllida* with only slight embarrassment, and he had none when he got home about telling Miriam, with Jenny in attendance, everything about his unscheduled visit to the pretend American. He also told his wife, not for the first time, of his growing qualms about his secret employment of a member of the public on police business, but that the Peter Piper Agency, with Miss Moon in particular, continued to serve him so well he had no intention of ceasing to call on it if and when he felt they could help an investigation in the future.

'Anyway, love,' he said, when they were getting ready for bed, 'I only use them when they're there already because they've been hired to investigate a situation that turns into a crime.'

'You're paying them yourself, aren't you, Maurice?'

'What else can I do?'

'Darling, we're well off and we're thrifty, and it doesn't bother me. Nor you, it seems to me, these days. And you're still tackling nine cases out of ten the conventional way.'

'Bless you for reminding me.'

Thoughts of Phyllida Moon's intriguingly strange career, and efforts to imagine how it could fit with a marriage, helped to keep at bay thoughts of the missing schoolgirl and what might have become of her, and Kendrick fell asleep more easily than he had managed since the case began, although all through it, and through his jumbled dreams, he was listening for the telephone.

By the morning its continuing silence reawoke his sense of frustration, and as he made his way to the offices of Hardman and Andrews, he felt bleak and dour.

Joe Hardman had been told by telephone to expect the Chief Superintendent and his team and greeted them with a subdued sparkle, still bright enough to remind Kendrick that his first sight of the man had put him in mind of the handsome gypsy of folklore.

'So why the sudden intimate interest in us all, Chief Superintendent? Or perhaps you can't tell us that at the moment? Ours not to reason why, ours simply to roll up our sleeves, or open our mouths, or whatever?'

'Life would be a lot simpler for the police, Mr Hardman, if members of the public were always so understanding. I can at least tell you that an object has come to light that we have reason to believe has some bearing on the murder of Mrs Jordan. We need to take samples of DNA from everyone who had regular contact with her simply as a routine means of eliminating them from our inquiries. I trust there will be no objections here from you or your staff to supplying us with them?'

'Goodness, no. After the phone call from police HQ I spoke to all members of staff and everyone's agreeable. There are just a couple of our junior members who are hoping you'll take a swab rather than prick their fingers for blood. One girl, I know, has fainted in the past at the sight of a needle . . .'

'It's to be swabs, sir, so no need for anyone to worry. Now, let me introduce the members of our forensic team who are here with me to take them.'

In view of Hardman's oblique warning, Kendrick suggested that the swabs be taken with the donors sitting down, and nobody passed out. The process didn't take long, and when it was over and Forensics had departed with their booty, Kendrick asked Hardman if he might have a further word with him in private.

'Of course, Chief Superintendent. I'm due, and very ready, for a coffee, and I hope you'll join me.'

'Thank you.'

Hardman touched a button. 'A cafetière this morning, please, Jill. And two cups. Now, Chief Superintendent, is there some further way I can help you?'

More truly relaxed this time, Kendrick thought. Less of the bright bonhomie, which could have been brought on by nerves. That would point to Hardman's innocence. Or, of course, a guilt he was now more confident of being able to conceal . . .

If the DNA on the handkerchief didn't match up with any of the swabs taken, if for God's sake it turned out to be animal rather than human, was he going to mentally arraign every innocent soul who had had regular contact with Sandra Jordan? This was the part of his beloved work he hated, this process whereby he found himself, for a while, seeing human beings as objects that might, or might not, be inimical, rather than his own blood brothers and sisters who could suffer as he could. Joe Hardman had cared for Sandra Jordan for a while, had worked with her as friend and colleague until the moment of her death, yet it was only now, looking into another face that had thinned and hollowed over the past days, that Kendrick remembered to feel sorry for the man. It didn't – it couldn't – prevent him from using his probe on the exposed quick.

'Mr Hardman,' he said, trying to sound conversational, 'you know from the media that Mrs Jordan's daughter has disappeared. Did you—'

'I know from her father, Chief Superintendent. I had dinner at the Golden Lion a couple of nights ago with Hugh. He appears to have no idea at all where she may have gone.'

'Or whether she went of her own free will.'

'That worries him most of all, of course.'

'How well did you know Susan, Mr Hardman? Do you have any thoughts on where she might be? Anything that could give us a lead? We went over her home and garden, of course, but no sign that she'd even been there. Anything you may have seen or heard when you were visiting the family? A favourite place of hers, say. Or some friend who lives outside Seaminster . . . According to her father she hadn't reached a stage of having a life outside home and school, but sometimes children speak with less inhibition to non-members of their family.'

'That's very true, Mr Kendrick; but I saw very little of Susan – only, so far as I can recall, when I went for dinner to the house. But she was always pretty easy with me, perhaps because I could see she was the sort of girl who resented being treated as a child and I always talked to her as if she was grown-up, asked her opinion on things, and so on. Ah, here's the coffee.'

The men sat silent while the youngest member of the staff, Jill Barlow, cheeks burning red and lower lip trembling, saw to their requirements.

'Jill was very fond of Sandra,' Hardman said, when the girl had left. 'But then, everyone was. But Susan . . . She resented her, I'm afraid. It was too easy to see.'

'Did this upset Mrs Jordan a great deal?'

'Oh, yes. Not that she said much, but I know – knew . . .' Hardman paused and bowed his head for a moment. 'I knew her well, and I could tell . . . She was always saying it would get better. Hugh seemed to handle it well, by the way; he was very fair. Oh God, Mr Kendrick, I hate talking about friends and colleagues as if I've been spying on them. Can we leave it there?'

'Of course, sir. You've been very helpful; I appreciate it. And the good coffee.'

'It was Sandra's choice.'

'I'm very sorry, Mr Hardman.'

Although he was anxious to get back to the only possible source of news, Kendrick felt so troubled he dismissed his driver and walked back to the office along The Parade.

Phyllida, filling the day in fitfully at home, found herself longing for a routine case she could engage her mind on. She would get them, of course, and Peter had promised her more, and more interesting cases than he had ever yet put her way, but she had come straight back to what the nation was now calling the Jordan Affair and been instantly absorbed by it. The one disadvantage of her unique role was that merely to be in the office she had to assume Miss Bowden or remain strictly out of sight, and she had had to agree with Peter's tentative suggestion that there was no merit just at that moment in either choice, particularly as Maurice Kendrick (she couldn't yet quite manage to think of him by his first name only) had indicated that he felt it might be helpful if she would continue for the time being to spend her evenings at the Golden Lion Hotel as Mrs Parker.

Days spent in little more than anticipation of evenings hang very heavy, particularly with the scope they allow for introspection. There was little or nothing to be done in her frost-bound garden and Phyllida, used to attending automatically and efficiently to the order and cleanliness of her home, tried to chastise herself for the comparative chaos currently surrounding her – without much effect beyond a sluggish display with vacuum and duster.

Languor and a general sense of impending doom accompanied her to the Golden Lion in the early evening, so that when the telephone rang at seven as she was about to descend to the Caprice Bar, she knew at once that Steve's sepulchral hallo was a preface to bad news and, as she heard

the gloomy relish of his tone, that he had been given the
job of imparting it by a considerate boss who was aware of
how much pleasure being the bearer of it gave him, with
its scope for the dramatic.

'Steve! Have you got some news for me?'

'Yep. Kendrick doesn't need to get Susan Jordan's DNA
from her father. He can take it from her own dead body.'

'Oh, Steve. So they've found her.'

'Yep. Correction, though. *I* found her.'

'*You?*'

'Yep. You know I had a half-day, and me and Melanie
were driving by the Jordan house and I just had the
thought . . . I'd have a look round there myself. Not
inside, of course, but it said in the reports about a wood
at the bottom of the garden. Melanie wasn't too keen, it
was getting dark, and the wood *was* kind of spooky . . .'

'I can picture it, Steve.' And his enjoyment of playing
detective in front of his adoring girlfriend, plus scaring her
a bit in the dusk with tales of what they might find.

Did find . . .

'I was further into the wood than Melanie, but she'd
moved a bit to the side and I heard her scream. She'd
fallen over something on the ground she was half on top
of, and when I pulled her off of it, it was this female body,
and when I shone my torch there was all this fair hair and
I recognised her.'

'Steve, I hope you went straight back to the car and
telephoned—'

'Yeah, yeah, I went and called Peter. He told me to sit
tight while he called the big chief, and it was what I was
expecting: I was to find the nearest call box and make an
anonymous call to the police.'

A wistful note had entered Steve's voice. Aware of his
craving for publicity, Phyllida understood it. 'If you'd told
them as yourself, Steve, your picture would have been in

202

every newspaper and on every television screen in the land. That would have been exciting, but it would have been the end of your career as a private eye, to say nothing of the Peter Piper Agency.'

'I know, I know.' And just in case he hadn't known, Peter had told him.

'So she went home after all. I wonder why the police searchers didn't find her.'

'Because they didn't look properly, of course,' Steve informed her sanctimoniously. 'Heads will have to roll.'

Seventeen

'*Nurse . . .*'
    '*Ah . . . I'm afraid he's gone, dear. Peacefully, in his sleep. Now, let me make you a nice cup of tea.*'

So here we go again, Kendrick thought wearily, watching the result of his sharp intake of breath spiralling away from him on the cold air as a tiny string of cirrus, with the strange sensation he had had before when he had stood beside the body of a missing child: the sensation that through all his hopes he had known that eventually this was how it would be. She was lying on her back – fully clothed, thank God – every detail of her cruelly sharp under the glare of the lights: the long blonde hair fanned out around her head, her bruise-coloured face a grimace with bared teeth and bulging eyes that he longed to stoop and shut. But as yet he was on hallowed ground; the team was only just moving into place, and after a long sorrowful look he stepped carefully back out of the bright circle and, blinking in the contrast of what for a few seconds seemed like total darkness, joined the little group of watchers already restrained by a line of blue-and-white-striped ribbon.

'What sort of person would come nosing about here, sir,' ventured the constable now beside him, 'and then refuse to give their name?'

'Some ghoul, Constable. There are plenty of them about; and we have to be grateful to this one.' And he was. No more grudging gratitude so far as the Peter Piper Agency was concerned.

'The area was searched, sir. Every inch of it, I swear. I can't think—'

'She'll have been moved, Constable. There've been a couple of nights. You've got a hell of a lot to worry about, never forget it, but not that.'

'Thank you, sir.'

So why move her here? Kendrick wondered crossly. The look of her face, the marks of the killer's hands he knew would be found under the scarf he or she had replaced over them – the murderer would have known there was no way it would appear the girl had chosen to take a walk in her own woods. He didn't have to wait for the doctor's preliminary findings: he had seen them for himself.

'Keep me in the closest touch,' he called over the ribbon. The man whose eye he had caught nodded, then blinked and put his hand up to his face as the first photo flash went off. Kendrick turned, his eyes now accustomed to the moonlit night, and made his way up the garden and out to his car. 'Any messages?' he asked his driver, as the man hastily stowed his tabloid.

'Nothing, sir. Sir . . .'

'I'm afraid it's murder, Constable; and yes, it's the Jordan girl, of course.'

'Sir, the area was searched.'

'I know, I know. She'll have been moved.' He'd probably be saying that in his sleep tonight. Kendrick looked at his watch. Half past eight. 'Go back to the station, pick up DS Wetherhead, then take us to the Golden Lion.'

It had crossed his mind to get Fred to do it, but he knew he had to be the one; and that this particular piece of news-breaking was as bad as any he had had to face in the whole of his three decades plus as a policeman.

Hugh Jordan received it in a silence that frightened

Kendrick more than a show of grief. At Fred Wetherhead's suggestion he had already been sitting down. Now he dropped his head in his hands and sat immobile and silent until Kendrick found himself forced to approach him, touch the clasped hands, and ask him if he was all right.

'All right, Mr Jordan?'

Kendrick had thought there was no more room for change in Hugh Jordan's appearance, but when the man looked up he was freshly shocked by the pain and defeat in the sunken eyes and the ivory-coloured lifelessness of the face.

'I'm so very sorry, Mr Jordan.' He'd told it all in one succinct sentence: death by strangulation, no apparent interference, lying on her back in her own piece of woodland. 'It would have been very quick.' But Jordan would know as well as he did that the panic and pain of the instant before death would have been the length of a lifetime. There was no comfort to be given, even though DS Wetherhead had filled the kettle from the bathroom and was popping a sachet of tea into a cup. Kendrick himself was suggesting brandy.

'Brandy . . . Yes, in the cupboard by the bed . . . the other side . . . Thank you.'

That was all Jordan said for the fifteen minutes or so during which they sat silent on each side of him. Kendrick wasn't happy about getting to his feet and saying they must go, and it was an enormous relief when Jordan's response was to drain his brandy glass and burst out crying. They sat down again while the crying lasted, DS Wetherhead making soothing noises; and when it had reached the stage of intermittent dry sobs, they got up again once Jordan had told them he was all right and they had elicited a promise from him to ring for service if he suddenly wasn't, or if there was anything he wanted that a hotel could supply.

'No hope of a result from Forensics tonight on the DNA samples,' Kendrick said in the car. 'So let's go home, Fred.'

The murder missed the seven o'clock news, but was an item at ten. Kendrick was glad to think of Hugh Jordan protected from the media by a well-run hotel; but it occurred to him to ring Miss Moon and ask her if she would suggest to the management that an eye be kept by the night staff on the back way in and the back staircase to deter reporters.

'You know those stairs pretty well, I presume.'

'Of course. I suppose . . . you broke the news to Hugh Jordan yourself?'

'I felt I must. It's the worst duty of policing. He was very quiet, almost as if he'd expected it. My sergeant and I were relieved when he started crying. I think it's too early yet for any attempt at comfort. Perhaps some time tomorrow . . .'

'I'll be in touch with him. Yes.'

'And off duty tonight. Goodnight, Phyllida.' The name was easier to say than he had thought it would be.

'Goodnight, Maurice.' So she was free to dismiss Merle Parker and cross the square. Just before Kendrick's call, for the first time in their working relationship, Peter had rung to tell her he would be there for as long as it took her to join him.

Kendrick concentrated on Jenny until her bedtime, and then Miriam opened some good wine and served him a delicious meal. They went up to bed early to make love, and to his surprise Kendrick slept dreamlessly until the summons of his alarm; but the old impatience was on him the instant he entered his office, and he was unable to resist for more than a few minutes his eagerness to know how near Forensics were to a result on the collected DNA *vis-à-vis* the handkerchief.

To his further favourable surprise he was told the result would be available by lunchtime, and at just after half past one, as he was throwing the major part of a sandwich into his waste-paper basket, a senior scientist arrived at his office to present it in person.

'It's very clear, Maurice. A million or so to one. I wish every job was as straightforward.'

'So do I, Tom. Thank you.'

Had he known this all along too? Kendrick wondered, as he stood for a few moments by his view, the report in his hand. A wind had come up since the cold stillness of the night when he had seen his own breath; the clear sky had lowered into cloud as the temperature rose, and the sea today was grey and restless.

He, though, was at relative peace, and to his immediate shame he heard something approaching cheerfulness in his voice as he spoke to Fred. 'We'll take PC Lloyd along with us. Seeing that it's an arrest.'

'The boss in?' DS Wetherhead asked the female array behind the counter, relieved to find no other customers.

'Well . . . yes. Who shall we say . . .' Three pairs of eyes flickered uneasily over the uniform.

'Thank you.' Kendrick at his most gravely authoritative, agreeably aware of his great height. 'We'll see ourselves through.'

'It's all right,' DS Wetherhead murmured, as the DCS led the way to the door at the back. 'Just carry on.'

Joe Hardman was alone in his office, sitting behind his desk studying some papers in front of him. He looked up in surprise at the three men, now in a row in front of him.

'Chief Superintendent! And team! To what do I owe this triple presence?' The eyes were sparkling, the mouth smiling, but Kendrick had seen the dart of fear.

'I think you know, sir,' he said, then stood silent as DS Wetherhead went through the spiel. 'Come along, then, please, sir,' Fred concluded.

Joe Hardman sprang to his feet, the sparkle a flash. 'This is outrageous! On what possible grounds—'

'On the grounds of a handkerchief with two sets of

bloodstains,' Kendrick told him. 'Modern forensics never lie, Mr Hardman; but we'll talk about it at the station.'

'Oh, God.' Hardman's hand went to the side of his chin. To the spot where he'd cut himself shaving. Kendrick and Wetherhead exchanged glances, each learning from the gesture why Hardman had bled.

'Come along, then, sir. You can ring for your solicitor when we get to the station.'

There was no more opposition. Hardman came round his desk, shook off the uniformed arm, but took his place in the small procession that made its way back into the reception area. There were some customers now, and ignoring the stares, Fred Wetherhead told the girls behind the counter not to worry.

'Business as usual, if you will, ladies,' Hardman said, on a smile from one to the other of them that Kendrick almost admired. 'Until lunchtime. Then you'd better shut up shop. Lynn will work out your money.' It was the code for *I shan't be back*.

'Mr Hardman . . .'

The procession was already on its way out to the street. Kendrick directed Hardman into the back of the car, between himself and DS Wetherhead, and the uniform chauffeur-drove them. Hardman didn't speak, and didn't move, for the length of the journey back to police HQ and still hadn't spoken when Fred directed him to a telephone. The solicitor, whom Kendrick recognised from previous similar situations, was there very quickly.

'So you cut yourself shaving, Mr Hardman,' Kendrick opened, when he and Fred were across the table from the accused and his brief. 'The morning Sandra Jordan was murdered. It will save us all a lot of time and trouble if you'll tell us in your own words what we already know.'

Hardman didn't turn to his solicitor. 'Yes. I cut myself. I remember now reaching out for a handkerchief to staunch the blood. Easily done; there wasn't much of it. I don't remember any more details, but when I was dressed I must have put the handkerchief into my pocket, not realising I was putting it on top of one already there. I think I do vaguely remember feeling a bit bulky.' Kendrick was aware of DS Wetherhead making an infinitesimal jerk backwards as Hardman's calm face was suddenly contorted with rage. 'Why the fucking hell I didn't investigate . . .'

His solicitor threw his client a raised-eyebrow look, and Kendrick wondered if Hardman had turned as swiftly from light to dark during his last conversation with Sandra Jordan.

'It certainly was unfortunate for you, sir. If you'd like to carry on.'

Hardman swallowed, and passed a hand over his face that took the rage with it. 'I knew Sandra was at home,' he resumed calmly, 'getting over the local lurgy. I just wanted to speak to her in peace, away from the office. I wanted to make her admit what it was so easy to see: that despite what she was always saying about Hugh Jordan being the love of her life, she was unhappy in her marriage. How it had turned her into another person, afraid of her own shadow. Whenever I visited the house she was tiptoeing about on eggshells: *Yes, Hugh; no, Hugh, three bags full, Hugh.* If that's love . . . In the office she was cheerful and confident, the way she'd been all the time before she met Hugh Jordan, not thinking every moment whether or not she was doing the right thing. It made me angry for her. And with her. But whenever I said anything, she just told me how much she loved Hugh, and wanted to please him, and that things would be better when she and Susan got to know one another . . . God, that cold little bitch!' Another look from the solicitor, which Hardman again ignored. 'Sandra hadn't a hope in hell. And I wanted one more try to tell her. And to tell her . . .' For the first time Hardman hesitated,

210

and dropped his eyes to the worn table top. 'To tell her,' he went on, after a few seconds' silence so total Kendrick could hear the faint whirr of the cassette, 'that I loved her. That I always had and always would.' Hardman looked up. 'When she left me for Jordan – because that's what she did, Chief Superintendent, whatever we pretended – I was gutted. We'd always acted as if our affair was just a light-hearted, take-it-or-leave-it matter between friends.'

'Why?' Kendrick asked.

'On my part . . . because I was afraid that was how Sandra really saw it, and I didn't want to blow the bubble away. Because it wasn't a bubble for me, you see; it was the real thing. And until she met Jordan I hoped that our surface attitude to one another was as much a cover-up of the real thing for Sandra as it was for me.'

'Even then, sir, you didn't tell Mrs Jordan how you really felt?' This from DS Wetherhead.

'And lose our working relationship as well? Oh, I made jokes; I said I was devastated, but I didn't dare make it sound serious, and she took that at face value, too.'

'And all the time the pressure was building up,' Kendrick suggested.

'I suppose so. When I went to see her – that morning – I was in a dreadful state. That could be why I took two handkerchiefs . . . I knew I was going to tell her what I felt, put our work together on the line as well as the remnants of our personal relationship; I knew I wasn't going to be able to help it. She came to the front door when I rang. She looked so frail and beautiful, I . . . I accepted her invitation to come in for a coffee, but as soon as we were in the sitting room I started on her.'

'Started on her, sir?'

'Started to tell her how I felt, how unbearable it was. I'd even decided that if the brick wall didn't come down, I'd suggest dissolving the partnership. I had no thought of harming her . . . But when she said her love for Hugh was worth any amount of worry about his daughter and about whether he loved her as much as she loved him – she even started going on about being jealous of his secretary – I was so . . . so *angry* I found myself grabbing hold of her and shaking her. Then she tripped and fell, and hit her head on the fender and didn't move. I swear to that. I didn't know whether or not she was dead, but I thought, She's got away from me again and . . . and the next moment I had that poker in my hand and was hitting her with it.'

'Thinking of anything in particular while you were doing it?' Kendrick inquired.

'Not *thinking*. But . . . feeling, I suppose, that she'd escaped me for the last time and that Hugh Jordan wasn't going to have her either. Oh, God, I don't know. I've been appalled ever since. In limbo. Nothing's been real. I never expected you'd catch up with me, Mr Kendrick, but I don't really seem to care that you have.'

'That you'll spend a lifetime in prison?'

Hardman actually shrugged. 'A lifetime without Sandra, and watching her make such a sad fool of herself, was hardly appealing.'

'What did you do – when you'd stopped hitting Mrs Jordan?' Fred Wetherhead inquired. 'If you . . . didn't care, why where you so careful to cover your crime?'

Hardman smiled. 'I believe the instinct of self-preservation is the strongest instinct we have, Sergeant; and as I've said, I wasn't thinking. So, I took a handkerchief out of my pocket and wiped the poker very carefully. Fortunately I'd weighed into Sandra before she made coffee, so the only other things I had to wipe were the inside and the outside of the front door, and I didn't worry too much about that because I'd been for dinner the week before. I must have pulled the two handkerchiefs out, and the one with the bloodstains fell on to Sandra. It could have done; I never looked at her again. I suppose that's where you found it.'

'That's correct, sir.' The faithful servant taking on himself the lie, Kendrick thought as he heard DS Wetherhead's endorsement. They would never know, now, if he was telling the precise truth, or if Susan Jordan had retrieved it from somewhere in hall or sitting room and applied it to her stepmother's head . . .

'The old woman started coming in from the conservatory while I was wiping the poker, and that nearly gave me a heart attack; but before I had to start thinking what to do about her, she gave a sort of shriek and fell down and didn't move. So I went ahead with wiping the door and she was still staring at nothing when I had a last look at her, so I hoped for the best.' Hardman leaned back in his chair. 'And that's it, boys.'

'And sometime on Wednesday evening,' Kendrick said, 'Susan Jordan came to see you, to tell you she'd seen you from the top of the staircase that leads down into the sitting room. Did she ask you for money?'

'What?' Joe Hardman had sprung forward, his eyes wide, his mouth shaking. 'Susan . . . You're accusing me of killing Susan? Dear God, I need a solicitor after all.' Hardman gave the man beside him a wildly beseeching look before turning back to the policemen. 'I haven't set eyes on Susan Jordan since I went to dinner at her house a few days before . . . before Sandra died!'

'All right, Mr Hardman,' Kendrick said. 'We'll leave it there for the time being. You'll be appearing in court in the morning, and I think I can tell you that any application for bail will be denied.'

'I didn't expect bail, Mr Kendrick, but I didn't kill Susan Jordan!'

There'd probably be no way of proving that he had, Kendrick reasoned, so perhaps it wasn't so perverse of him to be denying it. But the man's reaction to this second accusation was so wildly different from his reaction to the first, Kendrick found he couldn't quite ignore it.

He could put it on one side, though: there was a priority. 'Straight to the Golden Lion, Fred,' he said when they were outside the interview room.

'Can't think why Hardman expended so much energy on denying the second murder,' DS Wetherhead observed in the car.

'Nor can I, Fred. We'll chew it over later. As far as he's concerned it's academic. We've got him for life.'

Reception informed them that Mr Jordan hadn't left his room since the police visit of the day before. 'So far as we know, Chief Superintendent. We haven't kept a permanent watch on the back way out.'

'Will you ring up to him and tell him we're on our way?'

This time Hugh Jordan opened his door without asking who was outside it, and shuffled back through the lobby, still without speaking, as DS Wetherhead shut the door.

'We have some good news for you, Mr Jordan,' Kendrick said, as they took their places of the night before.

'Good news? Don't mock me, Mr Kendrick.' Jordan didn't bother to look at either policeman as he spoke.

'Of course not. Mr Jordan, we have proof incontrovertible that Joseph Hardman murdered your wife. He's been charged and is in custody. He's denying so far that he also killed your daughter but we're—'

'Joe Hardman killed Sandra?'

'He did. Without any doubt whatsoever.'

'*No-o-o-o-o!*' It was the roar of a wounded animal, blasting into every corner of the room, and both policemen sprang to their feet. DS Wetherhead put a hand on Hugh Jordan's writhing shoulder, but it was shaken off as Jordan too leapt up 'No!' he bellowed again. 'No! It was because she accused Hardman . . . changed to Hardman . . . that I . . .' Hugh Jordan sank back into his chair, closed his eyes and bowed his head. Then shot upright and stared in horror at Kendrick. 'I knew she was lying about Marjorie. I couldn't love Marjorie, but I respected her; I knew how true she was. So I knew it was a lie when Susan accused her, and it was when – it was because – she switched to Hardman that I was sure . . .'

Jordan bowed his head again and began to sob.

'What were you sure of?' DS Wetherhead asked him.

'That Susan had killed Sandra.' They had been dry sobs. When Jordan looked up there were no tears on his face. 'I was afraid from the start that she had, though I didn't face it. Then when she accused Marjorie . . . She was only a little bit late back from school that day Marjorie picked her up. She told me Marjorie'd offered her money to withdraw her accusation. I didn't believe that, either, because of knowing Marjorie. Suddenly I had to know the truth, had to get Susan to give it to me. I suggested we go for a run, creep down the back stairs and drive away from it all for a while. She liked the idea, but not so much when I told her I wanted to go home. She always hated that house; we moved there when I married Sandra. So she was sulky, but she followed me in and as soon as we were inside I sat her down and told her to tell me the truth. That I . . . that I knew she was the one who had killed Sandra. She went frantic. She denied it, and then she suddenly said, All right, I'll tell you the truth, it wasn't your precious Marjorie, it was Joe Hardman. I saw Joe Hardman, she said then, over and over again.'

'And it didn't occur to you, Mr Jordan, that she might have been telling the truth at last?'

'Dear God, no. The way she switched from Marjorie to Joe . . . it was confirmation to me of her guilt. I never thought—'

'You'd never thought, yourself, that it might be Joe

Hardman who had killed your wife? You'd commissioned a detective agency to look into her relationship with him.'

'Yes, but murder . . . It never crossed my mind it could be someone Sandra knew. Until Susan came out of shock and accused Marjorie I'd thought of some pushy salesman, some wandering nutter. Nobody with a name. And then when she named Marjorie I thought she was covering up for someone. Who could that someone be but herself? Joe Hardman . . . He meant nothing to her; she wouldn't have been covering up for *him*. Dear God. Susan told me the truth, and I killed her for it. I killed my innocent little girl, who loved and trusted me.'

'Innocent, Mr Jordan?' Kendrick inquired softly. 'Your daughter was attempting to ruin a woman she was jealous of. No, she didn't take a life, but she tried to take a reputation.'

'Not a capital offence, Chief Superintendent. I don't think I can bear it.'

Jordan slumped down in his chair, and for the second time DS Wetherhead fetched brandy. 'So what happened, sir?' he asked gently, when Jordan had choked over a couple of sips and the DCS's long legs were beginning to twitch.

'She was shouting all the time, *It was Joe Hardman, Daddy, it was Joe Hardman.* I'll hear her for the rest of my life. I had my hands round her neck. I think there were two things: I hated her in that moment for killing my beloved Sandra; it was an evil thing between my hands – my little girl! – and at the same time I saw the rest of her life in a flash as no life at all for a child. So . . . I just squeezed. My hands are big and strong; she hardly struggled. I put her in the little room behind the hidden door in the hall. It's an old house, and I reckoned your team wouldn't find the little catch of that hidden door when they came looking for her. The next night – late – I went down the back stairs, out of the back door of the hotel, and drove home again. I took her out, carried her across the garden into the wood and laid her down . . .' The anguished face turned to the DCS, the eyes entreating. 'Mr Kendrick, how can I lose this? How can I die too?'

'I can't believe it, Fred,' Kendrick said in the car. 'I actually told the man it would be a good idea for him to ask Reception not to put any calls through at night, to make sure he wasn't disturbed.'

'It didn't make any difference, sir. The girl was already dead and the delay in finding her didn't affect the case.'

'That isn't the point, Fred. I preach vigilance at all times and in all directions, and then don't practise it. Now, just about the last thing I want to do at the moment is talk to Marjorie Turnbull; but take us to Hugh Jordan's office.'

In the event DS Wetherhead did most of the talking, quoting Jordan as fully as he could remember wherever he had spoken of his secretary.

'So Hugh's belief in me was the death of his daughter,' Miss Turnbull pronounced, when Fred had finished.

Standing anguished before them, she made Kendrick think of the tragic heroine in the staging of an opera by Wagner. 'Susan Jordan ordained her own death,' he said severely, 'and caused you a great deal of suffering. I don't know what will happen to Mr Jordan's business, but are you willing to carry things on for the time being?'

'Certainly, Chief Superintendent. For as long as required.'

Magnificent Marjorie about to Hold the Fort.

'There's one other thing,' Fred Wetherhead said diffidently. 'If you can bring yourself, Miss Turnbull . . . I know Mr Jordan would like to see you.'

'Bring myself, Sergeant?' Kendrick had thought Miss Turnbull was standing as erect as she could, but now she drew herself up further. '"Love is not love which alters when it alteration finds,"' she quoted reprovingly. 'I've loved Hugh for years. To him I've been a loyal friend and a good secretary, and although I had foolish hopes when his first wife died, I knew in my heart it would never be any different. But I was blessed: I helped him all day and some-times I sang with him at night. His daughter behaved very wickedly, but how could I have harmed her? Hugh's daugh-ter? Anyone's daughter? Of course I shall see him. Please let me know when and where this will be possible.'

'We will, Miss Turnbull. Thank you.'

The Good Fairy, Kendrick thought as they left her. Not the Demon Queen.

'Shall I drop you at Dawlish Square?' DS Wetherhead asked as the car left the kerb.

'Via a wine lodge, Fred. And wait for me, if you will. It won't take me long to put them in the picture, and they won't need me to talk through the implications.'

By late afternoon Miss Bowden had been laid to tem-porary rest and Phyllida was back in her office. She was resting too when Peter rang. 'I thought we might have a little party tonight,' he said. 'Just you and me and Jenny and Steve, and the Chief Super's bottle of bubbly. I think late-ish would be nice. Ten o'clock? The idea's gone down well here, and Steve's even offered to run Jenny home.'

'I'd like that. Oh, Peter, I've just been thinking . . . Two unnecessary reports commissioned by two loyal and loving people. What a waste of their short time together! Tonight . . . I'd like to come as myself.'

'Of course. You're off duty for the rest of the day, anyway. I've got a nice case for you in the morning, by the way. Non-homicidal, I'll swear to it. See you at ten.'

'*As myself*,' Phyllida repeated aloud, lying back on her pillows and stretching her limbs. Before Jack she had sometimes wondered who that was, but now she knew; and before Peter's call she had had one from her stepson, asking her if he could come and stay.